THE MURLEYS
OF CLOUGHFUNE

THE MURLEYS
OF CLOUGHFUNE

Potato Farming to Copper Mining

SUE HURLEY MYERS

ISBN paperback: 978-1-7323095-0-0
ISBN ebook: 978-1-7323095-1-7

Cover Design: Rebekah Sather
Interior design: Ghislain Viau

To George
Our journey continues

Good God, what a brute man becomes
when ignorant and oppressed. Oh Liberty!
What horrors are committed in thy name!

—O'Neill Daunt, W. J.,
Personal Recollections of the Late Daniel O'Connell,
M.P., 2 Vols. London, 1848.

CONTENTS

ACKNOWLEDGEMENTS

I am grateful for the assistance of my husband, George Myers, who has been a faithful and insightful critic and has provided steadfast encouragement. I am also indebted to the many helpful people I met in Ireland. Ken Mason, unofficial genealogist, and his wife, Kathy, led me to valuable archival and ancestral information. The Castletownbere librarian, Dorothy Brophy, spared no effort in providing me with local publications and resources. A special thanks to my inspiring memoir group, especially Gerry DeJesu, Mal Ward, Kay Cima, Agnes McCarthy, Suzanne Rocanello, Fleur Jones and John Poignand for their unflagging support. Additional thanks to author Rose Connors, whose editing improved the story's clarity. I am also grateful to my son, Mike Myers, for making the maps showing where the Murleys lived and how they traveled to and from Mountain Mine. Sincere gratitude to George Snider, who generously gave me his extensive collection of Irish history books and materials.

The main sources for technical research about the copper mine and John Puxley were R. A. Williams's book *The Berehaven Copper Mines* (1993), personal tours of the Allihies mine ruins, and consultations with staff at the Allihies Copper Mine Museum. Other helpful resources were P.J. Dowling's book *The Hedge Schools of Ireland* (1968), and the valuable books of George Snider's Irish collection.

I also wish to acknowledge Daphne du Maurier's popular 1943 novel, *Hungry Hill,* a saga about the Puxley family, and its many hardships over five generations from 1820 to 1920. Du Maurier's story depicts copper mining from the point of view of English mine owners; *The Murleys of Cloghfune* offers a perspective from the point of view of Irish mine workers and their families.

INTRODUCTION

The Murleys of Cloghfune were a family interwoven in the six-centuries-long history of hatred between the peoples of England and Ireland. Before, during and after the Murleys' brief lives, Irish had killed, been killed, been colonized, rebelled and been subdued again and again. Religious enmity, beginning with the Reformation, was the foundation for those centuries of bloodshed among both Catholics and Protestants. Short of outright destroying the Irish, the English Penal Laws of the late 1600s set in motion years of Irish disempowerment and emasculation.

This historical novel follows the Murley family from 1813 to 1820 at a time of gradual repeal of the Penal Laws, along with the first wave of industrialization in southwest Ireland. Unlike Northern Ireland and England, where industrialization was well underway in the mid-1700s, the populace in southwest Ireland was in a state of ignorance and poverty, relying almost solely on the potato for sustenance.

In 1812, Englishman John Puxley visited the mountainous land of Ireland's Beara Peninsula and saw the potential for mining copper in deposits there that had been mined sporadically by indigenous people since the Bronze Age. He began a venture that changed the trajectory of the Murley family and hundreds of other farming families who labored at Mountain Mine.

I chose the Murley family as representative of this time of inexorable change because it is my family. I created the happenings of their daily lives based on five years of research, including an extended trip to the Beara, the village of Allihies and the townland of Cloghfune.

In the local Catholic Church in Allihies, tucked away in a thick two-foot-tall volume of recorded births, deaths and marriages, two names leapt out at me, inked in cursive 168 years ago, faded, but still legible: Dionysis (Latin for Denis) Murley and Johanna Twomey, married 5 February 1850, my great-great-great-grandparents.

Denis, my protagonist, would have been the father of Dionysis. All the Murley characters are fictional, though the family existed and lived in the townland of Cloghfune, based on Griffiths Valuation records. I chose to use the given names of certain real-life characters, such as Denis Murley; the mine owner, John Puxley; the temperance worker, Friar Theobald Mathew; Daniel O'Connell, the Liberator; and Father Walmsley, author of Pastorini's Prophecy.

The reader should assume that when the Irish speak among themselves, they are speaking Irish. Early on, translation is required between the English and Irish, but as the story progresses, when dialogue is between English and Irish speakers, the reader can assume English is being spoken. For the most part, I have omitted incorrect syntax by Irish speakers, for the sake of easier reading. When colloquial speech or altered syntax benefitted the dialogue, I used it.

CHAPTER 1

SUMMER HUNGER

August 1813

Padraigh Murley dropped to his knees, his deep-set blue eyes fixed on a thick mound of straw. Underneath lay the remaining potato harvest. Sweat beaded on his forehead. His temples throbbed. "Jesus, I need some big ones. Me chil'ren are hungry."

He pulled a flask of poitín from his overalls pocket and took a slug, then another. Seconds after gulping a third, he groaned and grabbed his chest. "Christ's sake, calm down. Summer hunger happens every year. This year ain't no different."

After taking another gulp, he returned the flask to his pocket. Groping blindly under the straw for the day's food, his hand emerged holding three small potatoes. He eyed the puny tubers. Forehead furrows stood out as he raised his eyebrows, making him look older than his thirty-five years.

Denis Murley, a short, tousle-headed boy of thirteen, squatted beside Padraigh. Denis soon retrieved two large potatoes. He held them up for his father to see.

Padraigh smiled, "Good, lad. Now take 'em to Ma. I'll find a few more."

Denis put the three small potatoes in the pocket of his overalls and held the two large potatoes, one in each hand. "Da, when are we going to the copper mine?"

"This morning—tell Ma we'll be needing some gruel."

Denis skipped toward the front of the two-room shanty where he lived with his parents and his three-year-old sister, Bridget, in the townland of Cloghfune on Ireland's Beara Peninsula. His round freckled face favored his mother, his square jaw and dimpled chin his father. When he smiled, his blue eyes smiled too, like his father's.

Don't know how me boy is going to grow if there ain't enough food, Padraigh thought as he watched his son walk away. *Guess I ain't been looking close enough. Skinny he is, but his overalls are way above his ankles. So he's a-growing, even if we're all getting hungrier.*

He spat. *I knew it—drenching rains, bone-chilling cold. Damnable weather. Surprised we got any lumpers left.*

Padraigh trudged toward the shanty's doorway, his eyes glazed, and his temples no longer throbbing. His thoughts of hunger were interrupted by the sight of Margaret, his wife of fifteen years, standing in front of their home. She held a bucket in one hand.

2

He avoided her eyes. "Not many lumpers left."

"Bonine Bo's still giving us milk," she said, holding up the nearly full bucket. "'Besides, Bella's near six months. Fattening up, she is. Big enough for market before we know it."

"That pig's time for market is coming quick if lumpers aren't ripe soon," Padraigh said.

"Should be just a few weeks more. Besides, you be getting mine work today. Better eat before you and Denny go."

He gazed at Margaret's tanned, freckled face, then lowered his eyes to her pendulous abdomen, recalling the midwife's visit the previous day. It was as if Mrs. Riley was still standing in the doorway, giving Margaret last-minute advice, "This is your sixth baby. It will come fast. When your pains are regular, have Denis come fetch me."

Padraigh's attention was drawn to Bridget, peeping out from behind Margaret's flowing ankle-length muslin dress. Winking at Margaret, he asked in a deep, lilting voice, "Where's me li'l Bridgee?"

Red tresses suddenly disappeared from view. "I think wee Bridgee wants to fool you, Da." Margaret spoke softly, but loud enough for Bridget to hear.

Silence.

The few seconds of silence were long enough for unwanted memories to flood Padraigh's poitín-laced thoughts. *Oh, Jesus. Why did you take me boys? Me Shamus, me Diel, me Leo. If them damn fairies are as evil as Maggie says, we got to*

3

be watching at every corner, in every tree, in every dust ball, all the time.

Bridget remained wrapped in her mother's skirts, clinging to folds of muslin, while she walked behind Margaret.

"Lass, you be hiding like I never saw you do."

Bridget didn't respond.

"You best be going soon's you eat," Margaret said as they entered the shanty. "The day's going to be as hot as the devil's own."

"Ready we are for going, and working, starting today."

Denis ladled gruel from a black pot on the stone hearth. "Da, you really think they'll let us work at the mine?"

"Thinking they will, lad. They need us. I hear they don't have enough of their own kind. Need strong men, like you 'n' me." Padraigh finished eating his gruel and stood, donning his wide-brimmed straw hat. Denis swallowed the last of his gruel, stood and pulled his tattered hat over his unruly brown hair. Denis's blue eyes squinted, then gave way to a broad smile. Padraigh's eyes brightened at the sight.

After they left, Margaret looked about for Bridget, who was asleep on a straw pallet close to the hearth. As she stepped toward the pallet, she tripped over Bella, who squealed at the disturbance. "Out you go!" Margaret coaxed the family pig outside with her booted foot. "Ain't much for you," she added as Bella trotted to the slop pile.

Bella grunted, following the odor picked up by her

4

well-attuned snout. She devoured the meager meal of soured milk, barley chaff, grass and fish leavings.

Meanwhile, Padraigh and Denis made their way to Allihies, home of the recently opened copper mine. Beyond the familiar path, strewn with rocks and flattened wild grasses, they walked across a rutted vale and ascended northerly into the rugged Bealbarnish Gap, huge craggy boulders on either side. Despite its spartan look from afar, the Gap was bespeckled with bell-shaped white and pink foxglove and patches of ubiquitous white hogwort.

A stiff northerly wind off the Atlantic passed through the Gap as they walked toward the sandy shores of Ballydonegan Bay. Allihies lay just beyond the Bay, its western boundary hugging the shores of the Atlantic. It was also home to Frank Twomey's pub, the only public house in the Allihies and Cloghfune townlands.

Stone-framed shanties were clustered along the wide, rutted path that served as the main road. A few more ramshackle shanties were scattered randomly over the surrounding terrain. Beyond the village loomed the gray sandstone peaks of the Slieve Mishkish mountain range. The destination, Mountain Mine, was perched on its southern slope, four hundred and fifty feet above the ocean.

As Padraigh approached the Bay, the sight of the foothills brought back boyhood memories of his father's anguished words: "Paddy, this land belonged to your great-great-great-grandfather. Fought noble, we did, at the Boyne, but we was beat. Me own da lost his five hundred acres to a bugger Royal captain. Truth is, they made us slaves."

Bedad! Nothing has changed. Same land where we try to survive, owned by Englishmen who won't set a foot in Ireland, same conniving middlemen, same threats of eviction.

If the copper mine don't work out, I got to be leaving the Beara to find work up north, else me family'll starve. Six more weeks to go afore the new crop's ready for harvest. Maybe this year will be different. If Twomey's right, a rich man from Wales, name of Puxley, will be needing mine workers.

As Denis strode nonchalantly beside him, Padraigh offered a silent petition. Me Denny, you must have a better life. Even if I die trying to get it for you.

CHAPTER 2

NO IRISH NEED APPLY

"Da! You hear that?" Denis asked.

"We getting close to the mine, lad."

"What're all them clanging sounds?"

"Not sure. Your schoolmaster said it sounded like nothing he's ever heard."

"Did he tell you how they did it?"

"Said they use a sledgehammer to break up big rocks, to find copper laced inside."

"Laced inside? What'd he mean?"

"Copper's green and is mixed in with big rocks. Hard to get at, he says."

Padraigh wiped his sweaty face with a dirty shirtsleeve as he and Denis walked up the steep hill toward the loud clatter. They soon reached a large, flat stone-strewn expanse of ground, a dressing floor. Denis's eyes widened as he saw young men wielding sledgehammers, splitting apart large rocks and workers pushing wooden-wheeled carts.

7

A few yards away, several women and children stood at a long wooden bench using smaller hammers to break fist-sized chunks of rocks into smaller pieces. While Padraigh and Denis stood watching, curious workers turned from their tasks to stare at them.

The silent face-off between Padraigh and Denis and the workers, was interrupted by a loud voice from a towering, thinly-built man, who barked, "Get back to work!" Those workers closest to the man, abruptly turned to their carts laden with large pieces of ragged stone and dumped them onto the dressing floor.

With arms folded, and a leather cap tipped back off his forehead, highlighting deep-set squinted eyes, the man strode across the dressing floor and stopped in front of Padraigh and Denis, glaring.

Padraigh looked into the man's eyes and spoke in heavily accented English. "Good morrow, sir. Me nem's Padraigh Murley. This lad 'ere's me son, Denis. Me 'n' me boy want work."

The man retorted angrily, "You'll not find work at Mountain Mine. No Irish here!"

Padraigh looked at him, expressionless. Almost immediately, his posture tensed, his eyes narrowed and his face reddened. A rhythmic tic began to pulsate on his temples. He pushed Denis to one side. With clenched fists, he thrust his face within inches of the man's and bellowed in Irish, "May the devil be a cat and bite your neck!"

8

"Get outta here! I'll never hire Irish," the man shouted back.

Dressing floor workers stared at the trio. Some smiled. Others were stone-faced.

Padraigh spat on the ground, grasped Denis's shoulder and, this time in English, cursed, "Go to the devil, you dog!" He turned away abruptly, pulling Denis along. "We'll not work for the likes of that arse."

They began the long trek down the mountain toward home. "Why does that man hate us?" Denis asked.

"He hates us 'cause we're Irish."

"Then he must hate everyone."

After a long silence, Padraigh explained, "Two years before you were born—1798 it was—Irish soldiers tried to take back our land. I was twenty when the Royal militias came through. We gave 'em hell, but we lost. Killed us, they did, without mercy. Women and chil'ren too. I'll never forget it. And I don't ever want you to."

"Schoolmaster Tucker don't want us to forget it either. But all I can think of is you leaving and the baby coming."

"I know, Denny, I know."

How can I leave Margaret and the unborn one? Maggie'll survive, begging or stealing, whatever it takes to feed the children. But Jesus, I don't want that. If them constables catch her stealing, they'll take Denny and Bridgee to the orphanage and put Maggie in gaol.

9

"I must be gone," Padraigh said, "but just for a few weeks. You will help Ma. Beg if you have to, but no stealing. Too dangerous."

"What about the lumpers the O'Tooles, O'Sheas and McCarthys are growing on our land? Won't that be enough for the rent?"

"If the lumpers grew like they should, them families would have enough to eat and pay us rent. Truth is, there's barely enough to feed them. Just like us."

"But it isn't right. And Schoolmaster Tucker says it isn't right."

"That all he said?"

"Said there's too many people who are poor and can't afford land. Farmers like us have to rent our land to others to grow enough food just to survive."

"Did he tell you that without them extra lumpers, we won't be able to pay our rent and we'll lose our land? Soon's we get thrown off, fifty more are lined up to take over."

Denis shook his head. "Didn't tell me that."

With a heavy sigh, Padraigh put his hand on Denis's shoulder. "Somehow we'll manage 'til harvest time. Just six more weeks to go."

When they arrived home, near midday, Margaret greeted them. "Did you get the work?"

Padraigh looked at the ground. "No. Won't take no Irish."

"Da cursed the man," Denis added. "Bad."

"I was hoping..." Margaret's voice trailed off.

Padraigh looked at her downcast eyes. Tears trickled down her ruddy, freckled cheeks. She said, "Denny, go inside and find your sister."

Denis headed for the shanty's dark entryway.

Padraigh moved close to Margaret and wiped away the tears on her cheeks with a sweaty finger.

Margaret looked into his eyes. "'Tis our fate, it is. Me own mother told me there's nothing can be done. English want us to suffer until there's no more of us. Or until we swear to be Protestants."

"Your mother was right about the suffering. But not about not fighting back. I was so angry this morning, I coulda killed the man, but something stopped me."

"Maybe it was the wee fairy sitting there on your shoulder. Thank the Good Lord for that."

"Weren't no fairy. It was something Schoolmaster Tucker told me. Said the way to fight back is to be educated. And part of that is learning to speak English."

"English won't do us much good," Margaret replied, "if we starve to death."

CHAPTER 3

BRIDGEE

Denis peered into the dimly lit earthen-floored main living space. "Bridgee! Where are you?"

Silence.

He scanned the rough-hewn stone and thatch-laced walls to see if she was crouched in the room's dark shadows. He looked under the rickety table next to the hearth and eyed the straw pallet that lay nearby. Reaching for the family's tin fiddle on the table, Denis strummed and sang Bridget's favorite song. "Where's me dancing girl?"

Again, there was silence.

He walked through a narrow doorway into the small room where the two Murley children slept on a wooden pallet covered by a worn cotton spread. Scant light entered through a tiny window. Beside a soon-to-be-filled wooden cradle lay Bridget, asleep on the earthen floor, her cheeks crimson, her breathing rapid. Denis reached down to touch her outstretched arm with the back of his hand. "No dancing today, little Bridgee," he whispered.

Returning to the living area, he yelled outside, "She's asleep, Ma. And hot she is!"

"Saw her playing with Bella early this morning," Padraigh said.

"But she stayed hidden. And no giggles when she heard your voice."

"This morning, she held her neck when she swallowed, like the porridge hurt her throat."

"Can you find Liam O'Rourke?" Margaret asked.

"Don't trust them fairy doctors. Never did. I can find Father Murphy."

"No! Too many children take sick and die. Can't take a chance. Need more than Father's prayers." Margaret turned from Padraigh and hurried inside. Denis was squatting beside Bridget.

"Father in heaven," Margaret said. "Evil fairies, don't take me wee Bridgee, me precious child. You already broke me heart forever. Have you no mercy?"

Margaret asked, "Did you walk over the fairy mound?"

Denis shook his head. "No, I never go over it. I remember what you told me."

Hands shaking, Margaret looked at Bridget closely. "I'm going to cast my eye," she said softly, "like Mrs. Riley told me, so I might know what's ailing me Bridgee. Her skin's not yellow like me boys, now in heaven, they are." She made the sign of the cross three times.

Margaret continued aloud as she pulled up Bridget's tunic. "Bridgee's skin is bright red. So's her neck, her chest and arms. Little bumps all over. Smaller than a flea bite, they are. Me boys' skin was dry and loose. Bridgee's skin is hot and sweaty and smells sour. 'Tis not the same as me boys. Their skin had a fishy odor. Least I know it's not what took them so quick. Thank you, Mary, Mother of God.

"She's not soiled herself, nor thrown up, and she even turned her wee head just now. Not the same as me boys, thank you, Lord Jesus. Did something in the soil make her sick? Something in the air? But the rest of us aren't sick."

Turning to Denis, she asked, "You're not sick, are you?"

Denis shook his head.

Then, she remembered. *No! Is the Lord punishing me for not wanting to have more children, like Father Murphy said? But why, God? Why would you make me Bridgee suffer?*

Peering intently at her crimson cheeks, half-closed eyes and placid expression, Margaret begged her to awaken. "Me Bridgee, you must open your eyes, so it is, you must."

She repeated her plea. Bridget moaned as her body trembled. Margaret remembered the shaking bodies of her suffering sons as they perished. *"No!"* she screamed.

Denis remained silent at Bridget's side.

Margaret leapt up, ran to the entryway and looked

outside. "I don't see the Banshee woman. I don't hear her wailing. Bridgee's safe. Least for now."

When Margaret returned, Denis asked, "What happened?"

"I feared the Banshee woman might be coming. So old she is, her white hair flows to her knees. When death is near, she takes to the sky, screaming so loud we must block our ears."

"Have you ever seen her?" Denis asked.

Margaret nodded gravely. In her hand was a straw Cross of St. Brigid that she'd grabbed off the wall near the entryway.

She knelt next to Bridget and touched her with the cross. "St. Brigid, I beg you, protect me daughter—your namesake—from the evil fairies."

Margaret then recalled what Mrs. Riley had told her when her three sons had become ill. Heart pounding, she looked at Denis. "Go to the brook. Get a bucket of water. Find two big clumps of sphagnum moss near the bog and bring them here. Quickly!"

"I'm going." Denis jumped up.

"Wait! Don't go over the fairy mound, and don't look up in the tree near the mound. Them evil ones may be just waiting to blast you."

Denis nodded and hurried out.

Minutes passed. Sitting at Bridget's side and clutching the cross, Margaret remembered with a shudder just like it was yesterday. *I was cutting peat wedges at the bog. Bridgee knelt next to me, playing like she does, squishing bog water from moss tufts. Just like them evil pookas to send a friendly old man from nowhere to try and take me child. Looked right at me and said, 'Good morrow, madam. I come from Ardgroom on me way to Urhan, but seems I's lost. Can you help me?' Didn't think nothing of it. Told him I grew up in Urhan and he needed to turn 'round and go the way he came. About two miles it was.*

That's when it happened. He looked at Bridgee. And now I see. He gave her the Evil Eye is what he did. Looked into her eyes and said, 'What a sweet lass you be.' Then he was gone. Never said, 'God bless you. My eye shall not punish you,' and he didn't spit. Never did, not even once. Mary, Mother in Heaven, he didn't do none of them things to break the spell of the Evil Eye.

Soon, Denis returned to the sleeping room lugging a bucket filled with water. Wordlessly, he put it on the floor next to Margaret, along with several large clumps of sphagnum moss.

Handing him a clump, Margaret said, "Here, Denny. Dab her legs with the wet sphagnum, while I cool her neck and arms."

"Like this?" Denis dipped the moss into the bucket and held it dripping onto the earthen floor.

"Do what I do. Not so much water dripping. You'll make mud, me fear."

As if blown in by the wind, Padraigh rushed in with the fairy doctor. O'Rourke's old black top hat covered all but a few wisps of his white hair and made him seem taller than he was. He wore baggy brown pants and a black suit jacket a few sizes too big. His deep brown eyes and ruddy, weathered countenance were well known in Cloghfune. He held a wand made of ash wood.

Clasping her hands together in prayerful thanks, Margaret bowed her head to O'Rourke. "Thank you for coming, Liam."

O'Rourke looked down at Bridget. "They already took her. 'Tis a changeling lying here. I must work quickly, for the hand of death is upon her."

"Oh, no!" Margaret cried.

"Shhhh. Please." O'Rourke held a finger to his lips. "I fear you may provoke a fairy blast. I have not the power to stop the wrath of a fairy blast."

Tears streamed down Margaret's cheeks. Padraigh put his arms around her. "Let us go so Liam can talk with the fairies."

"Yes," said O'Rourke. "There may yet be time, but they will only listen if I speak to them in private at the changeling's side."

Margaret, Padraigh and Denis left the sleeping room where Bridget lay and stood just outside the doorway. They listened to O'Rourke's incantations. After a few minutes of mysterious sounds coming from the room that sounded like different voices, there was a long silence.

Padraigh finally whispered to Margaret, "Who's he talking to, for Christ's sake?" He took a step toward the sleeping room.

Margaret grabbed his arm. "No! You must stay right here, or we may lose the only chance we have to get Bridgee back."

"I don't like this. Would've been better for Father Murphy to bless our suffering child." He reached in his pants pocket, pulled out his flask and took a long drink.

An hour passed before O'Rourke finally reappeared, hat and ash wand in one hand, his jacket draped over his arm. All Murley eyes fixed on him.

O'Rourke spoke calmly. "Evil fairies heard me every word. They're talking now, trying to decide whether to return Bridget."

He handed Margaret two small bunches of dried brown leaves and fragments of tiny, faded purple flowers. "This here's vervain. It'll make the changeling stronger so it won't die. When the changeling becomes stronger, your daughter will too. Up to the fairies to bring her back."

"What does that mean?" Padraigh asked.

"Can't be sure. They're an unruly, evil bunch."

Margaret looked at the vervain she held. "What should I do with this?"

"Put one stem with leaves and flowers in each of her hands and make fists so it stays in her palms."

"For how long?" Margaret asked.

"Long as it takes," O'Rourke answered.

Padraigh's eyes rolled heavenward. "What—"

Liam interrupted, "Now I must go. That'll be two shillings. One for me and one for the herb."

"Christ Jesus, ain't there anything else we can do?" Padraigh asked.

"Done all I can. Keep her cool like you're doing. Fairies don't like that. If they give her back, she'll need a lot to drink."

Padraigh dug deeply into his pants pocket and retrieved a shilling. "This is all I got. I'll owe you the other."

O'Rourke took the coin. "May the fairies know of your honesty, me friend, or I shall fear the worst for your wee sick daughter." Donning his hat, O'Rourke bowed to Margaret and walked out of the shanty.

CHAPTER 4

LABOR DAY

The morning after Padraigh and Denis were turned away at Mountain Mine, Colonel Andrew Hall, manager of operations, arrived at the mine. A retired Royal Marine, he was six feet tall and handsome with a muscular build. After reining in his purebred copper-brown horse, he dismounted and hitched the horse to a post in front of the recently completed Mine House.

Minutes later, John Puxley, owner of the mine, arrived in his one-horse four-wheel carriage. His post boy, Dillon, pressed the wheel brake and pulled sharply on the horse's reins, bringing the carriage to a quick stop. Jumping to the ground, he ran to the carriage door and opened it for his boss.

Ignoring Dillon, Puxley stepped down from the carriage, looked about and strutted toward the Mine House. Puxley's rigid posture enhanced his modest height of five feet six inches. He had a jutting chin and a sharp, straight nose between closely set dark brown eyes.

Over the din of the dressing floor, Hall yelled to the fast-approaching Puxley, "Good news, sir. Another large vein has been discovered in the open pit, near the east lode. Only problem is, it's buried under six feet of quartz. We blasted through yesterday and malachite stared back at us."

"That is good news, Colonel, but I need manpower to mine it. Workers won't arrive from Cornwall for at least a month. We'll lose a lot of money between now and then."

"Sir. I've got a plan." Sweat began to bead on Hall's forehead.

"There can be no delay. We need more surface exploration. Need to excavate an adit to intersect with the east and west lodes. More sinkings. This is our time, Hall. Are you with me?"

"I'm with you, sir. I plan to hire local men, women and children. The men will work open pit until we start sinking. Women and children will work above ground, sorting, jigging and buddling."

"No!" Puxley answered. "That'll never do! The Irish are uncivilized. They'll try to kill us. Besides, they don't speak English. How would we talk to them?"

"I've a friend, sir, name's Peter Lord, who served with me in the Royal Marines. Speaks Irish and understands these people. I'd like to bring him here, at least for the hiring."

Puxley stiffened. "No, Hall. They are a backward people. Not the Irish."

"Sir, I've thought a lot about this. Even though most of the Penal Laws are gone, the Irish here on the Beara have nothing except the potato. I believe they want a decent life like everyone else. Besides, we can pay them a lot less than the Cornwall workers we've already hired."

Puxley paused, considering the logic of Hall's last words. "Just get me some honest workers who'll do their jobs. I need them here by the end of the week." He turned quickly and strode toward his carriage.

"Yes, sir," Hall replied to Puxley's back.

By God, I can do this. I led men in battle and I'm still a leader of men. I'll find strong men who can wield a pick, sledge or shovel twelve hours a day, six days a week. I'll show puffed-up Puxley he's got the right man.

Hall walked toward his horse, intent on traveling to the nearby townlands to find workers.

"Another thing, Hall," Puxley called out from his carriage. "Before we bring up more copper, the road to Balleydonegan Bay must be built. Copper's piling up in the yard. Two of my ships sit empty in the harbor. Investors want answers." Without waiting for Hall's response, he turned to Dillon. "Let's go!"

"Yes, sir," Hall shouted. "I'll have those workers for you and get that road built." He took quick, long strides to his horse as the carriage pulled away.

It will be simple. Farmers plant their potato crop in March, around St. Patrick's Day. Potatoes won't be ready for harvest

22

until fall, early September the soonest. Last year's harvest is running thin. People are hungry. Before the men leave the Beara to find work, I'll hire them. And they'll be thankful to make half the wage of English workers.

Hall's confidence was offset by painful recollections. He thought again of Peter Lord, an Anglo-Irishman and his Royal Marine compatriot on a day fifteen years earlier when he'd learned of Irish inclination to lawlessness and revenge. *I need Lord here. He knows the Irish. Saved my hide that day, and other times too. I must find him, but today I must find workers myself. Where do I start? Now that the summer hunger is on the Irish, they drink their own brew at home. I'll go to them.*

Turning his horse southward, Hall slowly descended from the rocky terrain. He rode toward Allihies' main dirt roadway and stopped at Twomey's pub.

Frank Twomey was perched behind the makeshift bar, a wooden plank held up on each end by a wooden barrel. "Top o' the day to you, Colonel. Need some strong drink, do you?"

"Good day, Frank. Not today, but I do need your advice. I'm looking for locals to work the copper mine up yonder."

"Can't see Irish farmers being mine workers, but if there's money in it, who knows?"

"We're already excavating. You've met some of the Cornwall workers?"

"I have. Seem like good blokes, even though they're Brits and come from across the sea. Some townlands ain't too far from here—Cloghfune, Killaugh and Leanmore. Cloghfune's a good place to start."

Twomey gave him directions. Hall thanked him and continued his journey, riding past Ballydonegan Bay and up through Bealbarnish Gap. The terrain became more rolling and easier to traverse as he neared a shanty village overlooking Bantry Bay.

When he came upon an unusual outgrowth of beech trees and a line of uneven, low-lying hedges, he heard a man's voice and stopped to investigate. Upon dismounting, the only sound was the rustling of leaves swaying in the warm ocean breezes. He walked toward the copse of trees, taking in the sight. *Must be a hedge school. These people don't yet know the law has changed and these children can be educated openly. Information must travel slowly in this part of Ireland.*

Twelve children huddled on the ground next to the protective row of bushes. Ten boys and two girls. A man stood in front of the children. His ruddy complexion, white hair and beard, and slightly stooped posture posed uncertainty about his age. *Must be the schoolmaster, though he doesn't look like any teacher I've ever seen.*

The presumed schoolmaster held a well-worn book in one hand, *Child's New Spelling Primer.* He turned toward Hall, his arms outstretched as if to protect his charges.

"Have no fear," Hall said and offered his hand.

"Good morrow to you. Me name's Tucker. Most call me

24

Tuck," Thomas Tucker replied in English, grasping Hall's outstretched hand.

"I'm Hall."

"Hall, eh? Where you from?"

"Copper mine on the mountain," Hall said, pointing north. "I'm looking for workers for the mine."

Tucker pulled a flask of poitín from a dirty pants pocket, opened it and offered it to Hall, who declined. Tucker took a long swallow, capped the flask and returned it to his pocket. He turned to the children and, in English, said to a boy about nine, "Tadhg, practice the words on this page. Have each one speak out loud."

With a smile, Tadhg jumped to his feet, took the book from Tucker, and returned to the children, motioning for them to sit in a circle.

Turning back to Hall, Tucker said, "You may be too late. They're readying to leave the Beara to find work before the next lumper crop's ready. Truth is these folks don't even have spuds to pay me. Teaching these wee ones for free, I am. I got to move on, else I'll starve too."

Hall glanced at the raggedly clothed children sitting in a circle, reciting English words at Tadhg's direction. "Where are their parents?"

"Over yonder. See that patchwork of land and shanties there?" Tucker pointed to a large dip of land checkered with even rows of green plants growing in random stone enclosures.

"Much obliged, Tucker." Hall prepared to mount his horse.

"They know nothing other than farming."

"They can learn, can't they?"

"What do you know about 'em, Hall?"

"I was in the Royal Marines. Here on the Beara. I know plenty. But things have changed these fifteen years past. I can offer them work so they won't go hungry waiting for harvest."

"All good, Hall. Do you know why our population here on the Beara is so swelled we're on the brink of collapse? Do you know that we keep dividing our land and our landlords keep raising our rents and we keep having more children to feed? If we can't pay, we're out. If the price of spuds goes down, we're out. If our children get sick—well, you know the rest."

"I do know. Fact is, I need the farmers and they need the work," Hall said.

"Right you are."

"Tucker, I'd like to offer you a job. Help me talk to them in their language. At least until I get workers hired."

"Can't. My place is educating Irish children. The Penal Laws made it illegal for them to get an education and illegal for me to teach them. But don't worry. The children'll help you. Many know English, as I've taught them. Irish will always be in their heads and hearts, but they need English to survive. Their parents don't see that yet. They're embittered."

"What about you, Tucker? Are you embittered?"

"How could I not be? But me hope's with the children."

"I've no quarrel with that, Tucker. But right now my hope is with you."

"Aye, Hall. I'm trying to keep me own hope alive. Things are changing, but not fast enough. Some in the Parliament think that educating Irish children will make them loyal, forget about popery. Others think the Irish are only good for tilling the soil. So, Hall, what do you think?"

"I think there's hope for them working in the mine, earning money."

"Earning money would be new to these folks. I thought Puxley would bring in his own workers from Cornwall."

"He's doing that, but copper's being mined faster than the crews can ready the ore for shipping. Need more workers."

"I hear copper's like gold. Your King George is desperate to defend against Napoleon's ravings. And now he's at war with America. Can't fight wars without warships. And can't build a ship without copper."

"That's true. Copper's price has never been higher," Hall said.

There was a long pause. The two men looked at each other.

Tucker broke the silence. "Changing me mind, I am. Guess I can help you for a while."

"Can you come with me now?"

Tucker held up a hand. "A moment, Hall."

He returned to the children, who were reciting spelling words. "Thank you, Tadhg. Lads and lasses, class is over for the day. Keep practicing your words. We'll be reading next time."

One of the two girls spoke up in a soft voice. "Schoolmaster, me ma and da told me I can't come back for a while. No pence 'r spuds to pay you."

"I'll talk to your ma and da. You need to come back, little Rose, or there'll be no way for you to read, now will there?"

"I'll not be reading, Schoolmaster."

"Then, I expect you back. Remember, it takes time to build a castle."

The class chimed in unison, "Rome wasn't built in a day, Schoolmaster." The children rose from their heather-laced seats on the ground. Tucker gave each of his students a pat on the head as they filed out of their hedge enclosure and ran toward their shanties.

CHAPTER 5

RENEWAL

Hall walked his horse alongside Tucker as they followed the children toward the cluster of shanties. Nearing their destination, Tucker recognized Liam O'Rourke trudging toward them, his eyes fixed on the path.

"Good morrow, Liam," said Tucker.

Liam looked up. "Good morrow, kindly, Tuck."

"Did you heal one of me children?"

Liam glanced at Hall, hesitated, then spoke softly. "Hard to say. 'Tis a changeling."

"Who's the poor one?"

"The Murley lass," Liam replied. "We'll know by the morrow."

"Thank you, Liam."

"No bother, Tuck." Liam resumed his slow-paced walk.

Tucker recognized Padraigh up ahead, standing outside his shanty, flask in hand, talking and gesturing to neighbors.

29

"This may not be a good time," Tucker said. "If they've lost the child, we can turn 'round now."

"We've got to try," Hall replied.

"Wait here. I don't hear any wailing. 'Tis a good sign."

Leaving Hall a few yards away from the group, Tucker approached. "Padraigh Murley, how's your wee daughter?"

"Don't know, Tuck. O'Rourke says the fairies haven't decided whether to give her back."

"Sorry for your trouble, Paddy."

Tucker turned and pointed. "This here's Hall from the copper mine on the mountain. He's looking for workers."

Blue eyes blazing with fury, Padraigh flexed his elbows and clenched his fists. His temples were pounding. He strode past Tucker and faced Hall head-on. Hall's height did not slow Padraigh's threatening advance. The unsuspecting Hall stood silent as Padraigh hurled Irish epithets at him like lead balls shot from a blunderbuss.

Hurriedly, Tucker stepped between the two. "Now, Paddy, me friend, listen to the man. He's here to help you from your troubles."

"Evil's what he is!" Padraigh spat on the ground at Hall's feet, turned on his heel and stomped toward his neighbors.

Tucker put his hand on Padraigh's shoulder. "Paddy! You're filled with venom. You must say why."

Padraigh spoke passionately in Irish about what had happened to him and Denis hours earlier. Tucker translated the story for Hall, who said to Padraigh, "I'm sorry for how you and your son were treated. We need the likes of you, your son and others here. If you come to work at the mine, you will earn money. You won't have to leave your family. This is a chance for you and your son."

Padraigh scowled at the ground as Tucker translated Hall's apology and offer of work. Emboldened by poitín, Padraigh thundered, "For Christ's sake! I don't want me family to starve, but I ain't going to be treated like a damned cur!"

Hall stood a scant two feet from Padraigh, looking downward to meet his eyes and spoke, after which Tucker translated. "This work is for strong men who want to earn a living. You'll work with other men, topside and underground, to blast and bring up copper. I also need boys like your son—and womenfolk, too—to get the ore ready to send by horseback to Ballydonegan Bay for shipping."

Denis suddenly appeared at the open shanty door, "Da!" he screamed, "Ma needs you!"

Wide-eyed and raising both hands, Padraigh signaled for Tucker and Hall to wait. He dashed inside to where Bridget lay and sighed in relief to see her arms moving restlessly.

Then his eyes turned to Margaret's bent, rigid pose. He stood frozen until she finally turned toward him. "The baby's coming. Send Denis to fetch Mrs. Riley. You must sponge Bridgee when I can't no longer."

Padraigh nodded, his heart pounding. He hurried outside to where Tucker and Hall waited. As he approached, he took a long slug of poitín from his flask and faced Hall.

"Me wife's having the birthing pains and me wee daughter's near death. We want the work, but can't go 'til this is over."

Tucker translated.

Hall, eyeing the other men gathered at the Murley shanty, remained silent while Tucker and Padraigh engaged in an animated exchange in Irish.

Finally, Tucker spoke to Hall. "Padraigh and his son want the work. He wants to know when they must be at the mine."

"I need them in two days. Six thirty sharp."

Hall looked around. "Tucker, we need to talk to these other men and go to other shanties, too."

By the end of the day, Hall and Tucker had recruited sixteen workers—men and boys—with the expectation that more would follow.

CHAPTER 6

NEW LIFE

Denis burst into the entryway and announced, "Mrs. Riley be here soon's she can. There's another baby coming, she said."

Margaret lay on the straw birthing mat. "Find Mrs. O'Shea, me birth helper. Fast as you can." As another contraction began to envelop her, she yelled, "Hurry!"

"Ayyyeeee!" Margaret's scream pierced the confines of the shanty and sent Denis flying out the door. Margaret's face was contorted in pain, her eyes tightly shut. Two minutes later, as the rock-hardness of her uterus eased, the rest of her body relaxed. She lightly massaged her domed abdomen, whispering, "A little more, me baby. Just a little more."

Padraigh appeared from the sleeping room, where he had remained, sponging Bridget during Margaret's increasingly strong contractions. Perspiration glistened on his forehead as he peered at his disheveled wife on the birthing mat.

33

"For the love o' Jesus, where's your helpers?" He crouched down on the floor beside Margaret.

"Ayyyeeee! It's coming! It's coming!" Margaret howled.

Padraigh had no time to curse the absence of the midwife or Mrs. O'Shea. Seconds after the last contraction, another began. With a loud guttural noise, Margaret began pushing. Padraigh leapt up and scurried to support the baby's emerging head, his hands and arms shaking. "Blond hair I'm seeing."

Two more strong contractions followed. The infant's entire head, and then shoulders, appeared during the second, followed by the rest of its body. "A boy! 'Tis Colm!" Padraigh shouted as he held the newborn clumsily.

Margaret lifted her head and smiled at her newborn son. Seconds later her smile disappeared. "He ain't breathing! Turn him over!"

The baby lay lifeless in Padraigh's hands.

"Come on. Come on, breathe. Breathe!" Padraigh jiggled the newborn from one side to the other.

"Put his head down at your knees and pat his back. Pat him! Keep patting him!"

Minutes passed. Colm was bluish gray and not moving.

Padraigh continued patting the infant's back. He said softly, "Come on, come on, come on."

Suddenly, mucous spewed from the infant's mouth onto Padraigh's weathered boots. Before he could give another pat to Colm's back, the infant breathed in and for the first

34

time exhaled, releasing mucous and birth fluid. Then came a series of loud cries. Like a chameleon, Colm's bluish hue turned pinker with each breath and lusty wail. Margaret and Padraigh gave each other the kind of smile that seldom passed between them in their daily lives.

Holding out a faded towel, Margaret instructed Padraigh to swaddle Colm. "Don't worry 'bout the cord. Mrs. Riley'll tend to it."

Just minutes old, Colm continued to cry loudly while he was being wrapped by his fumbling father. Margaret propped herself on one elbow, her smile suddenly gone. "Now!" she screamed. "Baptize him right now. Them evil fairies will do everything in their power to grab our baby and leave us another changeling. They'll not do it. I'll kill them first, I will. I swear I will." Her eyes darted around the dimly lit room.

Padraigh looked at Margaret in wide-eyed amazement. "Och!" she screamed. "The fairies are getting ready to take him. Baptize him! Get the water afore it's too late." She held out her arms, beckoning to Padraigh. "Give him to me!"

"For Christ's sake, wife!" Padraigh exclaimed, handing Colm to her. "How am I—"

"Now do it, you must!" Tears streamed down her face.

Padraigh looked at Colm, now nestled quietly in Margaret's arms, his eyes closed. "He looks only a wee weary to me, he does. And weary he should be, I'm thinking."

"Don't matter." Holding Colm to her breast, Margaret started to sit up.

"Jesus, Mary and Joseph! Don't get up, woman!" Padraigh strode to the hearth, filled a ladle with cool water and quickly returned. Margaret had propped Colm's head over her arm, ready for the soul-saving rite.

"Ain't real holy water, like the priest has," Padraigh said.

"Don't matter!" Margaret yelled. "Do it now!"

Just then, the birth helper, Mrs. O'Shea, appeared in the shanty entrance, trailed by Denis. "Go to Bridgee, Denny. Go quickly and keep sponging her," Margaret said. Without a word, Denis hurried to the sleeping room.

Before approaching Margaret and the newborn, Mrs. O'Shea spat three times toward the pair, insuring Colm would be protected from the curse of the Evil Eye. "I stopped for the holy water. Couldn't come sooner. Me own baby moved today, and I feared me pains would start if I was with you when you had your pains. Didn't even know I was having another baby until today when it moved."

Listening to Mrs. O'Shea, Padraigh concluded, *This ain't men's work. Birthing's women's business. Nothing's going right. Fairies are in control. Wee Bridgee is fighting to return and take the changeling's place, and now Margaret thinks Colm will be taken by the fairies. What if she's right? I need Father Murphy here to talk sense. But he won't be back in Cloghfune until next week. Too late.* Still holding the ladle, Padraigh pulled the near-empty flask of poitín from his pocket and finished its contents.

"Here, Paddy." Mrs. O'Shea took the ladle and handed him a vial of holy water. "Baptize him with this."

With a frown, Padraigh returned the empty flask to his pocket and took the vial from Mrs. O'Shea. Then, pouring a few drops of holy water on Colm's forehead, he recited the familiar Christian rite: "I baptize thee in the name of the Father, the Son and the Holy Ghost." Margaret voiced a sigh of relief.

The placenta delivered on its own during the baptism. Mrs. Riley arrived at the shanty a few moments later. She spat on the floor as Mrs. O'Shea had, greeting Margaret and Colm and thrusting a worn wood-handled knife toward Padraigh. "Here, Paddy, clean it."

Relieved, Padraigh stood up from where he'd been kneeling next to Margaret and Colm, dunked the knife into the pot of hot water on the hearth and rubbed the blade between his fingers.

Mrs. Riley studied the umbilical cord still linking Colm to the afterbirth. She took two short pieces of twine from her pocket, knotting the first piece around the glistening, pearly-colored vessel an inch from Colm's belly. The second piece she knotted around the vessel about an inch from the first. Taking the knife from Padraigh, she cut through the umbilical cord between the knots and looked carefully at the placenta. "'Tis healthy." She placed the bloody organ in a metal pan and handed it to Padraigh. "Bury this."

He carried the pan with its contents to an edge of their potato plot. *How many more of these will I bury? Six so far. 'Tis too many children we be having. If Father Murphy is preaching the truth, we ought to be having a baby every year. He may preach different if it was him who had to feed 'em.*

Using his potato spade, Padraigh dug a hole three feet deep, laid the placenta in the hole and prayed aloud, "Lord, protect Colm from earthly evil as you receive his gift."

He made the sign of the cross, then filled the hole with dirt.

Meanwhile, Mrs. Riley unswaddled the now-sleeping infant and looked intently at him. "How soon did Colm first breathe?" she asked Margaret.

"Not right off, but after a while. Paddy patted him on the back."

Nodding, Mrs. Riley began bathing Colm in a basin she had brought with her. After drying him, she put a swatch of charred cloth covered with pig fat ashes over the umbilical stump and wrapped a cotton band snugly around Colm's abdomen to hold the cloth in place. "Keep this on for two weeks. I'll come by to check it after a few days."

Padraigh, now returned from burying the placenta, asked, "Mrs. Riley, can you check on our wee Bridget? Don't know if she'll be given back to us. Liam O'Rourke told us 'tis a changeling."

"Did he now? I will see to her."

After placing Colm in Margaret's arms, Mrs. Riley said, "I'll send Denis in to meet his brother."

Padraigh wearily lowered himself to the floor beside Margaret and Colm, when Denis burst in from the sleeping room. "Bridgee's eyes just opened! She looked at me! Da, come see for yourself!"

"I'm coming," Padraigh said, hoisting himself up.

Mrs. Riley was already at Bridget's side. "She'll come back, Paddy. But it'll take time."

Without a word, Padraigh knelt down and gently caressed Bridget's red, sandpapery cheek. As he reached for her hand, her fingers lightly grasped his outstretched index finger.

"Thank you, Jesus," said Padraigh.

"Can't be forgetting to eat, nor you neither, Denis," Mrs. Riley said. "There's some buttermilk broth, potatoes and fish, left by the Kellys and the O'Neils." Turning toward the main room, she added, "Now, I must go."

"Thank you, Mrs. Riley," Padraigh said.

He turned to Denis. "Me lad, fill a bowl of gruel while I carry Bridgee to the table. I will hold her while you feed her."

"But I haven't seen my brother yet."

"Quickly, lad. We need to hurry so them evil fairies don't change their minds."

Denis joined the now sleeping Margaret and Colm, who was enveloped in Margaret's embrace. Denis bent down, looking closely at Colm's face. "We'll be doing our chores together before long, little brother. And Bridgee too – soon as she's strong again."

He stood straight, turned to the hearth kettle and ladled a bowl of porridge. He took it to his father, who was holding Bridget in his arms. Padraigh propped Bridget upright in his lap and raised her sagging chin.

Both father and son watched Bridget slowly open her mouth when Denis prodded the spoon between her parched lips. She swallowed the porridge.

"A bit more, me Bridgee, then you can rest," Padraigh whispered.

Denis continued to feed her small spoonfuls of porridge until her mouth clamped shut. She fell back to sleep, breathing rapidly.

"Are you ready to work at the new copper mine?" Padraigh said. "We start in two days."

"But, Da, you said we'd never work there. Ever!"

"Och! Forgot to tell you, lad. So much has happened since this morning. Schoolmaster Tucker brought a man from the mine here, Hall by name, who has work for us. And other farmers, too."

"You mean you don't have to leave?" Denis asked.

"I wouldn't tell you if it weren't true. The Lord has blessed us today with Colm and work at the mine. Let's hope we'll soon be blessed again." Padraigh looked down at Bridget, asleep in his arms.

CHAPTER 7

NEW HIRES

Padraigh and Denis stood on the dressing floor at Mountain Mine, along with fourteen other newly recruited Irish workers. Farmers all, they were bearded and wore ragged shirts and overalls, worn boots, and wide-brimmed straw hats. Facing them were Colonel Hall, Thomas Tucker and two other men standing beside them.

Colonel Hall spoke first, "Good morning, gentlemen. Tons of copper are waiting for you to dig, above and below ground. Different than growing potatoes. We're going to show you how."

Hall waited for Tucker to translate his words into Irish. The workers stood expressionless, looking at Tucker.

Hall continued, "We already have Cornwall workers here who have dug tons of ore, ready to be shipped to England. Problem is, there's no road for carriages to take the copper to Ballydonegan Bay, where a ship is waiting. Captain Daniel Egan here next to me knows how to build a road and he's going to explain that to you. Next to him is Captain Richard Glasson. You'll be seeing a lot of him. He's going to help get you started digging copper. While Tucker translated, Padraigh's eyes widened, staring at the man called Richard Glasson. *Gentle Jesus, that's the bastard I could've killed.*

Daniel Egan was a foot shorter than Hall. His short-brimmed leather hat was pulled down low over his forehead, obscuring his eyes. Egan stepped forward and said, "Here's where I come in. You start today to build the road. It must be finished in two weeks. If you do what I tell you, we'll finish. If you're lazy, you'll be tossed. Without pay."

After Tucker's translation, omitting the threat, Egan instructed the men to gather picks, shovels and axes from a nearby pile and stand ready for a hard day's work—or be sent home.

Tucker's translation again softened Egan's hostile words. "Be ready for making a day's wage. Hard work it be, but the tools in that pile will lessen your load."

Hall said, "While you're working on the road, your sons will start work with the ground crews. This is where big ore chunks are broken into smaller and smaller pieces."

Egan interrupted. "Give me the micks now. Can't stand around idle. They don't need talking to. They need to bend their backs."

"Take it easy, Egan," Hall said. "They'll be bending their backs soon enough."

Egan's muttered response was unintelligible.

42

Clusters of workers were on the dressing floor, mostly Cornwallian men, their wives and a few children. Some worked in the open, while others stood in three-walled wooden sheds protected by a narrow overhang that served as a roof. Still others toiled at waist-high benches, open to the elements. V-shaped wooden troughs mounted on the ground in front of the workers' benches were filled with water pumped from the mine's open pits and from small natural reservoirs on the mountain slopes.

Several boys pushed wooden-wheeled carts, laden with large blocks of ore from the nearby open pit, to the dressing floor. Raggers, all strong-looking young men, took the carts, dumped out the ore, and returned the carts to the boys. Sledgehammers in hand, the raggers broke the large blocks of ore into smaller chunks.

Without Tucker to assist with translation, Hall spoke slowly to the five boys gathered around him, "Look at me, lads." He pointed to Denis, Seamus and Ryan, the biggest boys of the group. "You three are raggers." Then, to the remaining two boys, "You are pickers. Wait here for me to take you to your captain."

Hall pointed to a muscular Cornwall teenager a few yards away who wielded a large wooden-handled sledge-hammer. "Raggers. That is your captain, John."

John swung the sledge handily, breaking a three-foot-diameter chunk of ore into smaller, green-impregnated pieces that fell upon the stone-cobbled dressing floor. As he was about to swing his sledge at another large block of ore, Hall interrupted, "Hold it, John. These are the workers I told you about. Show them how to use a sledge."

"Yes, sir," John replied. "We got ore piled so high on the floor we could use ten more raggers."

"True, we're backed up. See if these lads can keep up with you. But first show them how, so they don't break their backs or lose an eye."

"Aye, sir."

"I'll send my translator over if needed, but these three understand English pretty well. Right, lads?"

Denis responded for the trio, "Yes, sir. We do."

The ragger captain handed a sledgehammer each to Denis, Seamus and Ryan, then ordered, "Watch me."

John demonstrated the grip needed to wield the most force. He lifted the sledge effortlessly over his head. Then, bringing it swiftly downward, he slid his right hand down the handle to meet his left at the handle butt and delivered a sharp smashing blow to the ore block. It split into several large chunks.

"That's how it's done. Do some practice swings." John pointed at the dressing floor.

Denis and Seamus smiled slightly and nodded. Ryan grimaced.

After the novice raggers had completed a few practice swings, John said, "That's good enough. Let's get started. Remember, big swings come from your body, not your arms. Straight down on those blocks."

In the meantime, Hall had walked with the two smaller boys to a covered shed adjacent to the dressing floor, where pickers were breaking up smaller pieces of ore using large hammers. As they approached the picker captain, Elia Haines, her small brown eyes remained fixed on the rocks strewn on a long bench. She was clad in an ankle-length gray dress, her hair tightly bound in a bun just above the nape of her neck. She quickly tossed some rocks into a trough and almost simultaneously tossed others over her shoulder onto a rapidly growing pile on the dressing floor.

"Good day, Mrs. Haines," Hall said.

Looking past Hall, she nodded. Then, after glancing at the two young boys, she returned her gaze to the rocks.

"You're in good hands, lads. Mrs. Haines knows copper better than most. She'll show you how to pick the good from the bad, right, Mrs. Haines?"

"And how'll I talk to them?" Mrs. Haines asked.

"They speak English fairly well. They'll be able to follow your instructions."

"If they don't, there'll be trouble."

"Trouble?"

"I'll not put up with the likes of Irish brats."

"But you said trouble. What did you mean?"

"If they can't do their work properly, I'll be penalized. I won't allow it."

"Mr. Puxley and I are counting on you to bring these boys along, and treat them decently," Hall replied. "Many more Irish women and children will be hired. If you want to continue to work here as a captain, do what's expected of you."

Mrs. Haines' face visibly tightened. She nodded her understanding and motioned the boys closer to the wooden surface of the picking table.

"Lads, follow Mrs. Haines' instructions. Do as she tells you." Without waiting for a response from the boys or Mrs. Haines, Hall turned and strode away to find Puxley.

CHAPTER 8

STANDING GROUND

At lunchtime, the newly hired raggers, Denis, Seamus and Ryan, found a shaded area under a lone birch tree, close to the dressing floor. They sat on the ground to eat their meals of potato gruel and tea. Denis said, "I'm sore, but I like smashing them rocks."

"Aye, 'tis not too bad," Seamus agreed, rubbing his overworked shoulder.

Ryan, the shortest and smallest of the three, looked at them through a tangle of dirty blond hair. "Don't care about sledging. And don't care about speaking English to them British thugs."

"But working here means our das won't have to leave the Beara," Denis said. "And that means no begging. Or stealing."

Seamus and even Ryan nodded in agreement.

Two English raggers, who looked older and were bigger than the three, approached. In profanity-laced English, the larger of the two declared their ownership of the shady

47

eating spot. "Ain't no room for more dirt. Get yer arses outta here, you feckin' Paddies."

Seamus stood and faced the two boys. "We was just leaving," he said in English. "Wonderin' we was why it stunk so bad." He held his nose.

Denis and Ryan also stood up. As the three walked past the two taunters, one stuck his foot in Seamus' path, tripping him. His fall to the hardened ground was hastened by a sharp whack on his shoulder. Lurching forward, Seamus struck his forehead on the jagged edge of a rock. He got quickly to his feet, put his hand to his forehead and then rubbed his eye. At the sight of blood covering his hand, he blanched and dropped again to the ground.

Denis rushed to Seamus' side. Blood spurted from a deep gash on his forehead. "Wake up, Seamus!" Denis yelled, shaking him by the shoulders. He looked up angrily at the English ragger who had hurt his friend. Then, to the other ragger, Denis screamed, "Get help!" The ragger hesitated, then ran toward the Mine House.

Ryan lunged at the ragger who had attacked Seamus, screaming ferociously in Irish, "You cat devil!"

The ragger yelled, "Crazy Irish midget! I'll kill you!" Swinging their fists and kicking furiously, they fell to the ground, rolling about, trying to land punches. Denis watched the fracas while he tended to Seamus.

Colonel Hall and Puxley were walking toward the dressing floor, discussing the number of additional raggers that would be needed, when they spotted the melee under the birch tree.

Striding ahead, Hall got to the pair quickly. Grabbing Ryan's shirt collar, Hall pulled him off the English boy effortlessly, as if he were pulling a shrub of heather from the ground. "What in Hades is going on?" Hall demanded.

Denis looked up and nodded toward the assailant. "Ask him."

The attacker, with a bloodied and torn shirt, sputtered, "They was just sittin' around, the lazy arses."

Hall looked at Denis and Ryan. They were silent.

Arriving at the scene, Puxley demanded, "I can't have this! Who are these boys?"

"These three are local raggers," Hall answered. "This is their first day." Nodding toward the other boy, he added, "That one is from Cornwall."

Daniel Mahoney, the mine doctor, joined the group, accompanied by the English ragger who had gone for help. Dr. Mahoney bent his large frame down to determine the extent of Seamus' injury. "He needs stitches—the cut is deep and wide. He fainted is all. Rouse the lad and take him to the Mine House."

"Oh, come now!" Puxley said. "He doesn't need stitches. He needs to get back to work."

"Without stitches, the gash will fester. Take much longer to heal. He won't be able to work."

Hesitating, Puxley returned Mahoney's gaze. "All right! Stitch him up, then send him back to the floor."

Turning to Hall, he continued, "This is not going to work. Did you forget that the English and Irish have killed each other for hundreds of years?"

"No, sir, I haven't forgotten, but we need workers. I will find them, we'll train them and I *will* keep order. It takes time."

"I have no time, Hall," Puxley bellowed. "I hired you to get this copper lode excavated and on a ship that has been ready to sail for three weeks."

"If you'll give them a chance, they will succeed."

"They better succeed by the time I return from Wales— or else." Puxley drew a deep breath, as if he were going to say more, but after a brief pause, he exhaled, turned and strode away, muttering to himself.

John came upon the scene. "Heard about the fight," he said to Hall. "Looking for my raggers."

"They're ready, except Seamus. Doctor Mahoney will fix him up and send him back to you."

"Good. Four more carts of ore need to be ragged before the evening bell rings."

Denis was still crouched beside Seamus. "I need to help me friend to the Mine House."

"No," Hall said. "You and Ryan go with John. We'll send Seamus back to the dressing floor soon as he's stitched."

As Denis helped Seamus get to his feet, John took a rag from his pocket and pressed it firmly on Seamus' bloody forehead. "Hold it there so it'll stop bleeding."

Seamus walked unsteadily with Hall and Dr. Mahoney toward the Mine House. As the raggers returned to the dressing floor, John said, "All of you were hired to break down ore, not to break each other's heads open. Keep your anger to yourselves, else you'll no longer be working here."

CHAPTER 9

REALITIES

Near quitting time, John shouted, "Hey, oh! Finish the block in front of you. Be here on the morrow. Six-thirty bell, same as today."

With a groan, Ryan dropped his sledge and looked at his reddened, blistered palms. Wincing, he crossed his arms, balling up his hands into protective fists.

"For tomorrow, wrap your hands." John said to the three new raggers.

Ryan stared at him.

John mimed wrapping his own well-calloused hands. Ryan nodded, then looked away, his hands still curled into tight fists.

Leaning against a post near the ragging area, Padraigh waited for Denis, Ryan and Seamus. *Me boy looks like he's been swinging that sledge all his years, instead of digging with a spud spade.*

After putting away their sledges, the three novice raggers joined their fathers for the three-mile walk home.

"What happened to you?" Seamus' father peered wide-eyed at the stitches on his son's grimy forehead.

"'Twas them Brits. They don't like us. And I don't like them."

"Me neither," Denis added.

"One was a dirty fighter. Tripped Seamus, but I laid into his arse," said Ryan.

"We just about finished lunch when two raggers saw us and came over to pick a fight," Seamus added. "They wanted more than the ground we was sitting on. Wanted our blood, they did."

Padraigh appeared calm, though his temples were pounding. "Sometimes fighting back makes things worse."

"What're you saying, Paddy?" Seamus' father asked. "I seen you in fits now and again. What if it was Denis got beat up?"

Padraigh hesitated. "Not sure."

"You don't want Denny to protect himself?"

"No, I ain't saying that. But we just started working here, and already a fight."

"Them Brits would just as soon kill us as not," Ryan's father added.

"You may be right. But if they want to get copper out the ground, surer 'n' the devil, they need us," Padraigh said.

Silently, Padraigh recounted his own first workday. *Never seen so many stumps, rocks, weeds, and pit holes in a quarter mile. Took eleven of us breaking our backs all day, but, by God, we got that bugger boss Egan's goddamned road started, even though he yelled at us all the day long. We'll show him, we will.*

Nearing Cloghfune, the men and boys paired off as they approached their homes. When Padraigh and Denis arrived at their shanty, they heard loud, angry cries. "'Tis Colm, Da. Something's not right. Crying loud as a squealing pig, he is."

Mrs. O'Shea sat outside on the birch bench, trying to cradle the squirming, screaming three-day-old in her arms atop her pregnant abdomen. The early evening sun cast a dim light on her worried face.

"For the love o' Jesus, what's wrong with him?" Padraigh asked.

"Been a terrible day, Paddy, it has. I'm feeling weak meself, I am. Baby's been crying too much. Won't take Margaret's milk. She's got fever and been bleeding."

Padraigh frowned. "Did you fetch the midwife?"

"No. Couldn't leave Margaret, nor Bridget, neither. The lass, she hasn't stirred much, not much at all."

Padraigh turned to Denis. "Go fetch Mrs. Riley. Tell her we need her."

"Hope I can find her." Denis trotted off.

Padraigh looked at Colm helplessly. "Mrs. O'Shea, can you stay awhile longer?"

"Me own chil'ren need me, and me baby inside is making

54

me tired, it is. Only so much I can do. But I'll be back on the morrow."

"Can you wait 'til I talk to Margaret?"

"Sure 'n' I will and bring Colm to her."

Carrying the still-screaming Colm in her arms, she followed Padraigh as he entered the dimly lit shanty. Margaret lay on the birthing pallet, her color matching the grayish-white sheet that covered her. Padraigh knelt at her side.

Eyes drooping, Margaret tugged on his shirtsleeve, pulled him toward her, and whispered. "The fairies ain't done yet. They coming to take Bridgee for good. They plugged me milk and are making me bleed."

"No, crazy woman. Ain't no fairies. Remember what Father Murphy told us? Be still now while I go check on Bridgee."

Margaret turned away and closed her eyes. "You are wrong, you are. So's Father Murphy."

After looking in on Bridget, Padraigh returned. "Our wee one is still with us. Very weak, but she knew me. Needs food 'n' milk, she does."

Margaret cried softly. "Colm needs milk, too. Mrs. O'Shea's been trying to help him nurse. But he don't get any. They going to take us all."

"Quiet, woman! There's no one will be doing that."

Denis returned home alone and went to his mother's side. "Mrs. Riley can't come now because she's helping birth Mrs. Dolan's baby down the way. Said she'd come early on the morrow. Said your milk's ready to flow today and you must keep trying to nurse. And drink as much as you can. Said nursing Colm will help your bleeding."

Mrs. O'Shea tried once again to position the crying Colm to nurse. Margaret's eyes opened wide as Colm latched onto her nipple and began sucking, tentatively at first, then more vigorously. A thin, whitish-blue liquid flowed into and around Colm's mouth. "Them fairies must have pulled the plug. Me milk is flowing now, it is."

Margaret, Padraigh, Denis and Mrs. O'Shea watched Colm's suckling success. Padraigh pulled the flask of poitín from his pocket, took a long drink and looked heavenward. "Thank you, Sweet Jesus."

"Denis, me lad, I fear you must be as hungry as me. Get a big bowl of gruel and share it with Bridgee. I be getting a bowl for me and Ma."

"Sure, Da."

"Then go lay yourself down."

"I will. Aside Bridgee, I will."

Rising well before dawn on Colm's fourth day of life, Padraigh milked Bonine Bo, replenished the peat fire and added milk and potatoes to the kettle. The evening before, he had brought three large pails of water from the nearby brook, one for drinking, the other two for washing their bodies and their utensils. He poured Margaret and himself a cup of sweet tea that Mrs. O'Shea had prepared. Handing Margaret the tea, he mused. *Takes at least an hour to get to the mine. Working all day, me back is breaking. Food's scarce. Margaret's weak. And Bridgee to worry over. Jesus. How am I going to do this?*

Colm had cried loudly and often during the night, but slept after each nursing. Most of the nappies that Mrs. O'Shea had made for him had been soiled. Looking at Colm, now asleep in his cradle, Padraigh caressed his swaddled backside. *Me boy is going to live. Now I pray to Jesus for Bridgee to come back to us.*

Padraigh woke the sleeping Denis. "Time to eat before we leave."

After feeding Bridget, Denis said, "She took some gruel, Da. Still breathing hard. Don't seem much like she's back."

Denis and Padraigh saw that Bridget's face was swollen, making her freckles look stretched and shiny. Padraigh shuddered. *This ain't me Bridgee. Maybe Margaret's right. Maybe them devil fairies did take her.*

Just as dawn showed itself and Padraigh and Denis were ready to leave for the mine, Mrs. Riley arrived. "May God and the Virgin Mary bless you, Mrs. Riley," Padraigh said.

"Good morrow, Padraigh. How're Margaret and the little one?"

"Both doing better. Her milk's flowing."

"The lass, Bridget?"

"She's astir, but barely. We're keeping the herb in her hands. She don't seem much better."

"She taking milk or water?"

"A little. Mostly milk, now and then."

"Wait until I look at Bridget, then you can go."

"Sure, and I will, but there's no carriage waiting to carry us. We got to be there before the bell rings."

Mrs. Riley went quickly to the room where Bridget lay. After examining her, she gathered Padraigh and Denis to Margaret's side. "Bridget'll get better in time. Keep coaxing her to eat gruel and tea. Not too much milk. Tea is better. Children sick like Bridget don't take milk well. Makes them swollen and puffy, like she is this morning. I'll check her again on the morrow."

"Should Denis stay here today and see that Bridget has her gruel and tea?" Padraigh asked. "Mrs. O'Shea will be busy with Colm and Margaret. Need nappies washed, bathing water and gruel for Margaret, too."

"But ain't you both readying to leave for the mine?"

"'Tis true, but we must do everything we can to help Bridgee live."

"But Da, I told Seamus and Ryan I'd be sledging with them today," Denis protested.

"Copper'll be there for sledging long after today, lad."

"Them Brits'll think I'm a... a dosser," Denis said, screwing his face into a grimace.

Margaret, silent to this point, said, "Denis, go with Da. Mrs. O'Shea'll be here, helping me and Bridgee. Now go. You must, I say."

Denis's face brightened.

Silently acquiescing, Padraigh knelt down to Margaret, caressed her cheek, and then beckoned Denis. The two left the shanty just as daylight began to break over the Beara.

CHAPTER 10

HARVEST TIME

Richard Glasson walked toward the group of eight workers and asked, "Where're the others?"

Padraigh answered, "Lumpers is ready. They be back soon's digging's done."

Glasson shook his head. "You arses. Don't any of you come back unless you're going to be here every day."

In silence, the men shuffled their feet and looked away from Glasson, his finger stabbing in tempo with each angry word he spoke. "See that pit? Filled with water from last night's rain. Can't do any blasting until it's emptied. Pump's broken. Use the kibbles in the tool shed to bail it."

The men all avoided Glasson's fiery gaze. "Get it done!" he snapped, "Now!"

Once out of Glasson's earshot, Padraigh said, "You're the goddamned arse. Least we don't have to see his puss until the pit's ready for blasting." The others nodded as they walked toward the nearby tool shed.

60

Hours later, Hall was talking with Tucker in front of the Count House when Glasson strode up, his eyes fixed on Tucker. "I told those lazy Irish not to come back if they don't plan to be here every day. Most of them stayed home to dig potatoes."

Hall frowned. "You can't do that, Richard."

"Yes, I can. And I did. We can't work our bargains when fifty Irish are supposed to be here and only eight show. Besides, more Cornwall workers are due soon."

"If you call seven weeks 'soon.' There's another delay. Their housing isn't finished. No Irish workers, no copper."

"At least the few Cornwall workers we have show up every day," Glasson said. "That's more than I can say for the Irish." He kept his eyes on Tucker as he spoke.

Tucker returned his stare. "Well, me friend, they built your road in two weeks, the first shipment of copper's crossing the Irish Sea, on its way to Swansea, and they're sledging and pickaxing in the open pits. Sure you did the right thing?"

"I know about you, and your so-called hedge school."

"Calm down, Glasson," Hall interjected. "Puxley left me in charge of all operations. Go back and tell those men we need them to come to work every day. But no threats. Do you hear me?"

Glasson scowled at Hall.

"Take Tucker with you, so they understand all of what you're saying."

"Don't need him. Besides, them dumb Paddies had no idea what I said."

"Yes, they did. I talked to them at the pit," Tucker said.

Hall interrupted. "Whether they did or not, make sure those workers know they have jobs or you'll be packing your bags. There's a lot to work out—potato harvest, flooding, supplies, blastings, sinkings, shipping. We can get it done, but we need Irish workers to do it."

Glasson gritted his teeth, turned abruptly and strode toward the flooded pit.

"'Tis men like him and the road maker, Egan, that tell me I must return to the children."

"Tuck, you're the reason I've been able to hire workers from the townlands. They trust you."

"I know. And I know that Glasson has scorn in every word he speaks to Irish men and womenfolk. The young'uns know it better than their parents, because they understand more of his words."

"Glasson's like many English—educated, Protestant, from an old English family—even an earl in his kin, so he tells me. I don't like his buggering attitude either, but I need his mining know-how."

"I still need to get back to me hedge school, so our children can learn to live in dignity."

"But I don't like losing you. When do you plan to leave?"

"Today, pushed by that hopeless arse." Tucker pointed to Glasson. "Besides, I need to return to me Poor Scholar.

He's been studying with me these past two years, and filling in teaching the six weeks I've been here."

"Why can't he continue without you for a few more months?"

"'Fraid it's not that easy. I'm his teacher while he's teaching students. When we both think it's time, he'll ask to challenge me. If it happens he knows more, he will take me place as schoolmaster, and I will leave to find another hedge school. I'm smarter than most, so I don't worry. Been that way long as I know."

"I understand, but I don't like it. You put a lid on workers' discontent like balm on an aching back."

"'Tis not a problem if workers are treated fairly. That means fair wages, too. Irish workers know they're paid less than Cornwall workers."

"I'll look into it," Hall replied.

"Before I leave today, I'll tell the workers what you said."

"Don't make any promises."

Tucker nodded and smiled. "I be remembering that. You be remembering I'm teaching the young'uns at me hedge school. That's where I'll be."

Hall returned Tucker's smile. "Good luck to you, Tuck."

"Luck to you, too, me friend," Tucker said as they shook hands.

Hall's attention shifted to the pickers' table, where Elia Haines sat alone, her face austere, tossing rocks forward and aft. "Good morrow, Mrs. Haines."

"The children ain't here, as you can see. I'm happy as I'll ever be."

"They're not here for a good reason."

"Knew they wouldn't last long."

"They couldn't do the work?"

"No, they learned quick enough what was copper and what was junk, but they squirmed, wiggled, talked. And they were messy, too. Distracting, they be."

"Just like children, were they?"

"Aye, I s'pose you could say that. More trouble than they're worth."

"They're home digging potatoes. It's harvest time. But they'll be back, with their stomachs filled. Good day, Mrs. Haines." Hall touched the brim of his hat and walked away.

Hunger, potato harvest, low wages. And Tucker quit. Where are you, Peter Lord, my Anglo-Irish compatriot? Dublin, I trust. I need to find you, my good friend.

CHAPTER 11

THE LETTER

Sitting at his desk, Hall reread the letter he had just penned to his longtime Royal Marine compatriot, Peter Lord.

27 September 1813

Dear Peter,

It has been some time since I thought about our military service here on the Beara. I have returned as a civilian overseer for a newly opened copper mine located in the Slieve Mishkish Mountains near Allihies. An English businessman, John Puxley, is the owner.

This time I am here to support the Irish, not quell their revolt, as we did in 1798. Even though it is hard to see any real change in this part of Ireland, I sense a new hope has come to this barren, rocky land since the mine opened four months ago.

Puxley agreed to hire Irish farmers as laborers. With the help of a local hedge schoolmaster, I've

65

hired fifty Irish workers so far—men, boys and a few women and girls. He has brought miners and workers from Cornwall, but their hiring and resettlement has been slow and costly.

The demand for copper is high and we have discovered the lode is huge. We are in need of a much larger cadre of Irish workers. Many are hanging back. We have already had fights and trouble between the Irish and the English. But no deaths. Yet.

I remember the lessons I learned from you.

Without your knowledge of the Irish peasants and their ways, I believe even more deaths would have occurred during the Rebellion.

Will you consider working with me again, this time to hire Irish workers and smooth the sharp edges of animosity and mistrust between the two groups?

Your friend and compatriot,

Andrew

Andrew Hall, Overseer

Puxley Mine Company

Hall folded the letter so there would be a free space to write Lord's address and affix his seal. Soon he was engulfed in remembrances of his last military campaign, when he and Peter Lord had been on assignment on the Beara Peninsula.

Like it was yesterday, Hall recalled their 1798 mission to ferret out pockets of escaped rebels after the Irish defeat at Vinegar Hill in Wexford County. On a particularly hot summer day, he and Lord were on horseback in the town of Enniscorthy. The horses had just negotiated a span of uneven rocky terrain when the men heard screams. "Help! They going to scalp me!" yelled a desperate captive who'd caught sight of the two soldiers.

The gruesome scene lay in a clearing under a small copse of tall beech trees. Three white-shirted men had overpowered a small thin man and tied him to a tree. One assailant held the struggling man's head immobile while a second crudely sheared hair from the captive's head with a scythe. A third man aimed a blunderbuss pistol at him. On the ground lay a metal bowl of smoking hot tar.

"Halt, you damned fools! Throw down that pistol. Now!" Hall yelled. Peter Lord repeated Hall's commands in Irish.

The three attackers stepped back when they saw Hall and Lord pointing weapons at them. The man with the pistol stood firm.

"Damn them Whiteboys!" Hall said as he glanced up at the dark roiling clouds overhead. Without warning, a streak of jagged lightning lit up the sky. Simultaneously, a deafening clap of thunder erupted. A nearby tree flashed momentarily, both halves of its split trunk toppling to the ground. Rain pelted everything.

The attackers cowered, their shoulders hunched and their heads lowered.

The two battle-trained horses started to rear. "Easy, boy. Easy, boy." Hall and Lord tried to calm their mounts, pulling the reins to prevent them from bolting.

The three offenders were now at the mercy of the violent thunderstorm. "Let that be a message from God to each of you," Lord said.

Shaking in terror, the victim said, "I'm a middleman, come here to evict these men and their families. Ain't paid their rent for nearly a year. Out by tomorrow or else."

"Who told you to evict them?" Hall asked.

"The owner, James Pierce."

"Where's Pierce?"

"He don't come here. Lives in England."

"Untie that man now," Hall fumed.

Once released, the victim fled.

"I'd like to talk to them, to get more information," Lord said. "All right with you, Andrew?"

Hall frowned, but he nodded.

"You with the blunderbuss! Put it away if you want to see your wife and children again," Lord shouted.

The drenched gunman hesitated before lowering his pistol.

Lord walked toward the trio as the rain slowed. "Any of you been pitch-capped before?"

"No, but we know plenty who have been. By your brave Royal soldiers."

"Hot tar burns the scalp down to the skull, you know that?"

"That coward deserves far more," one of the men answered.

"They'd sooner burn our cabins and let us starve," another added.

"Do you know any other ways to get what you need besides robbing, mayhem and murder?" Lord asked.

"Look what they done to us. We're about to be without land or cabin. Might's well be dead."

"Well, you're not dead, are you? Where will your families go after eviction on the morrow?"

The soaked offenders stood mute.

Finally, one spoke up. "The poorhouse. I've got me five children—one just born—all ages to ten, they be."

Two others told of wives and offspring they would be leaving.

"You're all under arrest," Lord said. "But, God willing, your families will survive."

Following the arrest of the Whiteboys, Lord and Hall headed back to their quarters in Wexford. During the ride, Lord said, "These men were desperate, thinking they could make things right by killing whoever offended them. Even if they succeed, they fail."

"Can't let them get away with murder, Peter."

"No, of course not. Even though thousands of Irish have been slaughtered in England's quest to conquer them."

"Whose side are you on anyway, Peter?"

"On the side of fairness, but there is none. My father is English, a Member of Parliament. My mother is Irish. She raised me. I know both sides—a different history than you know. Their families will not survive if they have no crop to eat, no place to live. I don't trust the constabulary, but less so that thieving middleman, who nearly got himself pitch-capped."

Hall was still staring at the letter when his thoughts returned to the present. *I need Lord to help me keep order between the Irish and Puxley's people. Puxley's people, eh? Am I one of "Puxley's people?"*

CHAPTER 12

MASS ROCK

In a secluded setting about a mile from the Murley farmland, a craggy outcropping of rocks jutted up among a small cluster of trees. To one side of the outcropping was a large table-like rock. It served as Father Murphy's altar, Mass Rock.

The congregation stood on uneven rocky ground interspersed with grassy scrub. Many were closely huddled to ward off penetrating gusts of cold wind.

Families and friends were talking quietly, waiting for Father Murphy to begin Mass. The Murleys stood in the front of the gathering, along with other families who held infants.

Three-month-old Colm lay concealed in a heavy blanket in Margaret's arms, save for a wisp of blond hair that peeked out. Padraigh held the sleeping and swollen Bridget, bundled in his arms. Denis stood between his parents.

The diminutive priest wore a thin ankle-length white alb over his black suit, and a stole of green satin draped about his neck extended in uneven halves to his knees.

Father Murphy looked more like an altar boy than a priest in his oversized priestly garb.

When he took off his three-cornered black silk biretta, his shaggy nape-length brown hair blew in the wind around his pale, youthful face. His piercing blue eyes scanned the congregation, pausing briefly on each worshiper.

In a loud tenor, the priest began. "Good morrow, me brethren. We're grateful for this glorious Sabbath day and the blessing of our newest children. Our feet may feel chilled, but our hearts are filled with the warmth of the Holy Ghost. We welcome the gifts of our loving Savior in the names of Colm Murley, Daniel Mulligan, Camille O'Shea, twins Christina and Margaret O'Neil, John Padrig O'Rourke, and me own wee nephew, Shawn Murphy. This is our greatest glory—growing our Catholic community."

Father Murphy stepped away from the altar and approached the infants. He blessed each one with holy water, making the sign of the cross on each forehead praying, "May the Lord Jesus Christ, who loves all children, bless you, and keep you in His holy care, now and forever."

Each parent, in turn, said "Amen."

Father Murphy paused and clasped his hands in a prayerful pose. "'Tis unfortunate one is born in our congregation who has no heart nor soul for the Lord's blessing. I remind each family gathered here, having children out of wedlock is a sin, indeed, a mortal sin. Join me now in silent prayer for those lost souls."

The congregation stirred. A few glanced nervously about. Some nodded slowly. Father Murphy bowed his head for a long minute, then said, "Me brethren, I know of forced tithing to the Protestant Church. 'Tis the law, so you must. But I ask each of you to give a coin so I may keep the holy flame burning for your souls. I ask this not for me, but for our Catholic Church and Jesus Christ."

Father Murphy paused, then continued, "Many more of you are here at Mass, and the Good Lord blesses us this day. He sees the wee Bridget in her father's arms, struggling to get better. He sees Riobard Murphy taking too much of the drink and failing to be here this morning. The Lord knows of the merrymaking at the wake of Sean O'Leary last week. Remember, 'tis a sin to indulge in impurity at a beloved's wake. 'Tis a sin to sing and dance while mourning a dead soul. Our Lord in heaven knows what you are doing."

Some in the congregation lowered their heads. Others looked straight at the priest with inscrutable expressions.

"He knows me ways, too. I am one of you. I was born here on the Beara twenty-eight years ago, child of a farmer, just like you. Me calling came early, it did. Parents, keep your hearts open to a calling for your sons. Pray for the priestly vocations to guide our growing flock. Remember, too, your daughters, and listen for their calling to the convent. All are needed in Christ's name. Amen."

A few scattered "Amens" followed.

After Mass, the churchgoers broke into smaller groups and began walking back to their homes. Seeking relief from the cold wind, Father Murphy removed his stole and alb and was donning his heavy coat when Schoolmaster Tucker approached. "Thank you, Father, for your prayers and blessings."

"You are welcome, Tuck."

"No blessings for the wee one, Mary Callahan, Father?"

Father Murphy stiffened. In a soft voice, not his preaching voice, he said, "No, Tuck. A sin's a sin. The road to heaven isn't paved with illegitimate children."

"But you know both families, Father. They're not bad people. You were not here to marry young Katherine and Jack until the baby was nearly due. The families quarreled. And now both are living at their own homes as before. No reason for shunning, is there?"

"Yes, there is."

"Why?"

"Because these farmers don't know the difference between folklore and the Catholic faith. Now it's no longer a crime to say Mass, we must strengthen the Church, build a moral force. It takes a sermon like this one to help me flock learn to obey Catholic rules. The Archbishop called me and others back to the seminary a month ago. He told us what we must do. No churching of unwed mothers and their babies. Catholics must go to Mass every Sunday and Holy Day, and confession, too. No more wakes that turn into hijinks and orgies."

"You're looking to turn all us sinners into saints, eh, Father?"

"No. I want disciples. Disciples who'll learn the faith and practice it, not run around spitting in the wind to foil evil fairies."

"I understand, Father, but you need to know other facts if you don't know already. You haven't been back here for long, have you?"

"Nearly a year, Tuck. Graduated Maynooth January last."

"'Tis harsh here. Poor, ignorant farmers. You know that?"

"Were you listening to my sermon? I grew up here."

"There's another faction, Father. Aside from the flock you are trying to make obey and give money to the Church, there's a new gang of Whiteboys in these parts. That means trouble, Father. Used to be they'd go after the middlemen and estate owners, or their animals. They wanted revenge for being gouged again and again, first by rents they couldn't pay, then by tithes to the Protestant Church. I don't want to see any harm come to priests who're holding out a hand for money at Sunday Mass."

"But, Tuck—"

Tucker interrupted, "Hear me, Father. A priest friend from Cork visited me at hedge school this week. Told me Whiteboys warned him to return the money he collected in the Mass basket. Belonged to the farmers, they said. Priest refused to return it. They came looking for him, beat him up. Took all his tithings and more. Don't want that to happen to you, Father."

"'Tis me vocation. I'll not be bowed by misguided souls. We been tormented too long, stunted. Now that the law's moving in our favor, we must rope in our flock."

"May be true, Father, but Whiteboys hear you asking poor farmers for money, they may rope you in. Or worse."

"I am ready. I am here to serve the Lord and our people."

Tucker shook his head. "Isn't there any way you can help save the soul of wee Mary Callahan?"

"I cannot waiver. People here on the Beara have to learn to be true to Catholic teaching."

"'Tis a shame. Going to be a painful life for that innocent one."

"I will pray for her. That's all I can do. Good day, Tuck." Father Murphy placed the biretta on his head and, raising his right hand, blessed Tucker with the sign of the cross.

"That's all, Father?"

The priest did not answer. He draped his alb and stole over his arm and walked at a brisk pace toward his two-room stone parsonage. The parsonage stood apart from the ramshackle shanties in Cloghfune, about a quarter of a mile from the Mass Rock, near his parents' home.

Once inside the parsonage, Father Murphy felt the warmth of the hearth's peat fire, still aglow from early morning. Lingering next to the hearth, he thought about his own superior lodging compared to that of his parents and his three sisters. They lived in a dilapidated shanty, elbow-to-elbow with six other family members.

I couldn't help it if my parents said I had a priestly calling from God. What's wrong with being favored, aside from the misery it caused my brothers and sisters, and me too, because they taunted me every day? If I hadn't been the one chosen to attend hedge school, I wouldn't be here today. I'd not have become a Poor Scholar. I'd not have been able to study at Maynooth Seminary.

Now I am entrusted with a flock of poor sinners. Archbishop says I must use fear and shame to help them be true to Church teachings. And I must collect tithes, too, with all its danger if the Whiteboys come 'round. I pray for wisdom.

CHAPTER 13

AFTER MASS

Denis broke the silence as he and his family walked home from Mass. "Da, why doesn't Father Murphy like us anymore?"

Padraigh shifted Bridget to a more comfortable position. "Me lad, he likes us. Just wants us to do better."

"How?"

"By being closer to Jesus and the Church."

"He acted mad. Didn't bless Bridgee like he usually does. Is she being punished, too, like little Mary Callahan?"

"No, 'tis different."

"Why? Neither one did anything wrong."

"Guess you'll have to ask Father Murphy."

Denis looked up at Bridget, her eyes open, her head resting on her father's shoulder. He flashed a smile at her and beckoned with his arms. "Hey, little Bridgee, come down here!"

Bridget's soft murmur sounded like his name.

"She knows me! She wants to get down, Da!"

"Patience, Denny. One day soon, maybe she will."

Inside their shanty, the Murleys sought warmth and solace at the hearth, still emitting heat from the glowing peat ashes. Margaret handed Padraigh the blanket bundle that held a crying Colm while she removed her coat and sat in a chair by the hearth. After loosening her smock and bodice, she retrieved Colm and deftly put him to her breast. His hungry cries were replaced by gulping sounds.

Margaret stroked Colm's forehead. "There, there, love. Don't rush. We've time."

"I hope you are right, me Margaret," Padraigh said from the far side of the hearth.

"About what?"

"That we've time. That cheating arse Sutchins came 'round yesterday. Raising our rent 'cause we rebuilt them stone walls for the subtenants' plots. Rent's coming due in a couple of months."

"You must raise the rent for all the families."

"Won't do no good, it won't. They got no potatoes to sell, don't even have enough for their own broods to eat. And Declan's wife's near birthing. Lost count of their children."

"Six after this one." Margaret paused, then raised her eyebrows. "I heard they're still looking for workers at the mine. Earn money they would. They got to pay their share, else we'll be evicted, too."

"'Tis true. I told Hall about the O'Toole brothers and the others subletting our land. He wants to talk to them and any others I know. I'll start now with the O'Tooles. Denis, stay here and help your Ma with Bridgee."

"But I want to go with you, Da."

"Bridgee needs you here, she does."

Taking Bridget from his father's arms, Denis rested her swollen body on the hearth, holding her upright. "She don't seem like Bridgee anymore."

"Lord willing, in time, she will," Padraigh replied.

"The Lord ain't willing, Paddy, and you know it." Margaret's voice was loud and angry. "Been three months since she took ill. She's getting weaker and weaker. Eating poorly she is, not playing or dancing or even talking."

Padraigh thought, *I do know it*. But instead of answering, he pulled the flask from his pocket and took a long drink.

"Still a changeling, she is. Did you pay the fairy doctor what we owed him for the vervain?" Margaret asked.

"Haven't seen him. Besides, I don't have a shilling to pay."

"Well, I do." She took two shillings from her smock pocket and handed one to Padraigh. "Take this to Liam O'Rourke before you go to the O'Tooles. Maybe he can break the spell."

"Where in the love o' Jesus did you get two shillings?" Padraigh didn't wait for an answer. "Don't matter, I ain't paying him no more. I don't believe he did anything, except squeeze us."

Silently, Margaret rocked Colm in her arms, rhythmically rotating her torso left and right. Her rosy cheeks defied the darkness that reigned in the Murley shanty. Finally, she looked at Padraigh. "You're wrong. Bridgee's still alive, ain't she?"

"Look, a doctor works at the mine, a real doctor. Just for mine workers, but maybe he'll help our Bridgee."

"He won't know nothing about the fairies taking me wee child."

"Jesus, Mary and Joseph, woman! Forget them damned fairies!"

"Can't. And you are foolish to forget them. Pay Liam O'Rourke before them fairies take her for good."

"I won't. Pay him yourself." Padraigh took another long swig of poitín and walked out, brooding. *Always pressure, never lets up. That slime bugger Sutchins making himself a rich man. Forced tithes to the Protestant Church. Now Father Murphy and the Catholic Church want in too. Won't be able to pay the rent unless the O'Tooles and the others come through.*

Declan O'Toole stood outside his shanty. "Good morrow, Deck," Padraigh called.

"Good morrow, kindly to you, Paddy."

"I have news for you and Sean. He here?"

"No. Gone to Bally Bay. Scouring the rocks for dulse. Never knew about that red seaweed 'til we come to the coast. Helps fill empty bellies."

Padraigh nodded. "How you be getting along?"

"As good as the day is going to get. Saw you and your little ones at Mass. And what am I not a sane man to hear the good Father Murphy be asking us cottiers for money? Did I hear him correct?"

"'Fraid you did, Deck. Guess he don't get money from the Bishop, or the Pope neither."

"Some around here know we supposed to give money to the people who need it most. Not the Pope 'r the Bishop."

"Just so happens I got good news about making money. You interested?"

Declan's deep-set brown eyes widened in surprise. "Not much else matters if me chil'ren ain't got enough to eat. Course I'm interested."

"Man named Hall wants to talk to you and Sean about working at the copper mine. Lots of copper needs to be dug up. Blasted, too."

"The mine, eh? Heard you're working there. Back-breaking, ain't it? What's the pay?"

"You won't get rich, but you'll feed your family, keep a roof over your heads. I'm making near two shillings a day, depending on the copper we able to dig."

"Dunno, I don't, Paddy. But me and Sean will go see the man. Hall's his name, you say?"

"Right. Your boy, Ambrose, may be able to work there, too. How old is he?"

"Ten."

"That's young, but they need workers. Me boy, Denis, thirteen years, is working. Getting on okay, he is."

"What about school?"

"Has to wait. Don't like it, though. Father Murphy said he'd like to help children who work at the mine. Maybe have classes on Sundays, in English, after Mass."

"Won't help much if he keeps taking money from poor folk who're barely surviving."

"What're you thinking, Deck?"

"Us cottiers are one step down from you. We got nothing. We don't like seeing money taken from us and put into the priest's pocket."

"If you have some idea of going after that money, it'll come back to bite you. And if you get caught, they'll be a-coming after me, Margaret and the children, too."

"It ain't a bit fair, is it?"

"I'm warning you, Deck, best stay away from Father Murphy."

"Don't take to warnings much, Paddy."

The men eyed one another. Padraigh nodded, turned, and walked back home.

CHAPTER 14

CHOICES

Bridget lay on a straw mat, in a fitful sleep, breathing noisily. Margaret sat next to her, stroking her forehead, nursing six-month-old Colm. Denis and Padraigh had just finished breakfast and pulled on their woolen caps, ready for the trek to the mine.

"Denny, I need you here to help with chores. Bridgee is failing," Margaret said.

"But I'm s'posed to go with Da," Denis said, lunch pail in hand.

"He's needed at the mine," Padraigh added, "Can't you get a helper? Maybe Mrs. O'Shea."

"No, I can't. Mrs. O'Shea's baby's ill. Open your eyes and ears, Paddy. Bridgee's in trouble. Gasping at times, she is."

"But Da's right, Ma! They don't like it when raggers ain't at work."

"I can't help Bridgee if I'm feeding Colm, fetching water, milking Bonine Bo, cutting peat, and gathering seaweed. She needs me. Now."

84

Margaret grasped the handle of the milking pail and held it out to Denis.

Denis kept his hands at his sides for a long moment. Eyes downcast, he finally took the pail, put down his lunch pail and stomped out of the shanty.

"Telling his cap'n that he won't be working today won't be easy," Padraigh said.

Grasping Padraigh's arm, Margaret pulled him toward Bridget. "Not just for today, Paddy. Look at our child. I need Denny to stay here 'til she's better. Or..."

Padraigh watched the labored rise and fall of Bridget's chest and listened to the gurgle of each breath. He looked at her sallow skin and her swollen body.

"She ain't taking much gruel," Margaret said. "Chokes easy. Takes a long time to swallow. Almost seems like she can't."

Padraigh breathed a heavy sigh. "She's very sick, I know. But she's strong. They're bidding new mine jobs today. If I don't leave now, I'll lose out."

"If Denny's here, I can manage."

"Be home soon's I can."

"Don't be lagging at Fitzie's shanty, nor Twomey's neither."

"Won't. Must go."

"Wait. What about the mine doctor? Maybe he'll see Bridgee? Mrs. Riley says there's nothing more we can do. And Liam O'Rourke's not been back."

"He likely ain't been back because we owe him a shilling. And I told you, I ain't paying him. I'll ask the mine doctor today, but I don't think he'll see her. She ain't a mine worker." Lunch pail in hand, Padraigh left for the mine.

In the quiet of the shanty, save for Bridget's ragged breathing, Margaret looked down at the nursing Colm. Drops of milk trickled from the corners of his mouth. Suckling contentedly, his blue eyes widened and met Margaret's. Colm was the first to smile.

Despite her desperation, Margaret returned his smile, pulled him close and hummed a lullaby from her childhood.

The next day Margaret rose before sunrise. She nursed Colm, then put Bridget in the special chair Padraigh had made so she could lie in a half-sitting position. "Ah, there's me strong wee lass. Pretty she be." Margaret fed Bridget slowly, tiny spoonfuls of potato gruel. "Swallow, Bridgee. It'll make you strong."

Bridget opened her eyes.

"She hears me. I know she hears me! Oh, thank God!" Smiling, Margaret added, "And when you get strong, we'll have fun like we used to, me wee love."

Bridget continued to look at her mother.

"Dancing and singing and running. You'll see!"

With the next spoonful, Bridget closed her eyes, coughed hard, and forcefully expelled a mucous glob and most of the gruel she'd eaten.

"Rest for a while, me Bridgee," Margaret said as she cleaned up. "I'll try again before we leave." Tears filled her eyes, spilling over.

"And where is it you're going, woman?" Padraigh asked.

"You still don't see, do you? Bridgee ain't getting better. I know no more how to help her. Maybe the mine doctor can help."

"Didn't see him yesterday, so couldn't ask him. Can't you wait a few more days?"

"A few more days I fear will be too late."

"What if he won't see Bridgee? Or ain't at his office in the village?"

"I know he will see her."

"And how is it you know?"

"I held the Cross of St. Brigid last night and prayed, I did, and she answered me. I feel it. The doctor will see her today and cure her."

"Is it now Father Murphy's words I'm hearing? You think St. Brigid's Cross is able to outrun them evil fairies?"

"If I could find me fairy helpers from when I was a child, they would know how to bring Bridgee back." Tears flowed in little rivulets down Margaret's cheeks. "We must try to save our little flower any way we can."

"And we will. But remember what Father Murphy taught us. Fact is, Jesus, Mary, Joseph and the Holy Ghost may not be able to save her."

"I have faith. They and all the saints in heaven would not take Bridgee from us."

"Maybe." Padraigh looked away.

"St. Brigid's Cross will guide us to the mine doctor today."

Close to sunrise, the Murleys set out for Allihies. Padraigh carried Bridget while Margaret and Denis took turns carrying Colm. When they arrived at the newly constructed office of Dr. Mahoney in Allihies, Denis turned to his parents. "I'm going to the dressing floor. Hope John will be happy to see me no matter I ain't been there for a while. I'll tell Colonel Hall you can't work today, Da, but you'll be back tomorrow."

"Right, Denny."

"Bye, Colm. Bye Bridgee." Denis poked her puffy cheek. With a wave to his parents, he trotted up the mountain trail toward the mine.

The Murleys stood in front of the office, waiting until midmorning. When Dr. Mahoney appeared, Padraigh spoke first.

"Good morrow, Doctor. Me daughter is sick. Has trouble breathing. Can you help her?"

"I'm not the village doctor," Dr. Mahoney replied. "I've seen you before, Murley. Aren't you supposed to be working?"

The doctor's eyes moved to Bridget. He pulled back the cover from her neck and chest. With each breath in, her neck muscles became tight, while her ribs stood out like ridges on a washboard. "Bring her inside."

In the office, Padraigh held Bridget while Dr. Mahoney examined her. He shook his head. "It's not good news I have. Her heart is failing. Water in her lungs is making it hard for her to breathe. She's swollen because her kidneys aren't strong enough." The doctor held up a thumb lancet. "She must be bled. It's her only hope."

Margaret shook her head repeatedly.

"Her death will be painful if she is not treated soon," Dr. Mahoney said.

"If you can save her, you must do it," Padraigh answered.

"Me midwife, Mrs. Riley, told me that taking blood, like you say, can kill. She says 'tis dangerous."

"You came to me for help. This is what I can offer. It's the best treatment we have."

Padraigh ignored Margaret's protests. "Thank you, Doctor. When can you help our wee daughter?"

"It must be now. Her blood humor is poisoned." Mahoney took a metal basin from a wooden cabinet and wiped the thumb lancet with a dry towel. "Murley, hold her arm tightly. No movement. Once I pierce her vein, blood will drain into the basin here. Need to bleed an ounce. No more, no less."

Dr. Mahoney pierced Bridget's vein, deep in the fold of her arm. Blood rose to the skin surface and dripped slowly into the basin. Dr. Mahoney periodically squeezed her arm to increase the sluggish flow of blood.

Bridget did not react. Margaret bent close to her ear and whispered, "Me precious one. Don't give up."

After the bleeding, Dr. Mahoney wrapped a bandage around Bridget's arm. He told Margaret and Padraigh, "If you see blood on the bandage, press hard on it. Do you understand?"

They nodded.

"Nothing more I can do," Dr. Mahoney said. "I must take leave now and go to the mine. Too many come to work sick."

Margaret dressed Bridget, stroked her matted red hair, wrapped her from head to toe in her blanket, and handed her to Padraigh. Bridget melded into her father's arms, resting her head on his broad shoulder. Margaret donned her coat. She picked up the sleeping Colm and nestled him into her arms for the long walk home.

CHAPTER 15

DIVERGENT POWERS

Denis was returning from the brook with a pail of water when his mother called from the doorway. "Denny, be looking out for Liam O'Rourke going to O'Shea's. Ask him to come here. He may still be able to help our Bridgee."

"But what about the bleedin' yesterday?"

"She's not better. Weaker, she is," Margaret said, turning to look at Bridget lying near the hearth.

"Liam O'Rourke didn't help her neither," Denis said. "Don't think he knows nothing about evil fairies."

"Knows them better than most. Now do what I say."

"I be watching for him from the bog 'cause we need more peat." Denis handed the pail of water to his mother.

"Come back straightaway."

"Soon's I've enough peat."

Margaret remained in the doorway, watching anxiously for O'Rourke. Soon, she saw him walking toward the cluster of shanties. When he was close enough, she called out,

91

"Good morrow, Liam O'Rourke. Please come see me Bridget. She ain't no better."

"Good morrow, kindly to you, Margaret Murley. Afore I see your suffering one, do you have a shilling owed to me?"

Margaret reached into her pocket and retrieved two coins. "Here's one for before. And this one is for today." She dropped each coin into Liam's palm.

"Thank you kindly," Liam said. He put the coins in his pants pocket and followed Margaret inside.

Bridget lay near the hearth, a child unlike the one he'd seen weeks earlier. She was struggling to breathe. He turned to Margaret. "Your daughter won't come back without more vervain. 'Tis a tea she must drink. Vervain is stronger when it's in a tea."

He handed Margaret a small cloth bag pulled from his waistcoat. "Make a tea from these leaves and give her a few sips often as you can. She'll get stronger and the evil fairies holding her will get weaker. But the cost of these here leaves is more than the stems."

"The extra shilling I gave you is all I got."

"Then you will owe me another."

"Aye. Me Padraigh will be paid soon and I will pay you."

"She will get better, but you must be patient."

"Thank you, Liam."

Nodding, Liam touched the brim of his hat, turned and walked out.

Margaret prepared the vervain tea, roused Bridget and gently tried to prod her lips open with a small spoonful. Bridget did not open her eyes or move her lips.

Denis returned to the shanty. "I saw Liam O'Rourke leave. What'd he do?"

Margaret held up the cup of tea. "Gave me vervain leaves to make this tea."

"Sure and it won't do nothing if she can't drink it."

Ignoring Denis, Margaret turned again to Bridget and touched another tiny spoonful of tea to her lips. "Me precious child. You should not suffer as you are. I beg you to drink this tea."

Denis bent down to Bridget's ear and sang softly. "Bridgee, where did you go by chance? Hurry home to finish your dance."

She moved her head slightly, her lips and eyes closed, her breathing forced.

Turning toward the doorway, Margaret froze. "I hear them clanking chains of death."

"Don't think so. I see Father Murphy coming. Maybe you hear his footsteps," Denis said.

"Good morrow to the Murleys," a voice from outside called out. "God bless you. 'Tis Father Murphy calling."

After concealing the vervain tea behind Bridget's pallet, Margaret rose. "Good morrow kindly, Father. Come in, if you please."

"Thank you, Margaret. I came to give your wee ones the Lord's blessing."

"'Tis good you came."

"Did I see Liam O'Rourke on his way just now?"

Looking at Bridget, Margaret's face flushed. "You did see him, Father."

"Me child, salvation is found in the Church. The Lord will not forsake you nor your family. Turn away from the fairy doctor. His offerings are useless. Heathen, they are."

Margaret lifted her head, looking into Father Murphy's eyes. "May be true, Father, but I see no miracles coming from the Church."

"Ma! Bridgee ain't breathing!" Denis cried out.

Gasping, Margaret grabbed Bridget's shoulders, shook her hard and screamed. "Noooooooo!"

Bridget began breathing again, but slower and deeper.

Father Murphy took a vial of consecrated oil from his pocket. "Let us kneel. I am going to anoint her."

As he completed the traditional prayers for the dying, Bridget stopped breathing again. "Do something, Father!" Margaret cried.

Denis interrupted. "She's breathing."

"Mother of God!" Margaret blurted. "Your blessing, Father, you saved her!"

"No, my child," said the priest.

Bridget had turned a pale, ashen color. Her breaths came in gasps, farther and farther apart.

94

As they continued to kneel at Bridget's side, Margaret thought, *If she had swallowed Liam's tea, she would live, but she can't. Can't swallow. Father Murphy can't change her sickness neither. He can say all the prayers he wants, but my baby is dying.*

A few more minutes had passed when Bridget stopped breathing again. "Oh, Jesus, bring her back to me!" Margaret cried.

The room grew eerily quiet. Tears streamed down Margaret's cheeks as she tenderly caressed her child's face. Bridget did not breathe again.

CHAPTER 16

GRIEVING

Father Murphy and Denis kept a silent vigil over Bridget's lifeless body. Margaret looked intently at her daughter's half-opened eyes. "Me Bridgee, I hear you, I do."

"What's she saying?" Denis bent over and turned his ear toward Bridget's face.

"Rest, me children," Father Murphy said. "Bridget is home. Weep only for yourselves. Bridget is happy in heaven, she is."

Margaret bowed her head and closed her eyes. *How can me Bridgee be home when she is taken from me? I am an empty vessel.*

Margaret took Bridget into her arms and swayed gently, her tears dropping on Bridget's face. Daylight shined through the window. "Da's on his way home, Denny. Bring the bench inside. I must get Bridgee ready for waking. No keening until she is ready."

"Why's that, Ma?"

She whispered into his ear. "Keening will rouse them evil fairies. Take her soul, they will, if she ain't ready."

"But Father Murphy has already blessed her," Denis whispered back.

"Don't matter."

Still kneeling, Father Murphy prayed. "Lord, guide your flock to accept Catholic beliefs so that they may know keening is but a pagan ritual."

Margaret didn't respond.

Denis brought the bench inside and placed it near the hearth. Margaret spread wool matting on the bench, laid Bridget on it and bathed her from head to toe with pig ashes and water. She covered Bridget's body with a flaxen cloth and, finally, placed a copper pence on each of her closed eyelids.

She whispered again to Denis, this time more softly, "'Tis to pay her way to heaven over the River Styx, no matter what Father says."

Ignoring Margaret's ritual, Father Murphy remained kneeling in prayer.

"Candles," Margaret said. "We must have candles."

Father Murphy rose. "I will go to the parsonage and bring back incense and candles. When Padraigh and the others return from the mine, we will begin Prayers for the Dead, for the heavenly journey of Bridget's soul."

"I saw yarrow and ragwort alongside the peat bog," Denis said. "I'll pick some and bring them back for Bridgee."

Father Murphy nodded. "Do that, lad. They are still in bloom. Fragrant they are."

Eyes closed, Margaret rocked to and fro as she knelt next to Bridget. "You are my heart, broken it is." She raised her head and released an ear-piercing cry.

Within minutes, two women entered the shanty and knelt at Margaret's side. When the three began keening, Colm awoke and screamed, his arms and legs swinging wildly.

Denis picked him up. "Let's go find them flowers."

As Padraigh neared home that evening, the keening sprouted goose bumps on his neck and arms. He ran to the shanty as fast as he could. Inside, Denis and Colm sat on the earthen floor, next to Bridget's body. Margaret and the two women stopped keening, but continued to hover over Bridget. Flickering candles gave an eerie glow to her white covering and the flowers surrounding her. Padraigh fell to his knees and embraced her. "Oh, me Bridgee, me Bridgee."

Margaret pulled Colm and Denis to her and the family fell into each other's arms, physically entwined for the last time.

After a while, Father Murphy approached them and began to pray. "Take Bridget into Your Heavenly Arms, Merciful God, where she will no longer suffer. Hear our prayer."

"Amen," Padraigh said.

Father Murphy spoke gently. "Neighbors are gathered outside. We must invite them in and begin prayers now."

"'Scuse me, Father. Need to talk with me wife before we begin."

The priest nodded. "A few minutes, then." He stepped outside.

"Why didn't you wait for me before you started the keening?" Padraigh asked.

"Couldn't wait. Keening had to start soon as Bridget's body was ready, or the evil ones could take her soul."

"Who're these keening women?"

"They're from here. They knew. Everyone knew."

"Who's going to pay them? Good fairies?"

"I made sure we'd have money for our children. Our three boys had no keening, nothing but a cloth over them. Weren't right, it just weren't."

"You hiding money from me again?"

"'Tis for our children, Paddy. For hedge school. Or"—she pointed at Bridget—"this." A steady stream of tears spilled from her eyes.

More neighbors arrived. When men and older boys entered the shanty, they took puffs of tobacco from clay pipes or a pinch of snuff. The air inside became smoky. The peat-laced tobacco odor, along with the fragrant flowers and incense, suppressed the smell of death.

Father Murphy returned to the grieving parents and whispered. "Need to begin."

"We're ready, Father," said Padraigh.

"I be reminding you. No sinful frolic nor merrymaking, later and through the night."

Padraigh stood silent for what seemed like a long time. "Father, we're drowning in our grief over Bridget. These here neighbors are our friends. They share our sadness. And that means what it always has—remembering our precious lass, drinking poitín, talking about our land, farming, weather. Mining, too, I suspect. Might even play a game or do a dance. 'Tis expected."

"These ways must stop. People drinking too much leads to sinning they forget are sins."

Padraigh didn't answer. Margaret looked at the priest and said, "We'll try, Father."

When Father Murphy departed, the wake took its traditional turn. Padraigh and the men gathered in a vigil around a vat of poitín. One man said, "The little lass shall be missed."

"I shan't forget her dancing," said another.

"Why do the fairies have the power?"

"Innocent she was."

"Ain't no fairies. 'Tis the Lord. Punishment for her sin."

"Sin? Wee Bridget? How can you say that?"

"Father Murphy said it."

"Don't mean it's so."

"Said something, I think, about 'original' sin."

"What's that?"

"Means sinning for the first time."

Padraigh finally interrupted. "Look, my friends, there's no evil fairies. And my Bridgee did nothing wrong, unless it was a sin to grab food when she was hungry."

The men nodded.

Denis, Ryan and Seamus went unnoticed as they slipped swigs of poitín. The women drank tea mixed with poitín in cups that Margaret had saved. The voices from the Murley shanty became louder and louder.

Denis began to play the tin fiddle. At first, he strummed softly and somberly, then harder, until the music reached an ear-piercing crescendo. He alternately laughed and cried as he played Bridget's favorite songs. Seamus and Ryan joined him in a roaring cacophony that competed with the keeners. As the evening wore on, mourners shouted to be heard. "Father Murphy's changed, ain't he?" one man yelled to another.

"You mean, asking for tithes, like the Protestants? He needs to eat, don't he?"

"No, I mean being so strict. 'Specially not blessing the Callahan baby at Mass Rock, the one whose mother wasn't married when she birthed."

"'Tis wrong, it is."

"Sure and it is. Now, he says we must go to Mass every Sunday. Mortal sin, he says, if we don't."

"Where'd he get all them rules?"

"From the Pope himself, I'm told."

"Still don't seem right."

After sunrise, Father Murphy returned to the Murley home, carrying a small wooden casket on his shoulder. Margaret met him at the doorway with Colm in her arms. Her eyes were heavy-lidded, her hair unkempt, and she wore a rumpled, stained dress. "Good morrow, Father. Best you wait outside. We're almost ready."

"You don't look ready, and it don't sound like anyone inside is ready. Be at the cemetery in a half hour, me child, with Bridget and the others."

Placing the casket next to the door, he added, "Lay her in the casket and close the cover. I was going to lead the procession. Instead, I'll wait for you at the cemetery. Bridget's grave is dug and ready."

"Thank you, Father. We'll be there soon."

Father Murphy walked slowly to the new cemetery. *How can I do the Lord's work if people are ignorant and poor and don't follow the Church's teachings? Be they without hope of redemption? I must follow my God—the God of Faith, Hope and Charity. 'Tis true the greatest gift of all is Charity, and the hardest to practice when my flock won't obey.*

After the funeral Mass and burial, neighbors offered their condolences to the Murley family before departing.

Margaret, Colm, Padraigh and Denis lingered at Bridget's grave until a cold wind swept the shivering family toward their home.

CHAPTER 17

FORGING AHEAD

Late in the day, John Puxley strode into Dr. Daniel Mahoney's office, angry. "I pay your wages to take care of miners, not offspring of Irish workers. I hear you bled Murley's daughter."

Mahoney looked up from a report he was writing. "Yes, I did. I had no choice."

"You did have a choice. You should have sent the child back home with her mother and ordered Murley back to work."

"Easy enough to say that, but you didn't see the child." Mahoney stood, towering over Puxley.

"You shouldn't have seen her either," Puxley fired back, taking a step toward Mahoney.

Mahoney looked away from Puxley for the first time. "I was told she died the next day."

"Yes, I heard that too." Puxley paused, but not for long. "I can't have you stitching up Irish children either, like you did. I stand to lose a lot of money, as do my investors. We've too many problems. Water in the open cast, late coal deliveries. The forge can't be fired up properly with peat. We're short on blacksmith tools, short on blasting powder and candles. Accidents. And deaths, too. I can't afford to pay grieving widows condolence money, just can't. I need you at the mine full-time. Your office next to the Mine House is ready. Start up there tomorrow. You can use this space here for Cornwall families if needed."

Mahoney took a deep breath and folded his arms across his chest. "Good of you to see that I have two offices. But I'll not be here in the village if I'm to be at the mine full-time. The Cornwall folks, especially the women with sick children, won't be happy if I'm never in this office. Why not advertise in England for another doctor to practice here in the village?"

"Not a bad idea if I could find a doctor who would work for nothing. But, in the meantime, I want you to see only mine workers. No Irish children."

"But, John, Irish children *are* working at the mine. If I'm not permitted to treat them, your output will suffer."

"Damnit, Mahoney!" Puxley grimaced and his eyes became slits. Seconds passed before he calmed down. "Of course, if Irish children are injured at the mine, you'll have to tend to them. Otherwise, you are not to treat the Irish children."

Puxley pulled the brim of his hat down low over his

forehead, gave a halfhearted wave, and walked out of Mahoney's office.

John Puxley, you are a man pulled tight. A shrewd businessman. Your wealth and landed estate attest to that. But who are you? An instrument of progress, giving opportunity to these less fortunate? A leader of industrialization in this grim pocket of humanity? Or a heartless mercenary? And me, what am I? A healer or a pretender? God knows.

Mahoney returned to his desk and opened the report he'd been working on before Puxley stormed in. It was titled *Allihies Copper Mine Quarterly Medical Report, 1.10.1813 –31.12.1813—For the Benefit of Shareholders and Interested Parties.* He had completed the section on accidents and illnesses. As he reread it, he thought, *John and the shareholders aren't going to like this report, not at all.*

Accident and Illness Report

Fatal accidents:

- J. Jones, age 40, blacksmith, found dead in unventilated furnace room, carbon monoxide poisoning.
- L. O'Mayo, age 20, worker, third degree burns over 50% of his body following blast explosion. Died three days later.

Major accidents:

- K. Donnelly, age 25, blacksmith helper, sliver of hot zinc penetrated right eye, eye removed.
- H. O'Shea, age 13, laborer, toes of left foot crushed,

uncontrolled black powder blast. Three toes amputated.
- G. Murphy, age 15, laborer, broken arm, large stone fell from blast site. Set bone and splinted.

Minor accidents and illnesses:
- S. O'Day, age 14, laborer, deep gash forehead, altercation. Stitches.
- P. Murley, age 34, laborer, syncope, pneumonia.
- J. Sullivan, age 12, laborer, fainted, overcome by fatigue, fever. Sent home.
- R. Flynn, age 16, laborer, coughing up blood. Sent home.
- A. Donegan, age 20, laborer, severe reaction to wasp sting.
- D. O'Malley, age 31, laborer, asthmatic wheezing episodes in blast area.
- S. Doyle, age 29, laborer, deep gash right elbow from falling blast debris. Stitches.

Summary: Nearly all patients are local Irish workers. Accidents costly to manpower. Many local workers have lost weight. They suffer from weight loss, pallor and fatigue, adding to respiratory difficulties. Food intake of Irish is meager, many lacking nutrition needed for sustained heavy labor.

Recommendations:
1) Eye shields
2) Cloth masks and water at blast sites

3) Purchase potatoes and grains to supplement
   workers' diet

Mahoney put down his pen and rubbed his temples. *Too many accidents. Workers are in peril and they don't know it, compelled as they are to eke out a living. Inhaling mine dust and dirt every day will take twenty years from them. If they knew, what would they do? What should I do? Keep on stitching them up, setting their fractures, treating their wounds? Accept the suffering of these men, women and children in the name of industrial progress? I took an oath to help my patients and do no harm. How do I do that when my patients walk into harm's way every day, and science doesn't give me answers I need to cure them?*

Slowly, he signed in a heavy-handed script, *Daniel Mahoney, Mine Physician.*

Laying the pen on his report, he reached into his desk drawer and pulled out a flask of whiskey, uncorked it and took a long drink. Then another. And still another.

CHAPTER 18

BARGAINS

Padraigh's sleep had been fitful. He awakened early to a cold chill that had seeped through the thatch-laced walls of their shanty. After rekindling the peat embers and using most of the remaining peat for the hearth fire, he walked to the brook for water. When he returned, Denis was rubbing his hands together above the flickering hearth flame. "Da, why you up so early?"

"Big day, lad. New bargains to bid this morning. I'm hoping Cap'n Bishop's bid ain't as low as the last one."

"Me, too. Lots of things unfair. Like having to pay for tools that get broke."

"And no matter how hard 'tis to get ore out the ground, we only get paid for how much copper's in it. Seems like 'tis getting more and more unfair."

"Why's that, Da?"

"The company just finished building cottages for Cornwall folks, east of the mines. So, I expect there'll be a lot

108

more of them coming in days ahead, getting paid more than us. Bringing their families, too, they are, and building a school. And them Protestants building a church, right in the village."

"What about us?"

"There's a gang of us now, more 'n' seventy workers. The mine needs us. If Hall can't get us better pay, we be asking him in a different way."

"What way's that?"

"Don't worry about that just now, lad. We going to make them bosses understand we know what's fair."

"Don't they already know?"

"They know."

"Sure doesn't seem like it."

"We need to be at the mine early, so go to the bog quickly and bring back as much peat as you can. We're nearly out."

After chores were done and the shanty had shed its chill, Margaret, Denis, Padraigh and Colm sat at the small table near the hearth, eating potato and barley gruel.

"Can you sew up more of them copper sacks?" Padraigh asked Margaret. "They get torn easy. Hall's paying a tuppence for every twenty sewn."

"Sure and I will. Them tuppence help."

"Aye, they do, but our cottiers aren't bringing in extra crop – because there isn't any. 'Tis on our backs, it is. Seems there's never enough."

After Padraigh and Denis left for the mine, Margaret began darning. Colm played at Margaret's feet, randomly spreading the thirty or so copper sacks on the floor. Glancing up over the doorway, Margaret's eyes came to rest on the straw Cross of St. Brigid. She stopped darning and glared at it. "You're no saint! No saint at all! If you were, Bridgee would be here with me. Get out!"

Ignoring Colm, who had begun to cry, she ran to the cross, grabbed it and threw it against the wall. Retrieving it, she threw it again, and this time it skittered through the open doorway to the outside. "Out! You don't belong here."

She turned to Colm, picked him up and rocked him—soothing him, and herself.

Padraigh and Denis stood outside the Mine House with their usual team of six workers: a miner, two laborers, two raggers and a cobber. Other men, women and children were loosely assembled, waiting. Some were clad only in shirt-sleeves, without coats or hats. Many crossed their arms and hugged themselves, trying to keep warm. Inside the Mine House, Colonel Hall offered aboveground excavation bids to the mine captains.

In anticipation of a renewed bargain with Captain Bishop, Padraigh had gathered up a hammer, chisel, borer, and two kibbles for bailing water that had accumulated in the pits the night before. When Bishop emerged from the Mine House, he pointed to a few laborers Padraigh had never seen before and said, "You three. Come with me. Bring your tools."

Expecting to get a nod, Padraigh walked toward him. "Who they be, Cap'n?"

"They're from the hinterland up north," Bishop said, "Way inland. Fifteen of 'em been here since last week. They're willing to work for less than you locals. 'Tis business, Paddy. Don't need you on this one. But I still need your boy for ragging."

Padraigh's body tensed. His heart pounded and his temples throbbed. "Christ a'mighty, Cap'n! What the hell are we supposed to do? Work for nothin'?"

"There's plenty of work here, Paddy. I needed this bargain. These three agreed to the pay. They've been here every day since last week. Might remind you locals that *you* need to be here every day."

"'Tis goddamned unfair's what! Me child just died!"

"I know, and I'm sorry for your loss. You too, Denis," Bishop replied.

Padraigh's eyes glistened. He pulled a flask of poitín from his pocket.

Bishop shook his head. "No, Paddy, not now. Look, Richard Glasson is still inside bidding on an east lode job. He's short a hand. Ask if you can work on his team."

"Glasson? Bedad! Man's the devil himself!"

"Maybe so, but he can blast and excavate safer than any miner I know. And you need the job. Go now. I got work to do." With that, Bishop motioned to Denis, the three strange workers and the rest of his team to come with him.

Padraigh turned to Denis. "You get going. Meet right here after closing bell."

"But what if you don't get a bargain?"

"Don't worry, lad. I'll get one."

Putting the unopened flask back into his pocket, Padraigh waited outside the Mine House until Glasson and a few other captains appeared. Workers milled about waiting to be called, stamping their feet to ward off the cold.

Padraigh stared hard at Glasson. *Looks no different than he did six months ago. Hasn't grown fangs. No horns from his head. Not yet, anyways.*

"My crew!" Glasson yelled. "I need you over at the east lode. Now! Get your gear and move!"

Swallowing hard, Padraigh raised his hand high. "Cap'n Glasson, Cap'n Bishop says you're down a man. I been working with him for twelve weeks past. Will you take me on your bargain?"

"So, Murley, you're still around. Thought you'd have drunk yourself to death by now." Glasson winked at the other captains standing nearby.

Padraigh swallowed hard again. "Trying to make a living is all."

"I've heard about you, Murley. I hear you're not a bad worker. Least on the days you're sober and decide to come to work."

"There's reasons."

"I don't listen to reasons. When you have a job, you come to work every day. That's what my men do."

"Gimme a chance." Clenched fists at his side, Padraigh maintained eye contact with Glasson.

"I got big doubts about you, Murley, but I could use another hand. One shilling a day. Take it or leave it."

You dirty-arse bastard. Them's women's wages.

"I'll take it."

CHAPTER 19

OBSTACLES

"Worse than I thought," Glasson said.

His four-man crew stared at the blasting site filled with a sea of water.

"Going to take hours to bail," Glasson complained. "Start filling kibbles and pass them down the line to the sluice." He pointed to a wooden trough that led to open drainage down the hillside.

"Right, sir," Jones said. Shea, O'Neil and Murley stood grim-faced and silent. None wore clothing suitable for the cold, damp weather.

"We're losing half of every day to bail water. Damn rain doesn't happen in Cornwall," Glasson said. "Get to it!"

Kibble in hand, each man walked to the edge of the small lake that covered the work site. *Christ a'mighty*, Padraigh thought. *This'll take all day. Must be four feet of water in this pit*. He positioned himself at the water's edge and began filling kibbles, handing them off one by one to the next man, Shea. The loose soles of Padraigh's shoes invited water in.

Later, as he bent over to fill another kibble, he saw his hands and arms shaking. *Christ, ain't that cold. Me hands and arms are moving too fast.*

Glasson stood a short distance away, watching. "Keep it up," he said. As he turned toward the Mine House, "I'll be back." Two hours had passed when Shea turned to Padraigh. "What's the matter with you, Murley?"

"Nothin' I know."

"You're shaking all over, is what it looks like."

"Nay, I'm not."

Padraigh was breathing fast. His movements were erratic, halting. He looked down at his soaked shoes, then up at the gray sky. Cold raindrops stabbed his face. *Got to keep going. Can't stop. Jesus.*

Glasson returned to inspect the work site and frowned at Padraigh. "We working you too hard, Murley?"

"No, Cap'n." Padraigh's face was wan and wet. Glasson shook his head. "Can't you see this damned water? We still got to blast today."

"Murley ain't feeling too good, Cap'n," Shea interjected.

"If he can't carry his weight," Glasson bellowed, "there's no place for him here!"

Jesus, help me. Padraigh took a deep breath, his eyes rolled upward and he crumpled into a heap on the puddled ground at Glasson's feet.

Glasson looked down at him. "I should've known. Poitín poisoning. Pull him away from the water. We're way behind."

Shea and O'Neil dragged Padraigh away from the half-empty pit to dry ground.

Glasson looked closer and his eyes grew small, his mouth turned down at the corners. "Guess I better have the doc take a look at you. Damned weak Irish."

"I been next to him all morning," Shea said to O'Neil. "Knew he was ailing."

"He's breathing, he is. Maybe just fainted," O'Neil said.

By the time Dr. Mahoney arrived, Padraigh was lying on his side, conscious, still breathing fast as he stared vacantly at the ground.

"Didn't think I would see you again so soon, Murley. What happened?"

"Don't know. Just got some shaking."

"Have you eaten or drunk anything?"

"Not since before the sun come up."

"You think you can chisel and sledge for the rest of the day?"

"Don't know, but I gotta try."

"Been coughing? Or wheezing?"

"Some."

"Anyone with fever or rash that you know?"

Padraigh shook his head.

The doctor tapped on Padraig's chest and back, listening intently.

"You have pneumonia. You need to go home."

"Can't go home. Have to finish me bargain."

"Won't do you much good if you're dead. I'll tell your captain."

"Nay! I'll stay home the morrow if I still have the shivers."

Mahoney sighed. "Your choice. Drink as much as you can—sweet tea, water—whatever you have."

"Just happen to have some poitín in me pocket here."

"Sweet tea's better. Too much poitín and you'll blast off your fingers or your toes. Or worse." Mahoney turned and walked back toward his office.

By midafternoon, Padraigh was back on his feet and helped finish bailing. Glasson instructed the four men on the exact locations to chisel holes for blasting. An hour later, he returned to inspect. "Deep enough."

He handed Shea a bag of gunpowder. "Fill the hole tight, then push this pricker through the powder, far as you can. Pull it out and thread the fuse to the end of the hole."

You think we're idiots? Padraigh thought. *We been doing this near a year.*

"Then you want me to light the fuse?" asked Shea.

"No, no. I'll do that. I want to make sure no one gets blown up. After I light the fuse, I'll give the word for everyone to move quickly toward the dressing floor."

Padraigh broke out in another cold shivery sweat. *Day from hell. If I get out of this alive, no telling how I'm going to get to me bed. Might's well be a million miles away.*

Glasson lit the fuse and yelled, "Cover!"

The earsplitting explosion produced a shower of rock that rained down into the pit and filled the environs with a black sooty cloud.

"Good blast," Glasson said. "We got enough to sledge for today. Tomorrow we'll finish blasting. Get to it."

"Right, sir," Shea said. The four workers began picking, sledging and pulling large blocks of ore-bearing rock from around the blast hole.

At 6:30 the closing bell rang. As the men walked to the storage house to put away their tools, Glasson approached. He looked at Padraigh's stooped posture and gaunt, pale face.

"Took a chance with you, Murley. Don't come around here tomorrow if you can't put in a full day's work. I'll get someone else."

Can't let this son-of-a-bitch make me look like a dosser.

"Count on me, Cap'n. I'll be back on the morrow."

CHAPTER 20

PROGRESS REPORT

The main room of the new slate-roofed Count House was empty, except for a long oak conference table where John Puxley and Andrew Hall sat to prepare for an investors' meeting. Designed by Puxley with investors in mind, the Count House had been completed only days earlier. It stood out from other mine structures, with its wide front porch and two large windows overlooking the Atlantic on each side of an oversized double-door entrance.

"How was your trip from Llethrllestry, John?" Hall asked.

"Well enough. My wife is not yet able to travel, so I will be here only until after the meeting tomorrow. Then I must return."

"I hope Sarah is improving."

"Yes, my hope as well." Puxley looked down at his hands and paused only briefly. "What are the hiring numbers that I am to share with investors?"

"Cornwall workers, including captains, number forty-five. And as of today, we have seventy-five local workers, all laborers. Nine of the locals are women. Eleven are children, ages ten to fourteen."

"Seems like a lot of local workers. Do the numbers match production? How many shipments have been sent to Swansea?"

"Four. The fifth is almost ready," Hall replied. "The problem is water. Recent rains have been fierce, slowed us down. The one sump pump we had broke down. Two more should be coming in from Cork next week. For now, the men have to bail with kibbles."

"I don't like it," said Puxley.

"I don't either, but we can't blast when water is up to our knees. Truth is, we need all the workers we can get, more excavation above and below ground."

"You have a plan for that?"

Hall nodded, "Yes, sir, I do. Keep up the open cast quarrying, order more pumps, more kibbles. At the same time, start forging an adit that will take us underground to the east-west lode. Glasson and Egan agree we must use both methods, above and below ground. The first four shipments were about seventy-five tons each, so you can see what these workers can produce."

Puxley raised his eyebrows. "Not bad, not bad. But it may not offset costs. I fear this business is not as profitable as I thought it would be. Makes me wonder if it's worth the trouble."

"Takes time, John. One problem is the grumbling I hear about local laborers being paid less than Cornwall workers."

"I'm more concerned about grumbling from the investors. What do I tell them tomorrow about the additional expense of going underground?"

"Tell them it's necessary. We have good reason to believe this lode is extensive. Once we've paid the initial costs from the proceeds of the copper we've already shipped, investors will reap dividends. For now, we need more gunpowder, fuses, candles, lumber and mining tools. We're building linhays over the work areas so the women and children on the dressing floor can keep working in rainy weather."

"If you're right about the size of the lode, the dividends will compensate the investors. But what if you're wrong? Then what?"

"We've come through a lot these past months. I believe the decision to excavate an adit to go underground is the correct one. Glasson stakes his reputation on it. And now we have the manpower to do it."

"I hear different. I'm told the locals come to work when they please. We're behind in our bargains, supplies are barely enough. And the locals are so poor we'll have to supplement their diets through the summer so they can finish a day's work."

Hall shifted uneasily in his chair. "Many of the workers come from miles away. Some walk more than three miles to get here. They need a place to live close by, same as the Cornwall workers and their families."

"Too expensive," Puxley said. "I'll hear no more of housing for Irish workers. Not now. August will take us through a year. After we see our bottom line, I might consider it."

Puxley stood to leave. "Anything else I should know before tomorrow's meeting? If not, I'm going to Dunboy, try to make sense of what my children are doing these days."

Yes, Hall thought. *Your investors should know about wages, working conditions and accidents.*

Instead, Hall said, "Remind them the demand for copper will stay high as long as Little Boney is bent on conquering all of Europe."

Puxley headed for the exit of the Count House but stopped to pull an envelope from his coat pocket and hand it to Hall. "By the way, a letter addressed to you has been sitting on my desk. Posted a few months ago. Just came across it."

CHAPTER 21

THE LETTERS

Hall looked first at the return address and the post date, then flashed a look of annoyance at Puxley's back as he left the Count House. Hall returned quickly to the conference table, sat down and tore open the envelope.

October 5, 1813

Dear Andrew,

Your letter was a welcome sight. If I had my way, I would begin travel today from Galway to be your translator and aide at the newly opened copper mine. But my life has taken an unfortunate turn since our Royal Marine days. Read this, good soldier, and you will understand.

I read with great interest about your current employment with the Puxley Mine Company. You say life on the Beara Peninsula is the same as it was fifteen years ago, but I am confident that with your leadership, an important opportunity has unfolded.

Mining will allow poor farmers and their families to become less reliant on the spud. I've seen what happens when their main crop falters, as it did in 1807, and before that in 1800. If farmers continue to depend on fate, superstition and Irish luck, I fear far worse will happen.

When you studied at the Royal Military Academy years ago, you were taught about England's centuries-long oppression of a backward people who were deemed to be ignorant brutes, thieves and murderers, incapable of leading moral, productive lives.

All that, written by the victorious English. John Hooker comes to mind. He believed Catholicism was satanic worship and the cause of Ireland's backward ways. We both know it was Parliament's Penal Laws, designed to get rid of the Irish altogether that cemented Ireland's fate.

I had the rare opportunity, as the son of an Irish mother and an Anglo-Saxon father, to learn for myself the world of tenant farmers and their families. We were a rarity because we lived on our estate and managed the land without middlemen. My mother offered long leases to Irish farmers and frowned on subletting. She taught me Irish, her first language, and the beauty of Gaelic culture and its people.

You asked me to help smooth the sharp edges between the Irish and English at the mine. There is no one answer for that, but remember what I've told you in the past. The Irish are people like you and me. They want to be free. They can be submissive, apathetic, or outlandish and loud. Be wary. Irishmen's rage can rise to the surface without warning, especially when they believe they are being treated unfairly.

Remember, too, that oppressed people keep score. Some seek revenge, others detachment. The Irish try to sustain a level of control. But, in a mine setting, they will be controlled by outside forces. If they are treated fairly and with respect, those sharp edges will become smoother. Fair pay and fair working conditions are important. You can be a force for change, a catalyst to heal old wounds.

When I retired from the military, I studied law in Dublin at Trinity College. My father wanted me to follow him into Parliament. Instead, I joined a Dublin firm that specializes in Irish property rights and practiced there for the past decade. It will take many lifetimes of legal work to undo the damage done by feudalistic land takings over the past five hundred years.

Two years ago, my health began to fail. I lost weight, tired easily, ran fevers and had swellings in my neck. A doctor in Dublin finally told me that I have a cancer they call lymphoma. They operated and removed the largest tumor, but within a few months, I was back where I started.

Mothers are not supposed to take care of their grown sons, but that is what has happened. I now live with my mother on her estate. I've embraced this sanctuary and the peace it brings me. Autumn has touched my soul, as I watch the elms and birches shed their leaves. They will return after the winter. I have accepted the fact that I will not.

My time is near. God willing, I will keep to this world until I hear from you again. If that is not to be, please do not forget me. It is my dying wish that I remain with you in spirit and give you guidance for your task ahead.

Yours in Anglo-Irish brotherhood,

Peter

Andrew read Peter's letter twice, then sat back and closed his eyes. He pictured his friend when they rode together, a strong, sure-saddled Royal Marine. Already six months had passed since Peter had written. No time for delay.

April 20, 1814

Dear Peter,

Your letter took months to arrive in my hands. Your disease rocks me to my core. Despite your suffering, you gave me valuable insight into the problems I face at the mine.

It is one thing to teach mining skills to Irish workers, quite another to see the realities of their lives.

The number of Whiteboys on the Beara is on the rise, but they are far too few to make a difference. Yet they raise havoc, just as they did when we were stationed here, choosing to steal, maim and even murder because their colonialized voice was crushed.

I fear that violence will increase as the Whiteboys learn about the pay discrepancy between the English and Irish worker. But I also see many Irish and English workers who get on well with one another, having found some common ground in their toil. It is the miners and the crew captains, who have trouble accepting the Irish worker.

You and your beliefs are the foundation upon which I will continue my work.

I remain your devoted friend.

God bless you.

Andrew

CHAPTER 22

BREATHING

Margaret sat outside on the birch bench, singing softly to Colm as he nursed. Hearing Padraigh's labored breathing become louder and louder, she stopped singing. "I hear the devil inside your breathing, I do," she said when he came into view.

"And what do you know, woman? Bedad! Ain't no devil."

"What, then? You're not better since the spring past, and now 'tis August."

"Aye, sucks me energy, it does." Padraigh's wheezing hit a high-pitched whistle with each intake of air.

"Coughing and breathing too heavy you are, in case you don't know."

"I know it, woman, and try not to remind me. 'Tis a day of rest, and after we return from Mass, that's what I aim to do."

"Have you seen Doctor Mahoney?"

Padraigh nodded. "He told me breathing problems are more likely now because we ain't in open quarry no more.

Being under grass, there's always dirt and dust in them caves. Gets in me lungs, it does."

"Other workers having trouble?"

"Some are. Others no. Doc said some do better with bad air than others. Said I may get better, may not. Said if me cough gets worse, or I see the blood, I need to go back to him."

"What will he do?"

"Don't know."

"Saints in heaven protect us, could be white plague like what killed your own ma and da. Put us in the nether region, it will, if you can't work at all."

"Stop your wailing, for Christ's sake, Margaret. I've not seen no blood. I got a lot of work left in me before that copper dirt finishes me off."

"Finishes you off? What is it by that are you meaning?"

"Meaning nothing. Forget it."

Colm, now a plump one-year-old, stopped nursing and wriggled to the ground from his mother's lap. He looked up at his father.

Padraigh reached down to pat his head. "Aye, me wee lad, you are growing strong. Maybe you will be the one to answer our prayers."

"Won't be worth much if you're not with us."

"Lord willing, I'll be with you."

"There's other ways to get prayers answered," Margaret said. "I been thinking, if our tenants pay rent with their mine wages, we'll be able to keep our leasehold. Means you can quit the mine. Be better for your breathing if you come back to farming."

"Can't. Truth is, the rent keeps going up. Doubled, it has. That gouging middleman, Sutchins. Need the mine work just to keep up, we do. Until the O'Tooles, O'Neils, and Sheas started working at the mine, we were short every time rent was due. Least now, they're paying from their mine wages so we ain't going to get kicked out. Not today, anyway."

"But your breathing is too hard. Ain't good."

"You don't understand, wife. Not easy going down the hole every day. Labor fit for a slave. But will be worth every painful breath I take if the same life don't happen to Denny and Colm. Or our children not yet born."

"May come a time when your breathing can't keep up with your working."

"'Tis a risk I must take. I've been thinking, too. About Denny. Says he likes ragging, but he needs learning. Tuck is willing to take Denny on as his Poor Scholar. Thinks our boy is smart enough to be a clerk or a teacher one day. With me working the mine, we can pay for his schooling until he knows enough to start teaching or clerking."

"May be good for Denny, but not for you, if you keep working under grass. You are stubborn like a goat." Margaret sputtered.

"'Tis for you and our boys. I'm working to give us a better life, like me da tried, God rest his soul." Padraigh made the sign of the cross.

"You have already, Paddy. But what if Denny wants to keep working at the mine?"

"I'll not give him a choice."

"Won't be easy if he don't want to."

"I know. He got himself a backbone since he's been ragging. Like his ma he is now." Padraigh bent down and kissed Margaret on the forehead. "'Tis time to ready for Mass, it is."

CHAPTER 23

DIFFERENT PATHS

The evening air was warm, with an earthy aroma of potato blooms that wafted toward the Murley shanty, muting the usual stench of human and animal odors. Padraigh and Denis sat on the birch bench, watching Colm crawl on nearby rocks.

Padraigh asked, "When's your bargain done?"

"A week more," Denis answered.

"Hard enough work for you?"

Denis flashed a smile. "Been ragging about a year, Da. Seamus, Ryan and me are a lot stronger. Used to be the Brits would out-sledge us. Not anymore. They ain't bothering us no more either."

"Always want to be a ragger?"

"No. I want to go in the hole with you when Colonel Hall says I'm big enough."

"Way you're growing, won't be much longer. When you was a wee one, I remember you wanting to learn English

132

words, listen to stories. And you looked at Tuck's school books like you wanted to jump inside them."

"'Twas true, it was."

Padraigh and Denis followed Colm's explorations as he perched on a mound of weeds and heather, patting his hands together, babbling, "Mamama...dadadadada."

"What did you like most about school?" Padraigh asked.

"Schoolmaster Tuck. He told us things I never knew before. Like the story about Táin Bó."

"I heard of Táin Bó. Long time ago, it was?"

"A real long time ago, even before Catholics came here. It was about a famous Irish queen. Soon as she married the king, he made her jealous because he said his bull was bigger than hers. She was so jealous that she started a war."

"Why you think they had a war?"

"Schoolmaster Tuck said the queen would lose face if she didn't go to war."

"Do you agree?"

"No. Nothing I ever thought of before. But I liked the story. 'Twas exciting, it was."

"Sure and I know that, me lad. Do you miss those learning times?"

"Some. I'll go back later, after I'm done working at the mine."

"'Later' could be a long time from now. A time I may not be around."

Denis looked into his father's eyes. "Where you be going, Da?"

"Not going anywhere soon, lad. Point is, copper mining is dangerous. 'Tis so. There's better ways to make a living, but you need learning. Schoolmaster Tucker has a place for you at hedge school as the new Poor Scholar."

Denis sat upright and shook his head. "Me? A Poor Scholar? I can't do that. Not when me and me friends are ragging every day. Me captain won't be liking me not being there, neither."

"'Tis hard to think of not being with your friends, but learning to read and speak the English is what you must do."

"I don't need more English, nor learning, to do me work."

"May be true. But you need a lot more learning to live a better life than the one you have now."

Denis returned his father's gaze. "I can't do that now. Not now, Da!"

"You need to learn why we're living this way, why we have no voice, how they robbed our land and took away our rights."

Denis flushed with anger, shot to his feet. "You don't understand. You don't. I want to work with me friends!"

"Lad, you must know more than ragging, pickaxing and blasting. You must learn our past and know better the ways of our land and our people."

Denis crossed his arms.

Padraigh stood up to face Denis. Arms still crossed, Denis glared at his father.

"Look around you. See us as we are. Poor, overcrowded, sick, treated like dirt at the mine. We're not dirt. Like me own da said, 'Ain't right.' And it ain't. Schoolmaster Tucker is expecting you. I told Colonel Hall no more bargains after you finish this one."

With tears filling his eyes, Denis stamped his feet like a raging bull. "I'm not going! I'm not!"

"You be going, as I've told you." His temples pounding, Padraigh picked up Colm and walked into the shanty.

Margaret was sitting near the hearth, darning a copper sack. "You best not push the child."

"He needs pushing, so I'm pushing. Before it's too late."

Margaret kept her eyes on the tattered copper sack and said no more.

CHAPTER 24

POOR SCHOLAR

Denis stood facing Schoolmaster Tucker inside an abandoned barn, recently converted to a hedge school, about a half mile from Father Murphy's parsonage. Refurbished by Tucker, Father Murphy and a few parishioners, the barn provided a spacious rectangular classroom with a packed dirt floor. The stone hearth in the center of the classroom was vented through an opening in the thatched roof. Spaces in the wooden walls were filled with a straw and mud matrix to keep out moisture and cold drafts.

Off the classroom, a small room that had been used to store tools was converted to a sleeping room furnished with a cot, a small desk and a chair. Compared to the shanties in Cloghfune, the school was an elegant structure.

Denis had grown taller, with gangly arms and legs compared to his torso. His cherub-looking face had subtly elongated, making him resemble his father more.

"Ah, me Denis. Are you the same lad sitting by those hedgerows yonder years back? You are growing like ragwort rising in the sun, you are."

Denis gave Tucker a half-smile. "Aye, sir. 'Tis still me."

"So you're going to be me Poor Scholar?"

Denis's smile vanished. "Me da's making me."

"I see. Do you know any Poor Scholars?"

"Only Dorian, your Poor Scholar when I was at hedge school before."

"Ah, yes, Dorian. Fine scholar he is. Had a calling, he did. Left a few weeks ago to enter Maynooth Seminary."

Denis brightened. "Then I shouldn't be here, 'cause I don't want to be a priest."

"There's other ways of being and knowing, me lad. You can study to be a schoolmaster like me, or maybe a clerk."

Denis shrugged. "Never thought about it. Don't even know what a clerk is."

"A clerk is someone who knows numbers, works in a shop, or sells potatoes, barley, oats, flaxen or wheat. You might have a gift for work like that."

"We only have enough potatoes to feed ourselves, none to sell right now."

"Maybe not now, but with more land cleared, you could produce enough crop between the Murleys and your cottiers that your da may want to sell some. Need to know arithmetic to figure out how much it costs to grow crops, what to charge and how much crop is needed to make a profit."

"Don't seem likely. Me da works at the mine. So do the O'Tooles, O'Neils and Sheas. 'Tis our women and children do most of the farming."

"That can change."

Denis gave Tucker a somber look, then scanned the rustic expanse of the dark classroom and the large wooden headmaster's chair placed close to the hearth. Two small openings for windows on each end of the room allowed in a little daylight. On the floor was a familiar semicircle of gray slates, each about the size of a peat square, a sharpened stone next to each.

"Being a Poor Scholar is being in training," Tucker said, "so you can maybe take me place one day. You must learn our history so you can pass it on to others and to your own children one day. Takes time to learn it."

"How long?" Denis asked.

"No saying. Like Dorian, you start with literature."

"But I can barely read."

Tucker placed a hand on Denis's shoulder. "You will learn, lad. To know where you are going, you must learn from where you came. Hundreds of years ago, Ireland and England could have been sisters, but ignorance, fear and religious hatred doused any hope of that. War stories are written by the victors, not the vanquished. You will need to be learning to understand what really happened to Ireland and why."

Denis nodded slightly, but his expression remained grave. He asked Tucker, "Was Ireland always the loser?"

"No. The story is long. And the final chapters are nowhere near written."

About twenty young students, mostly boys, entered the school. Each sat beside one of the slates.

"Good morrow, lads and lasses," Schoolmaster Tucker said with a broad smile. "I have a surprise for you. Beside me here is Denis Murley, your new Poor Scholar. Let's see how much you can learn from him. He'll be asking you lots of questions and teaching you reading and arithmetic."

Denis smiled self-consciously at his audience, looking briefly at each child. They returned his looks with earnest expressions.

That was me years back. I knew nothing then. Don't know much now. Wish I was at the mine, ragging.

His eyes lingered on those of a carefree-looking girl, about ten years old. *Looks like Bridgee might look if she was still alive.* Gradually, Denis's somber expression relaxed and they exchanged smiles.

CHAPTER 25

DOWN UNDER

"You shorted me," Declan O'Toole said.

The mine accountant and paymaster, James Parker, stood behind his pay window in the Count House. "This here is what you bargained for, O'Toole. You're lucky you got what you did."

"Feeling mighty unlucky since I been working here near a year. Was expecting me full wage. Can't pay rent and feed me family with this."

"Nothing I can do. You owe the company five shillings, two pence for damaged equipment and a sack of barley."

"What the hell? Pick handle broke. Not my fault."

"Can't help you." Parker glared, then tilted his head to look at the long line. "Move on. You got a bone to pick, go see the colonel."

Declan glared back. He snatched up the one pound note and ten pence, walked away from the pay window, and shoved the money in his pocket. He barked angrily at the queue of men and boys who'd been waiting behind him. "Christ a'mighty! They robbing me!"

Weary, dirt-smudged faces stared at him.

Declan's eyes narrowed and he lowered his voice. "Any of you are Whiteboys, meet me at Twomey's tonight, eight o'clock."

More stares.

"Any others want fair wages, but ain't Whiteboys, don't matter, come anyway." With that, Declan buttoned his coat, donned his cap and stomped away. He spotted Padraigh beginning the long descent from the dressing floor toward Cloghfune. "Paddy, wait up."

Padraigh turned and waited.

"How you be doing?" Declan asked as he approached.

"Good as can be when the air isn't friendly to breathing. Heard you yelling at Parker. Get your bargain pay?"

"I got it all right. Shorted me, saying I owed money for broke tools. Robbing us, they are. Having a meeting of Whiteboys tonight and any others feel they're being suckered. Can you come?"

"What're you planning? Pitch-capping Parker?"

"We don't get paid for the work we do. 'Tis a known fact. Cornwall workers get paid more. Stealing from us is what they be doing. If it ain't Puxley and Hall, then it's the Protestant tithes. And Father Murphy's got his hand in our pockets, too."

"I know it, but stealing from them will get you arrested, maybe hung."

"I'm sick of it. Keeping us paupers. Slaves more like it." Declan raised his arm and smacked his fist hard into his palm.

"Look, Deck, use your head. I know you and the White-boys have them blunderbuss pistols. That ain't no way to get better pay."

"It's getting worse, it is. Hall's done nothing to help us. A puppet is what he is. Says whatever Puxley tells him to. Acts like he's a fair man, but he's not."

"For a Brit, Hall's not bad. I've seen much worse, I have. What's in your head, Deck?"

"Methinks you are too high and mighty, Paddy, figuring you're too good for us cottiers. We rent your land in this rocky hell, can't even scrape out a living with the spuds. Now we're killing ourselves at the mine and still can't pay the rent."

"You got it wrong, Deck. We're the same, we are."

Padraigh offered his flask to Declan, who uncorked it, tipped his head back, and swallowed a large mouthful. He handed the flask back to Padraigh, who took a long drink. "Never felt high and mighty. Never did. I was born here on the Beara. I see the English and their ways, trying to break our spirit. Nearly broke my father when they took our land years back. I got a leasehold, but a pittance it is. So you see, I'm no better off than you. But me spirit's not broke. Not yet anyways."

"Not true we be the same, Paddy. Me and me family were spalpeens years past. Lived off the land in the hills, we did. No way to live. Another baby on the way. That'll be six wee ones to feed. Run out of patience, I have."

"Mrs. Riley been by to see your wife?"

"Not yet."

"When's the baby coming?"

"Not for a while she tells me. She thinks sometime next March."

"Deck, if you go off with Whiteboys and start plundering the mine, you'll land back in the hills. Else in gaol."

"Can't live like this, I just can't."

"Don't be forgetting you and your brother each owe me three months' rent. You can pay with potatoes like before, or shillings." He looked hard at Declan. "Don't be letting me down, Deck."

"Don't you hear me? You are either thick-headed or a coward. They cheating you, too. No cur can cheat me and get away with it."

"Ever hear of a strike?"

"No, I ain't heard of no strike."

"Workers get together and agree to stop work. Been a year and a half since the mine opened. There's now near two hundred workers, not counting captains and miners, and all but about seventy are Irish. If we tell Hall and Puxley we won't work unless we're paid fair, they'll talk. They stand to lose a lot of money."

"How can we do that? Takes too many Irish to agree, and most are cowards anyway."

"Takes time. Instead of getting out your blunderbuss or setting fire to one of the mine houses, start talking up a strike."

"Don't know nothing about a strike." Declan's voice was filled with rage.

"Tuck told me about them. First one happened more than twenty-five years ago. A cotton mill in Scotland, it was. Workers were poor, just like us. Got unfair wages, just like us. Owners wouldn't listen, just like these here."

"What'd they do?"

"Weavers they were. Called themselves the Calton Weavers. They stopped working 'til they got higher pay."

"What happened?" Declan asked.

"In the end, six of them weavers got killed, but it started something. Tuck says it started a movement. Gave workers power, power they badly needed, just like us. But it took time, it did."

"'Tis time I don't have."

"You best think about it before you do something stupid."

"Humpff!"

The two men did not speak during the rest of the long walk home.

CHAPTER 26

PAYROLL

Biting gusts of cold wind pierced Colonel Hall's greatcoat as he hurried toward the Count House. Puxley's carriage was close by, empty save for his post boy sitting atop the driving seat, clutching his cloak closely around him.

Once inside, Hall's eyes scanned the four men sitting at the conference table. "Good morning, gentlemen."

Puxley and Parker nodded.

Mort Downing, the mine courier, looked up, then at his clasped hands on the table.

"Morning, Colonel," said Jonas Cooper, a local constable who knew Hall because of previous worker disturbances at the mine. "What's happened, Jonas?" Hall asked. "You wouldn't be here if there wasn't trouble."

"Right. This isn't a social call. Mort here was held up yesterday. Haven't caught the culprits yet, but we will. Mort, tell us what happened after you met with Mr. Puxley at Dunboy Castle."

"I packed my saddlebags with the money Mr. Puxley gave me for today's payroll. Three hundred pounds, it was. Because of all the trouble with the Irish, he gave me a pistol, just in case. I put it atop the payroll money inside the saddlebags."

Cooper interrupted. "Why didn't you carry the pistol in your jacket or on your saddle?"

"Not used to carrying a pistol, or using one neither. Didn't want to take it at all, but I know trails and roads aren't safe these days."

Cooper nodded. "Go on."

"I was halfway between Dunboy and Allihies when two men darted in front of me. Aimed pistols at me and threatened to shoot. 'Git off yer horse,' said one of them. Hard to understand. English it was, but Irish by sound. Both wore masks and long white shirts. Both bearded. Couldn't hold their pistols still, they were shaking so."

Downing took a deep breath. "With a pistol in hand, one of them told me to take the saddlebags off the horse. Fearing for my life, I had trouble unhitching 'em. Guess I was more angry than scared, because soon as I opened a bag, I quick grabbed the pistol, and pulled the trigger. Shot one of 'em in the shoulder."

"Then his partner shot at me. Missed me, but the shot must've grazed the horse, because he reared up all crazed and ran off, with the saddlebags and the payroll still in them. The thug ran hell-bent into the bush. Left his partner on the ground, bleeding and groaning."

"Did you recognize either of them?" Hall asked.

"Yes, sir. The man I shot was Declan O'Toole. Not sure who the other one was. The shot must've took O'Toole's breath away, 'cause he couldn't get enough air, so he threw off the kerchief that was his mask. The only thing I could do was press my jacket on his wound to stop the bleeding. In misery, he was. I left to get help, hurried to Allihies and found Cooper here."

"Thanks, Mort." Cooper turned to Puxley, Parker and Hall. "I sent Constable Appleyard to the scene with a horse and wagon to arrest Declan and take him to the gaol in Castletownbere. Appleyard arrived at the scene about two hours later, but the only sign of O'Toole was Mort's bloodied jacket. Two constables are out now, trying to find the horse and saddlebags. So far, no horse, no money, no O'Toole."

Parker spoke up. "I remember more than six months ago O'Toole came to my window to pick up his pay. Furious he was because I deducted the cost of a broken tool and a sack of barley. He yelled to other workers in line, talking about a meeting of Whiteboys at Twomey's. Haven't had any trouble from him since then, but he always looks angry when he gets his pay."

"Where's he live?" Cooper asked.

"In Cloghfune," Hall responded. "Rents from Padraigh Murley, as does his brother, Sean O'Toole. They must have a dozen children between them. Been working at the mine about nine months now."

"What does it matter who rents from whom?" Puxley asked. "I told you, Hall, the Irish are no good. Rob and murder whenever it suits them."

"Right, John," Cooper responded. "Nothing's changed. The Irish are as depraved as they were before the Union. Them Whiteboys think they can get away with maiming cattle, destroying property, and stealing. And now the mine. They'll keep at it until we send them all to the Queen's prisons in Australia or Barbados."

Puxley sat up straight in his chair and pounded his fist on the table. "Damnable Irish! I'm handcuffed. They're stealing from me like I'm a blind man. Hall, it was you, damn your hide, who said you'd find honest, hardworking men. Give them an opportunity, you said. That *is* what you said! Admit you were wrong. Dead wrong!"

"If you remember, John, I also said it takes time."

Though the Count House still held a chill, Puxley was sweating. He unbuttoned his overcoat and stood. "Time? How much time? How long did it take them to steal my payroll?" Puxley pounded the table again and again. "Damned Irish! Damned Irish!"

He glared at Hall. "How long does it take to pay rent on my estate? Hundreds live there. They haven't paid rent for over six months. Farmers keep subletting, women keep having brats. My middleman nearly got killed trying to evict a family who hasn't paid rent in more than a year. Can you tell me, Hall, how much damned time does it take?"

"I don't know. Maybe until we pay them a fair wage. They'll be at the payroll window later today. Let's deal with that first."

"Yes, John," Parker said. "Andrew's right. We must deal with that or we'll have a riot on our hands."

CHAPTER 27

AMBROSE AND DILLON

Puxley paced the perimeter of the Count House. Cooper, Parker, Hall and Downing remained at the table, eyeing him. Finally, he said, "Gentlemen, Englishmen never give way to injustice or terror. We will resolve this ugly matter before the next investors' meeting in two weeks."

"If it is humanly possible," Hall said.

"How much money do we have in the safe?" Puxley asked Parker.

"Not enough. Likely short about a hundred and fifty pounds."

"We'll take a look soon as we're done here. Constable, how do you plan to proceed?"

"First, I want to talk to Sean O'Toole this morning."

"He's under grass until evening bell," Hall said, "though Declan's son, Ambrose, is here, working on the upper dressing floor."

"That's where we'll start. Can you take me there, Colonel?"

"Of course. But the boy doesn't speak much English. Only been at the mine about nine months, same as his father and uncle."

"I'll be here with Parker for a while," Puxley said as the pair got up to leave. "On your way, check on my post boy, Dillon. Send him in. Warmer here."

"Right, sir," Hall said.

The boy was huddled inside the carriage, where his boss usually rode.

"Dillon, you're wanted in the Count House," Hall said.

The boy's surprised face appeared at the open window.

"Mr. Puxley says you'll be warmer inside."

"Rather wait out here, sir. Ain't too cold for me."

Hall raised his eyebrows. "Do I detect an Irish accent, lad?"

"Born in Dublin, I was, sir. Raised in strange circumstances. Knew me Irish first, but now know English better."

"How'd you meet your boss?"

"Last year, Mr. Puxley was at a horse fair in Dublin. I was there, too. A groom I was. He saw I could handle horses and said he was looking for a driver. Afore I knew it, he bought the carriage, the horse, and me."

"Where are your parents?" Hall asked.

"Died when I was five. 'Twas the fever. Two of my sisters lived. A brother died. Many others died. There was no one to take care of us. My sisters and I were sent to a

Dublin orphanage run by the nun sisters. They made sure we learned Irish and English, too."

"Like working for Mr. Puxley?" Hall asked.

"Sure 'n' I do. He's stern, but fair. I never get beat. Have enough to eat, a place to sleep. I'm almost sixteen. I'm grateful to Mr. Puxley. His ailing wife, too."

Yet another side of John Puxley, Hall mused.

"I'd like you to translate for a mine worker who speaks mostly Irish. Think you can?"

"I better check. Mr. Puxley might be getting ready to leave."

Hall and Cooper exchanged glances. "I'll go check with him," Cooper said. He sprinted to the Count House and returned a minute later, nodding.

"Hop down from there, Dillon. Let's go find Ambrose," Hall said.

The heavy blows of the raggers' forceful ore strikes became louder as they neared the dressing floor. The lead ragger stopped sledging as they approached.

"John, we're looking for Ambrose O'Toole," Hall said.

"I moved Ambrose and two other cobbers over to the middle dressing floor. Had trouble this morning. Was going to tell you about it, but figured Doc Mahoney would."

"I've not heard," Hall said.

"We added the five raggers you hired last week. All showed up this morning. I assigned them to work alongside the regular raggers and the cobbers, like usual."

"What happened?"

"One of the new raggers got too close to the cobber crew. Hit the ore block at an angle and sent off a stone sliver like it was shot from a pistol. It pierced a cobber's cheek. One of the Murray boys, Thomas. He was only a couple of feet away and the sliver got him just as he was swinging his hammer. Never seen anything like it."

"Is the boy alright?"

"He was scared. Gored he was. Dr. Mahoney took out the sliver and stitched him up. Thomas was mighty upset, only ten years old. Sent him home for the day."

"How many times do I have to say this can't happen again? We've got to stop these accidents."

"All about size and space, Colonel. Raggers are big, they've got to be. Cobbers are smaller, like their hammers. Once I saw what happened to Thomas, I sent Ambrose and the other cobbers to the middle dressing floor, to work with the buckers and spallers. Their hammers are smaller and there's more room there."

Hall nodded. "How about Ambrose? How's he doing?"

"He's doing what's expected of him. He's only eleven."

"Does he measure up with the other cobbers?"

"He did when he first started. Lately, he's been coughing a lot, acting tired before the end of the day. That puts pressure on the others."

"Does he come to work every day?"

"More often than not, he does."

"Constable here wants to ask him some questions."

"He done something wrong?" John asked.

"No, just want to talk to him."

"You might have trouble. He don't say much, English or Irish."

"We've got some help here," Hall said, pointing to Dillon.

On the middle dressing floor, Ambrose was swinging his hammer sharply in short arcs, knocking off bits of white quartz waste from the ore chunks in his work pile. His blond hair and freckled face were covered with ore dust.

Looks mighty serious for such a young lad. And his pants look like they'll fall off if he takes a deep breath. "Hello, Ambrose, lad. Constable Cooper here has some questions to ask you. And this is Dillon. He speaks Irish. He'll say in English what you tell us in Irish. Understand?"

After translation, Ambrose met Dillon's eyes for an instant, then shrugged. His "aye" was barely audible.

Hall led the small group off the dressing floor to a rock outcropping, away from other workers and the hammering.

Looming over the diminutive Ambrose, Cooper asked, "Where is your father?"

Dillon translated.

Ambrose looked at the ground and shrugged again.

"Look at me!" Cooper ordered.

Ambrose glanced up, then returned his gaze to the ground.

"When did you last see your father?"

Ambrose shrugged yet again, still looking at the ground.

"If you don't tell me the truth," Cooper said, "it'll be bad for you and your father."

Dillon translated.

Ambrose shook his head. With flushed cheeks, and a trembling lower lip, he extended his hands with palms upturned, as if pleading for mercy.

"Dammit, backward Irish brat!" Constable Cooper bellowed, "This is a waste of time."

"Easy, constable," Hall said. "That's enough with the boy."

"I'll talk to O'Toole's wife and what's-his-name, Murley."

Hall sent Ambrose back to the dressing floor. "Finish your day's work, lad, and go straight home."

After translating, Dillon went off-script, out of earshot of Hall and Cooper. "You afraid to say more?"

Ambrose started walking back to the dressing floor. His nod was nearly imperceptible.

CHAPTER 28

JUSTICE

Hall and Cooper walked their horses on the rough terrain leading to Murley's land. Once they reached the fields beyond Bealbarnish Gap, a panoramic view lay before them. The Slieve Mishkish Mountains to the north gave way to a huge swath of verdant fields, interspersed with furrowed rows of dark brown soil, the fecund bosom for another season's potato crop.

Hall craned his neck as the mountaintop came into view. A number of rills cascaded down its rocky façade, morphing seamlessly into a larger stream toward the mountain's base. The stream silently expanded and became a bubbling brook as it passed between shanties, haphazardly constructed on either side.

"You know where O'Toole's place is?" Cooper asked.

"Beyond the Murleys', toward the bay."

"This is God's land, not for Irish."

"Truth is, for centuries past, it was their land," Hall said.

"No more. Now the Irish can barely scrape out a living."

"Justice takes time, Constable."

"What do you know about Cloghfune, Colonel?"

"Some. I recruited quite a few workers here."

"Like the O'Toole brothers?"

"They were among the hires."

Cooper nodded. "I don't believe it's possible to take the Irish from the fields and give them real work. They're dishonest."

"If I agreed with that, Constable, Mountain Mine would be closed."

"I see their weak moral fiber all the time. Couple weeks ago, I oversaw an eviction nearby, along with another constable and the middleman, Daniel Sutchins. The farmer pleaded with Sutchins for more time. The bad crop last year put him and his family near starvation, he said. There were no potatoes to use for rent. Not our fault he's too dumb to rotate crops and put manure down. We got them out, but their resistance was fierce."

"Anyone get hurt?"

"No, but we had to burn 'em out."

Hall remained silent. *I hate your beliefs, Cooper, but I am no better. I have exploited the Irish, to get ahead with Puxley. Now, I'm bound to help you imprison one of my workers for the indefensible act of robbing Puxley's payroll. If Declan O'Toole was a free man, he wouldn't be out in the wilderness alone, maybe dying, or dead. If only Peter Lord were riding with me.*

"Murley's is close by," Hall said. "Let's stop there first, see if Murley's wife can tell us anything. Then we'll go on to O'Toole's place."

Margaret opened the door as the two men drew close. Eighteen-month-old Colm was asleep in a cloth sling harnessed over her shoulder.

"Afternoon, ma'am. Colonel Hall here. And this is Constable Cooper."

"Good morrow, kindly. What you be wanting?" Margaret asked in English.

"We're looking for Declan O'Toole. When did you see him last?"

Margaret shrugged.

"Does Padraigh know anything about O'Toole?"

"At the mine," she answered.

Hall nodded, then turned to Cooper. "Best we ride on down to O'Toole's."

"She's hiding something," Cooper said.

"Maybe, but let's go to O'Toole's."

Cooper nodded and added, "Murley's probably involved, too."

"One step at a time, Constable. Up ahead are the O'Toole cabins. Declan and his family live in one, Sean and his family in the other."

Tufts of weeds and heather marked the entryway to each mud and thatch cabin, separated by about fifty feet. Each had a narrow doorway and one window.

Declan's wife, Coleen, was returning from their potato plot. She and her eight-year-old son, Odel, and seven-year-old daughter, Camille, had been planting the spring crop. As Hall and Cooper approached slowly on horseback, she pulled each child to her and stopped. The children melded into their mother's skirts on each side of her pregnant abdomen.

Cooper dismounted about twenty feet away. "Does Declan O'Toole live here?"

No answer.

"Are you Declan O'Toole's wife?" Hall asked.

"Aye," she said, pulling her children closer.

"Where is he?" Cooper approached with long strides.

Coleen retreated a few steps back with her children, as if they were one. "Not 'ere—th' mine," she answered with a quiver in her voice.

Two toddlers ran out of the shanty, each clad in a ragged shirt. A small pig squealed and waddled out alongside them.

"Declan's probably inside." Cooper advanced toward the shanty doorway.

"Nay, he ain't!" Coleen shouted.

"You heard her! She says he ain't in here." Sean O'Toole walked out of the shanty.

Cooper drew his blunderbuss, aiming it at Sean. "Who're you?"

"Sean O'Toole," the stocky Irish farmer said through gritted teeth.

"We're looking for your brother."

"Can't help you. Don't know where he's at."

"No? You might figure it out at Castletownbere gaol."

Hall stepped in. "Where were you two days ago, in the afternoon?"

"Here, helping with planting. Stayed home from the mine to plant."

Coleen pulled her four young children closer.

"We need to take a look inside Declan's place and yours. That alright with you?" Hall asked.

Sean nodded. "Go ahead. You got the pistol."

Hall and Cooper completed the search, then returned to Coleen, her children and Sean.

"Declan O'Toole was shot during a robbery yesterday," Hall said.

Coleen gasped.

Sean stared hard at Cooper. "I don't believe it. Declan ain't that that crazy."

"It's so," Cooper said to Sean O'Toole. "Mr. Puxley's courier saw him plain as day."

"How can he be sure?" Sean asked.

"He's dead sure."

"Tell Declan it'll be a lot easier on him if he finds us before we find him," Cooper said, and added, "And we will find him." He and Hall mounted their horses and cantered past the Murley shanty on their return trip to Allihies.

As soon as Cooper and Hall were out of sight, Coleen, Sean and the four children ran to the Murleys' shanty and went inside. Margaret stood at the entryway to the room where Bridget had once lain ill. Inside, Declan lay on a straw pallet. His face was ashen, his eyes closed, his left arm immobilized with a flaxen rag stained with pink odorous drainage. He groaned and writhed involuntarily.

"Didn't take them constables long to find you," Sean said.

Declan stared toward Sean. "They arrest O'Neil?"

"Constable didn't say he's been arrested," Sean said. "Didn't even mention O'Neil. That may buy us some time."

"No time to buy. I got to get moving," Declan said weakly.

Coleen stroked her large abdomen. "You are too weak to get moving anywhere. And our baby is coming any day now."

Declan struggled to sit up but fell back on the pallet and closed his eyes. "Is it a crime to want a fair wage? Puxley gorges and we near starve."

"Shhhh. You must not go, Deck," pleaded Coleen. "I need you here."

"No. Constables will be back for sure, and you'll all be arrested for not turning me in."

Again, Declan struggled to sit up. He collapsed back onto the pallet and fell into a restless sleep.

CHAPTER 29

DECLAN

Covered with dust and dirt, Padraigh and Ambrose trudged home from the mine, their progress slowed by Padraigh's painful limp. Bealbarnish Gap loomed before them when they encountered Hall and Cooper on horseback. They stepped out of the pathway into the adjacent brush. While Hall and Cooper reined their horses to a stop, Ambrose disappeared behind Padraigh.

"Good morrow, Colonel," Padraigh said with a wave.

"Good morrow, Padraigh. Did you hear about the robbery yesterday?"

"I did. 'Tis a shame. We was paid by half today. Parker said there was nothing else he could do, but…"

"We're looking for Declan O'Toole," Cooper shouted. "The father of the little bugger hiding behind you. O'Toole got shot during the robbery. Caught red-handed, but escaped. Where were *you* yesterday afternoon, Murley?"

162

"Under grass." Padraigh's temples were pounding, his breaths came fast.

"If you see Declan, urge him to turn himself in," Hall said. "Make it easier on him. No telling what shape he's in."

"What happened?"

"Got shot pretty bad."

From behind Padraigh, a grimy blond red-faced comet streaked toward Cooper with both fists swinging. "Fairy devil! Fairy devil!" Ambrose screamed in Irish.

Padraigh surged forward, clamped his hand on Ambrose's shoulder. "Hold on, lad. Quiet."

Keeping his grip on Ambrose, he looked at the Colonel. "If I see Declan, I be sure to tell him what you said."

The two horsemen moved on.

"Where's your da?" Padraigh asked.

Ambrose shook his head. His tears turned the dust on his face into a thin mud. "Don't know. Ain't been home for two days."

When they arrived at the shanties a short time later, Padraigh ruffled Ambrose's mop of hair. "Try not to worry about your da. We'll find him."

Head bent, Ambrose turned and trudged toward home.

"What be happening to you?" Margaret asked, staring at Padraigh's limp.

"Bedad. Was under grass and coming up the ladder. Weak rung. Noticed it on me way down, but forgot about it. It broke and I fell. Landed hard on me knee and ankle."

Margaret examined his injuries. "The mine's full of danger. Got to be more careful."

"Humpf."

"Got troubles here, too," Margaret said. "Declan showed up after you and Ambrose left this morning. Bleeding and weak he was. Coleen and I figured it'd be safer for him to stay here, in our sleeping room. Constable Cooper and Colonel Hall just came by and searched Deck's place. Sean's too. Lucky they didn't search here."

"Lucky! Woman, we'd all be in gaol if they found Deck here!"

Padraigh limped into the sleeping room. "For the love o' Jesus, Deck, I wish you had listened to me. You can't stay here. Too dangerous. They'll be back. You got to get to the hills. 'Tis the only way."

"I know it, I know it," Declan muttered.

"Cooper and Hall stopped Ambrose and me on our way back from the mine and told us you been shot. Better let Ambrose see you. He's upset and scared."

"I'll fetch him," Margaret offered.

"Fetch Coleen, too," Padraigh said. "Be careful what you say to the lad. He don't know when to tell the truth and when to lie."

"Where's the money?" Padraigh asked Declan.

Declan closed his eyes. "Last I saw, it was still on the horse. Took off like a sheep in heat."

"O'Neil with you?"

Declan nodded. "He got away. But unless he made it to back country, they'll find him."

Coleen returned with Ambrose and bent over Declan. "If you want to live to see our baby, you mustn't run. Wound won't heal unless we get them lead balls out. Must be a million of 'em festering."

Ambrose moved close to his father and whispered, "Da, please don't go."

Declan, breathing fast and faint, grabbed his son's hand.

"I fear the constables may return soon and search all the tenants' cabins," Padraigh said. "Ours, too. You'll be safe tonight in the shed up yonder, where Bonine Bo grazes. Tomorrow, we'll figure out what to do."

"I want to stay with Da," Ambrose begged.

"No, lad, best you stay with your ma," Padraigh said.

Early next morning, Coleen stood outside in a cool mist and watched Ambrose run back from the shed where Declan was to have spent the night. "How's Da?" she yelled.

"He ain't there."

Massaging her abdomen through her flannel smock, she bent down to Ambrose. "Get yourself ready to work at the mine. Act like nothing's wrong. 'Tis what we must do."

"But what if Da's bleeding and calling for help? I got to find him."

"No, you mustn't."

Sean joined Coleen and Ambrose and spoke in a hushed voice. "O'Neil found his way here late last night. Woke me. Needed help to move Deck."

"Where is me Deck? I must talk with him."

"Can't tell you. A Whiteboy leader is trying to help Deck and O'Neil escape. The magistrate is fed up with the mayhem and property damage done by Whiteboys and he's bringing more constables here to find them. Deck is at the top of his list."

Coleen buried her face in her hands. "I cannot bear to think Deck will be put in gaol. Or hanged!"

"You must keep faith. Nothing more we can do for now, or we'll put Deck in more danger," Sean explained.

Ambrose clung to his mother.

"We must make things seem as normal as possible, lad," Sean said. "You and I will leave for the mine this morning at the usual time. Can you be strong, Ambrose?"

With tears filling his eyes, Ambrose nodded. Sean put his arms around the boy's small shoulders and pulled him close.

CHAPTER 30

HEDGE SCHOOL LESSON

Students sat in small groups eating lunch as Denis eyed the window behind them. Cold rain splattered through the opening onto the dirt floor. *No other way. Too much has gone wrong already.*

"Lads and lassies," he said, "I must be away this afternoon. We'll not meet again until Monday, when Schoolmaster Tucker returns."

"Awwwww."

Denis ran his fingers through his long, unruly hair. Despite the warmth from the peat fire, he shivered.

Twelve-year-old Rose raised her hand. "Poor Scholar Denis, 'tis raining hard outside. May we stay here and read our stories? We'll be quiet."

"Sorry, Rose. Not today. You must keep learning. But for today and tomorrow, at home."

Another "Awwwww."

167

How can I turn these children out? I can't. They should stay. But that can't be. What am I to do?

Finally, Denis forced a smile. "Remember, even if you're not here sitting by your slates, studying the poets, or history, or philosophy or literature, you can be learning all the time."

"That's hard to do without you and Schoolmaster Tucker," another student said.

"I know. But we're going to try something new. Before you return next week, think of something that puzzles you. About numbers, or the sun or the moon, or anything. Think hard and we'll learn the answers when we meet again."

As soon as the students had departed, Denis hurried to Master Tucker's sleeping room, where Declan slept fitfully on Tucker's cot. Denis recalled what Master Tucker had said to him the previous day. '*Soon you'll be learning what books cannot teach. Declan is here. Got himself shot. If he's found, he'll be arrested. And I will be, too. You must not tell anyone he's here. That means your ma and da, too. Can you do that?*'

Declan opened his eyes and propped himself on his elbow with a groan. "Where's Tuck?"

"Went to find someone to help you get away, before the constables find you. Left early this morning, he did."

Declan groaned again. "Fetch me some of Tuck's poitín."

From a large vat in a corner of the sleeping room, Denis filled a flask and handed it to Declan. A few minutes passed before Declan attempted to sit up to take a drink.

"Don't think you should be getting up," Denis said.

"Nay, but if I don't be getting up and out of here, worse will happen."

"How'd you get shot?"

"Don't really matter now. Stood for what is right, I did. Took an oath to stop those who rob from us, middlemen, tithers, mine owners, all of them. You may understand, considering you're learning from Tuck."

"He's been telling me about them laws the English passed so we're without land or schools. Without learning, Tuck says we lose. We have nothing to pass on. He said the reason we didn't win in 1798 was too many Irish unable to read and write, let alone lead a rebellion. Just wasn't there, even though the French tried to help us."

"He ain't far wrong," Deck said. "What else Tuck been teaching you?"

"That the reason the Americans won their revolution was because most of them were educated and were a fighting force in spite of their differences. The Irish tried to do the same thing twenty years later, but landowning Anglo-Irish and millions of Irish like us couldn't come together to fight for freedom."

Teetering, Declan lay down again. "And me, being just like your da, got no learning or know-how. So it's Whiteboys who even the score. 'Tis what we do."

"Seems like it only gets you in gaol or worse."

"That's where I'm headed if I don't leave soon."

"Tuck said you must stay here 'til he gets back."

"Don't think I've got strength enough to run anyways. Maybe I'll rest some more."

"Sure and you should. Wondering I am if you heard about Daniel O'Connell?"

Declan shook his head, his eyes beginning to close.

"O'Connell is trying to help Irish like us get our rights back."

Declan was silent for a while, then asked, "What do you mean, get our rights back?"

"O'Connell wants the Irish to be able to be elected to Parliament so we'll have a say about how we live."

"Won't do me no good. Besides, may never happen. I only want the right to be treated like a human, not a bum."

"O'Connell would say we should get our rights back with laws, not a blunderbuss. He doesn't believe in violence. He was in France during their revolution, and some say he changed after he saw all the killing and suffering."

They were quiet for a few minutes until Declan said, "Tell me more about this here O'Connell."

"He's a learned man, not poor like us. Comes from high stock. Schooled in law. Some believe in him, lots of poor folks and priests, too. And some think he's dead wrong. He talks mighty well to large crowds. They listen, but it's not done much for us so far. It'll take—"

"Enough, Denis. I got to rest a while."

"Sure and you do."

Denis left Declan in the sleeping room. *Maybe the poitín will help him sleep 'til Tuck returns. Ma's counting on me to help turn the soil, get lazy beds ready for planting. She'll be wondering where I be. And I won't be able to tell her why I ain't there. Nor Da, nor anybody. Declan is in big trouble for trying to rob his way out of being poor.*

I'm still mad at Da for making me be a Poor Scholar. He knows I'm mad, too, but he don't say much. And I don't say much to him. Not like we used to.

Been with Tuck these past eight months. It's not so hard teaching numbers and spelling to the young ones. Helps me learn, too. But Tuck says that's not enough. Learn your history, he says. Understand, you must. But I miss me ragging friends, even the Brits.

When I hear about the history of our people, it makes me think I'm in a bad dream and if I try hard enough, I will wake up and it won't be happening. Tuck always puts a twist to things I learn. Not all Irish are poor, he says. Some rich Irish landowners treat their cottiers just as bad as the English landowners do.

But why is Tuck helping him get away?

CHAPTER 31

ELEGY

The postmark was February 20, 1815, from Carleen Lord, Galway, Ireland. Hall singled out the letter from a stack of mine mail.

Dear Andrew,

It is with great sadness that I inform you that my son, Peter, died on February 10 of this year. Near death but comforted by laudanum, he wanted me to convey his last words to you. He made a valiant effort to answer your last letter, the one about worker wages at the mine and the Whiteboys' threat. If Peter could have, he would have been there with you. I wrote down what he asked me to say to you. These are his words:

My good friend, I shall not see you again. As I lie dying, my brain is alive with thoughts of the work you have undertaken. Your efforts and those of John Puxley, give me hope that though my death is at hand, the Beara will not suffer a similar fate.

Until I heard from you last year, I believed the Beara was nearing its demise because of too little land, too many poor and centuries of unjust laws, leaving the Irish powerless.

Industrial labor is not new in England, nor in parts of Northern Ireland, but it is unheard of in southwest Ireland. It is a new start, fraught with danger that may sink the Irish worker further into indentured labor. But a different picture is possible. Jobs, for one thing. With jobs come wages, money in the hands of workers. Especially for the lowest workers, money to buy goods, a concept unknown on the Beara.

Wages bring improved housing, crop choices, opportunities for advancement and a better life. Progress will be slow, considering the deprivation the Irish have endured since the Penal Laws were enacted two centuries ago.

Some Irish were lucky enough to keep their holdings and flourish. Millions of others were without rights or education. Though many of the laws have been repealed, they dealt a soul-killing blow. I fear the Irish will not soon recover.

But they must. In time, they will learn about protests, work stoppages and strikes, if they are treated unfairly. With your guidance, they will learn what they must do to achieve peaceful change.

I shall remain with you in spirit always, faithful soldier. Do not mourn for me. I am at peace, thanks to your commitment to my people.

Yours in heaven,

Peter

CHAPTER 32

INJUSTICE

The sun had set. Denis heard a sound outside, walked through the darkened classroom and listened at the doorway. Uneven footsteps approached. *Please be Tuck. I got to get home.*

Denis opened the door.

The visitor spoke first. "What you be doing still here?"

"Hard to say." Denis turned away from his father and stared blankly at the stone slates.

"What you mean, 'hard to say?' Where's Tuck?"

Denis swallowed hard. "Don't know. Not here."

"Constables out all over. Come from County Cork, they did, and the locals too. They're determined to find Deck. Couldn't be that he's here, could it?"

Denis shook his head.

"Your ma was expecting you this afternoon. Planting's not done. You forget?"

Denis shook his head again. "Tuck asked me to stay, to study some literature. Wants to talk to me about it before students' next class."

"And what might that be about?"

Denis shifted on his feet. "It's a story about prisoners chained in a cave and what happened to them."

"Here in Ireland, is it?"

Denis shook his head. "No. Far away it be, in Greece. But could be anywhere, from a long time ago."

"Seems things don't change much, do they? What is it you be knowing about what Deck did?"

"Just what you and Ma talked about last night."

"If Deck is here and the constables come, you will also be chained up in a cave, right along with him and Tuck."

Denis's mind raced. *If I tell Da that Tuck and I are hiding Deck, makes me a rat. But what if Tuck don't come back tonight? If the constables search the school, Deck is sunk and so am I.*

"I wanted you to find this out on your own," Padraigh said, "but I'm going to tell you what you need to know, so's you don't get arrested. Or worse."

Denis crossed his arms and stared at his father.

"Tuck became a Whiteboy many years ago. Still is. Took a sacred oath, he did, to uphold Whiteboys' ways of revenge. Years later, when Tuck became a schoolmaster, he wanted to quit the Whiteboys. Tried, he did, but they said they'd kill him if he quit. Tuck told me they meant it."

"I've never seen white shirts here. Isn't he too old to do them terrible things?"

"Ever seen them public Whiteboy notices? One a few weeks ago threatened to burn down Father Murphy's parsonage if he didn't stop asking for money from poor farmers. 'Twas written by Tuck."

"How do you know?"

"He's the only one around here who can write decent, except Father Murphy, and you know he didn't write it. Tuck's still sympathetic to Whiteboys, he is."

"I don't believe you! Tuck's a schoolmaster, not a Whiteboy. Never a Whiteboy, else I'd have known." Denis's face was crimson.

"Listen to me, Denny. You will get arrested, possibly hanged, if one of them constables walks in."

"Deck ain't here."

"Lying is what you be doing. I smell Deck's wound. Strong as skunk spray, only worse. I want you to leave. Now!"

"Tuck asked me to stay until he gets back. I ain't going to leave."

"You will do as I say."

"No! You forced me to be his Poor Scholar. I'm not leaving." Padraigh limped into Tuck's sleeping room with Denis close behind, yelling, "No! No! No!"

Declan sat on the edge of the cot, his chin on his chest. A burning candle behind him cast a shadow on his tattered shirt, hiding the thick gray drainage from his shoulder wound.

"Time's running out for you, Deck," Padraigh said. "Won't take them constables long to find you here. You gotta leave. Now."

"Been trying to," Deck answered.

"Where's Tuck?"

"Went to get supplies and find O'Neil. Said we'd have to hide out in the hinterland." Declan slouched more and more, until he was lying down again with his eyes closed.

"For the love o' Christ, Deck. This here war on landholders and middlemen and tithers is as bad as the damnable English laws. You Whiteboys think you can make wrong things right by stealing and maiming, but you can't. Don't you understand that?"

"There's no battle but the one I'm fighting now. Can't give up. Nothing else left for me."

"Ain't true, Deck. You got a family, a baby coming. New hope."

"No hope for me. It's like I'm underground at the mine and the walls are caving in and I can't breathe."

"I know a hiding place," Denis said, "where he can stay until Tuck comes back. In a drumlin near Mass Rock. It has a big overhang that gives shelter and a small stream near it. So many bushes have grown over the opening, no one'll look there."

Padraigh nodded. "I know it. No more 'n a mile, but the path is hilly. Can you walk that far, Deck?"

"Sure and I can, if you help me."

"Denis and I will go with you."

Denis nodded.

"We'll stop here on our way back, let Tuck know where you are."

"I'll bring some of Tuck's dulce and potato broth. Anything else?" Denis asked.

Declan attempted to sit up. "Flask. I need the flask."

"Don't worry. I got it."

An hour and a half later, well into the night, Padraigh and Denis had settled Declan in the rock cave on a bed of moss and leaves, along with the wool covering borrowed from Tuck's cot.

"Expect Tuck and O'Neil tonight," Padraigh said, "but with your Irish luck it'll be on the morrow."

Declan forced a wry smile. He was shaking. A thin layer of sweat covered his forehead.

"Don't be leaving here, or they won't know where to find you."

Lying on his back, Declan inspected his confines in the dim light of one small candle. "Not going anywhere. Will you be telling me Coleen I love her and be seeing her soon's I can? Please be telling me Ambrose to be strong, as he must be. The same to Odel, Camille and the wee ones, Mary and Margaret. I'd be a happy man if I could see me new baby."

Declan managed a half wave to Padraigh and Denis as they left. "God bless you both."

"Keep faith, Deck," Padraigh replied. "May the Holy Ghost be at your side."

CHAPTER 33

THE CAVE

"The good Lord is seeing fit to part them clouds and help us see where in tarnation we're stepping," Padraigh said. He favored his game leg as they walked back to the hedge school in darkness.

"Leg not better?" Denis asked.

"Takes time, it does. Lucky it was just me knee and ankle and not me skull."

"Wish it was me working at the mine."

"You not liking being a Poor Scholar?"

"I like teaching and learning, I do. But 'tis not the same as being at the mine with me friends."

"True, 'tis not the same. You be using your head, instead of your body like the rest of us."

Denis nodded. "But how could Tuck be a Whiteboy? It's against what he wants for me and the students. Told me, he did, he wants us to be freed, like the prisoner from the cave story I'm learning about."

Padraigh asked, "Tuck thinks you are in prison, does he?"

"In a way. The story's about prisoners chained in a cave. They can't move and can only see shadows on the wall from the glow of a fire behind them. They think what they see is real, but it's not.

"One day a prisoner gets sent out of the cave. After he gets used to the light, he understands what he sees in a true light. Feeling sorry for his fellow prisoners, he goes back and tries to get them to come into the light. They don't believe him. Frightened they are, and they decide it is better to stay in the dark and be tortured than to be free."

"Not too smart, them other prisoners. Was that the end of the story?"

"'Twas, but Tuck and I talked a long time about it. 'Tis a parable. Means the story teaches a lesson. The lesson is that we on the Beara don't know the truth about how to live better."

"But how can that story be our story?" Padraigh asked.

"Tuck says it is. We are ignorant and living in the dark. Says we must start learning the new laws that allow Irish children to go to school and priests to say Mass. It will be hard at first, just like the prisoner whose eyes hurt bad when he first stepped into the light, but that is what we must do."

"Seems like a lot to ask of poor folks. Do you agree with Tuck?"

"I agree about learning. That's why I ain't as mad anymore about you taking me away from the mine. But I'm still angry some."

"You got a right to be."

"Even if Tuck's just writing them public notices, he's still a part of what the Whiteboys do. Makes no sense that Deck and Tuck are of the same mind."

"Smart as Tuck is, he's got a blind spot, just like Deck."

"What do you mean?"

"Tuck's been living on the Beara these past ten years. Keeps saying he's going to leave, but never does. He knows the hard times of so many Irish families and sees things getting worse. Maybe he thinks he's seen the light, when he's still only seeing shadows of the truth, like thinking the Whiteboys have a right to destroy property because us Irish are treated unfairly. Ain't that what the cave story's all about?"

"Could be it is," Denis said.

The moon was cloud-covered when they arrived at the hedge school. Denis went to the hearth, picked up a candle and lit it from a peat ember. There was no sign of Tuck.

"I'll stay here," Denis said, "case Tuck and O'Neil come back tonight. They'll need to know where Deck is."

"I be leaving for home, lad. In no time, the mine bell be ringing. Afore you sleep, make sure there's no sign Deck's been here. I be checking you on the morrow."

"Don't need to."

"Going to anyway." Padraigh left for home, limping badly.

Next morning, Denis woke to the sound of heavy rain coming through the windows and the smoke hole in the thatched roof. He shivered in the early-morning cold, grabbed a poker and stirred the ashes in the hearth, hoping to see a few embers. The ash pile was cold and dark. *Bedad, shoulda stirred it last night. Not going to be easy, starting from scratch in this wet.*

The sound of horses' hooves and a loud commotion outside made Denis drop the poker and turn from the hearth. "O'Toole! Come out now! You too, Tucker! Hiding a criminal's a serious offense!"

Denis's feet froze in place. He put his hands in his overall pockets and clenched his fists. *Father Murphy, Da and all the angels and saints, where are you?*

The door burst open and three men rushed in, each aiming a dragoon pistol at him. "Get your hands out your pockets, boy, or I'll shoot!" Constable Cooper shouted. "Identify yourself!"

Denis quickly raised his hands over his head. "D-D-Denis Murley. Schoolmaster Tucker ain't here. He left for Cork three days ago. Put me in charge."

"You lying bugger!"

"Check with me ma and da, Margaret and Padraigh Murley, over yonder." Denis pointed toward his home. "And ask me schoolmaster, Thomas Tucker. He be coming back today."

"If you're lying, will be bad for you. Now, lead us to O'Toole."

"If you mean Sean or Declan O'Toole, cottiers they are on me da's leasehold over yonder." Denis pointed again. "I ain't seen neither of them in weeks."

"Outside!" ordered Cooper. He then turned to one of the constables. "Keep an eye on this one while we search the place."

After searching the two rooms of the hedge school, the constables walked outside and mounted their horses. Cooper glared down at Denis. "No sign of O'Toole. If you are lying, Murley, you'll regret it. Ever hear of Tasmania?" Smirking, Cooper said, "They like lads like you on the chain gangs."

"Let's go!" The three constables turned their horses and rode away in the direction Denis had pointed.

CHAPTER 34

SHADOW OF JUSTICE

Padraigh rose before dawn, careful not to waken Margaret or Colm. Bearing all his weight on his uninjured leg, he gingerly lowered the other to the packed dirt floor. "Och!" He raised his leg so his foot dangled above the floor. *Bedad. How am I going to get through this day? Left a load of ore down that hole, needs picking and loading and hoisting. Thank the good Lord for the new horse windlass doing the hauling.*

Margaret stirred. "What you be doing?"

"Need to get to the mine. Sunday's on the morrow. It'll come and I can rest."

"Methinks you should stay home, rest yourself today. Your breathing doesn't sound good."

"Not me breathing, 'tis me leg. Got to make things look normal with Cooper and them other constables sneaking around."

"You did nothing wrong."

185

"Not sure about that, but Denny could be in trouble. He stayed at hedge school last night. I'm hoping Tuck came back with O'Neil and found Deck where we left him. No way of knowing. No school today, but Denny'll stay there until Tuck comes back."

"You think Deck will still be alive in that cave?"

"Hard to say. He was ailing bad last night."

"Serves him right. Poor Coleen, with all them children and another any day now."

"Don't be too hard on Deck, Maggie."

"What he did was wrong, it was."

"I know, I know. I think Deck was trying to find a way out, to live like he wanted. The unfairness was too much for him. He had no know-how, other than a rebel's way. Take what you need and feck the rules because the rules are bad."

"Don't make it right."

"It don't. And Deck's paying for it."

"We're all paying for it. Gone or in gaol or hanged he'll be. Coleen with no home and the baby coming soon."

"Going to be hard, it is. Maybe the Good Lord will see his way to help Deck and Coleen."

"I'll be asking the good fairies to help."

"Truth is, neither praying nor talking to the fairies has helped us much, now has it?"

Margaret looked at the sleeping Colm, then back to Padraigh. "Thought about it, I have. Still no reason to give up."

After a breakfast of potato gruel and sweet tea, Padraigh laced his shoes, groaning when he drew the laces tight on his injured foot. "Och!" *Walking to the mine is going to be hell.*

"Denny'll be home later, God willing. That goes for me, too."

"You must. Both of you," Margaret answered.

The quitting bell rang at the mine. The broken rung that had caused Padraigh's fall the previous day was gone. There was no replacement. As the workers climbed the ladder one by one and squinted in the light of the waning day, Colonel Hall stood at the entrance.

"All workers meet on the dressing floor in front of the Count House now. I've an important announcement."

Soon, nearly a hundred workers had gathered, mostly men, with dirt and dust caked on their faces and on their ill-fitting overalls. Underground workers still had wax from melted candles stuck to their leather caps.

Hall climbed the steps to the front porch of the Count House, placing him a few feet above the workers. "Mr. Parker will be at the pay window, ready to square up with each of you, money owed from the short payday."

The workers moved toward Hall in a swarm.

Hall held up both hands. "Hold on! Hold on! No need to rush. We'll be here until the last worker is paid." *And a special thanks to Mort Downing's loyal horse. He returned to Dunboy Castle from whence he had come, and rested awhile in the cove with saddlebags full of payroll money. Not a farthing missing. Thank God Almighty.*

"Did you catch the robber?" a worker asked.

"Caught one," Hall answered. "Closing in on two others."

"Three there were?" he asked Hall.

"Two at the holdup scene. A third is suspected of helping them escape."

Oh, Christ, please don't let it be Tuck. That'll lead 'em back to me Denny, thought Padraigh.

Laughter, smiles and backslapping abounded as the workers waited for paymaster Parker's window to open.

"Lucky we be for getting this extra pay."

"Ain't luck, ain't extra, 'tis what we're owed."

"Still seems extra to me."

"The missus won't know. Methinks I should spend it proper. At Twomey's."

"Aye, Twomey's it is."

Sean O'Toole stood in line behind Padraigh.

"Hey, Paddy, me friend, you coming to Twomey's?"

"Sure, that's where I be going."

Padraigh and Sean walked together toward Twomey's. In a whisper, Sean asked, "Where's Deck?"

Padraigh answered with his head down. "Last night we moved him to a cave under a rock overhang. 'Tis safe for now."

"Them constables were snooping around at our place yesterday."

"Deck wasn't doing good last night. Needed a lot of help walking to the cave. His wound looked bad. Smelled bad."

"Think them constables will be following us?" Sean asked.

"Without a doubt, they will."

"Let's stay at Twomey's awhile, maybe throw them off."

The men shoved hard-earned shillings across the bar at Frank Twomey and his wife, Joanne, for shots of whiskey and pints of beer. A trio playing fiddle, flute and accordion sat in Twomey's music corner, blending one rousing Irish tune into another. The bar filled up quickly as each mine worker brought his unexpected pay to celebrate.

As they walked into the pub, Padraigh scanned the drinkers and singers and saw Constable Cooper sitting at a table in a corner with two other constables. Cooper nudged the other two and nodded toward Padraigh and Sean.

"Christ a'mighty! They know we're here. Better split up. Leave separately, too. I got to check on Deck first then Denis at hedge school. No idea of Tuck's whereabouts. What if he's already been arrested?"

"You, me and Denis will be in as much trouble as Deck if they find out we helped him escape," Sean said.

An hour later, Padraigh left Twomey's through a side door, his gait unsteady. He pulled out five shillings from his pocket and realized he'd spent most of his make-up pay. *Maggie'll be carping. Chest pain, cough, bad breathing, gimpy leg, too much drinking, that's me burden. Least whiskey stops me pain for a while.*

Padraigh looked over his shoulder frequently. Finally, approaching the bushes and brush that covered the opening of the rock cave, he slipped through the branches. A sharp stench made him gasp and turn away. When he finally looked at Declan, he quickly crossed himself. *God rest his soul. No escaping for Deck now. Just like them tortured prisoners. Goddammit.*

Declan's face and neck were blue, his eyes and mouth open. Padraigh picked up the borrowed cloth that lay on the ground, gently closed Declan's eyes, and covered him from head to toe. Must find Father Murphy. Deck's *deserving of the Last Blessing. Must be buried soon. Thanks to Jesus it ain't summer.*

CHAPTER 35

BITTER JUSTICE

Denis stood in the doorway of the hedge school watching his father limp up the narrow pathway. "Is Tuck inside?" Padraigh asked.

Denis nodded. "Came back before sunrise. Sleeping now, he is."

"What happened?"

"Not sure. Tuck said he was behind Mass Rock, out of sight, waiting to meet up with O'Neil to give him provisions. Father Murphy happened by on his way to his parsonage. He spotted O'Neil coming toward Mass Rock all nervous-like. When Father asked what he was doing, O'Neil said he was on his way to meet someone and ran off. Tuck said he stayed hidden, waiting for Father Murphy to leave, but Father didn't leave for a while."

"This ain't sounding good," Padraigh said.

"Tuck's worried."

"He should be worried. One of the three Whiteboys was arrested. Must be O'Neil." Padraigh crossed his arms, looking harshly at Denis.

"How you be knowing that?" Denis asked.

"Hall said so. And why is it you didn't go home today like you were supposed to?"

"Schoolmaster Tucker asked me to stay. He didn't look so good this morning when he got here."

"What you be holding behind your back, lad?"

"Nothing."

"I asked you, what's behind your back?"

"Nothing."

"Not true. Show me."

Denis stood his ground, eyeing his father, and shook his head.

Padraigh moved quickly, yanking Denis's arms forward with one quick jerk. "For the love o' Jesus! What you be doing with a pistol?"

"Master Tuck gave it to me. Asked me to stay and protect the school."

"You mean if the constables come and try to arrest Tuck?"

"Don't know. He didn't say."

"Did he show you how to use the damn thing?"

"Showed me how to shoot it, he did. Told me it would scare away them constables."

"Tuck's dreaming if he thinks the constables would be scared of you."

"You don't think I could shoot?" Denis glared at his father.

"Can't say for sure. What I do know is you were sent here to learn, not to shoot a constable or anyone else."

Tucker appeared at the doorway, unkempt, his snow-white hair adorned with twigs and dirt. The front of his shirt was bloodied and his pants were torn.

"What in the hell happened, Tuck?" Padraigh asked. "Sent my boy here to learn. Had faith in you, I did."

"Knew it was risky to help O'Neil. Felt I had to. Would be worse if he got caught."

"Well, the worst did happen, it did."

"Agh. Afraid, I was. Knew he was desperate, but it was too risky to come out from behind the Rock while Father Murphy was there. He lingered, Father did. Had a lot to pray about, I imagine. By the time Father left, O'Neil was gone."

"Looks like you got beat up," Padraigh said.

"Trying to stay away from them constables. But wanted to find O'Neil to give him a sack of potatoes, pair of boots and a coat. It was dark, no moonlight. Hadn't gotten very far when I lost me footing on one of them rock overhangs up yonder. About a ten-foot drop and I landed on a couple of sharp rocks. Got banged up."

"You risked everything." Padraigh's voice was loud. "Your life, getting me boy arrested or killed. Hall said they're looking for a third man—you—who helped the thugs get away. Was it worth it?"

"You're naïve, Paddy. Would surprise you how many hedge school teachers support the Whiteboys."

"Well, they're a lot dumber than I thought. Me Denny ain't going to write no Whiteboy threats, nor carry a pistol, nor take any secret oath. Not over my dead body."

"You can't stop me from doing what I think is right," Denis said.

Padraigh paused and took a step toward Denis. "Tell me what you think is right."

"Staying here with Schoolmaster Tucker, being his Poor Scholar, him teaching what he thinks I should be knowing."

Padraigh looked away, his eyes tearing. *How can my son be swayed so strongly by Tuck? My son, who only wanted to work with his friends at the mine. Content he was. Happy, until he discovered a world of learning and new ideas. He believed me, listened to me and his ma. That lad is gone.*

Tuck tried to explain. "I had no idea that O'Toole and O'Neil were going to rob the mine payroll. A desperate act, it was. Deck was like a caged animal for a long time. After he was shot, O'Neil came here, desperate to get to the hinterland."

"Christ a'mighty, you're just like them thugs. Can't have me boy end up dead or in gaol."

Tucker stood as straight as his aging back would allow. "You asked me to teach your boy how to understand what has happened to our people, what pushes them forward and what holds them back."

"I didn't hold no bargain for teaching him about Whiteboys, or putting a gun in his hand. Just want him to be a thinking man."

"Don't act dumb, Paddy. Rebel groups are part of the landscape and you know it. They're too scattered to be any real threat, but they think they can punish the power holders. Many believe prison or death is better than living like a slave. Others outside the pale know how to band together to get what they need or to get revenge. Whiteboys is just one group, part of our world here on the Beara and elsewhere. Don't mean I'm going to recruit Denis."

"I don't see it that way," Padraigh said.

Denis interrupted. "I want to keep learning from Schoolmaster Tuck."

Padraigh's anger gradually subsided. "You do need learning, lad. So I'm going to take you to Declan. He lies in a cave, waiting for Tuck here and O'Neil. I want you to see Declan. He died in that cave last night. Alone."

CHAPTER 36

TENTACLES OF JUSTICE

Sean O'Toole, spade in hand, approached Margaret on the well-worn path that connected the Murley plots with the O'Tooles'. "Have enough manure, do you?"

"Believe, I do. Thank you kindly, Sean," Margaret said with a smile as she wiped a layer of sweat and grime from her forehead.

A few yards away Margaret glanced at Colm. "Me tad farmer, are you be knowing you're digging the very row I just planted?" She picked Colm up and carried him three rows away, setting him down where the soil had not been turned and aerated. His blond hair fell in damp ringlets as he toddled barefoot in the untilled lazy bed row.

Sean gave a wistful sigh. "'Tis time that passes too quickly. Two years ago in March since Declan died and wee Colm barely walking."

"I remember that awful time. You've been such a help to Coleen and her chil'ren. Missing the mine, are you?"

196

"Thought I would, but me calling's here. I owe it to Declan to protect his family, helping with planting, and making sure that middleman Sutchins don't harass Coleen and her family."

"With Paddy staying at mine quarters all week, we all be needing you," Margaret said.

"I miss seeing Paddy. How's he like living at the quarters?"

"He's not liking it, never did. I don't neither. Says at least fifty boarders to a room. So overcrowded I don't see how he sleeps. But walking six miles a day to and from the mine was hard. He keeps a cough and has trouble breathing, but he's working most every day, he is."

"Seems like Denny ain't around much. He staying at the mine, too?"

"Not ever, I hope. Denny is living at hedge school since Tuck was arrested. I want him home, but he says he must stay at school until the new schoolmaster arrives. Denny's nearly seventeen, so stubborn, like his da. Hardly know him anymore." Margaret's gaze shifted from Sean to Bantry Bay behind him.

Colm scrambled into a just-planted row, and Margaret lifted him up into her arms again. Protesting, he arched his back. "Me get down!"

Margaret held her grip on Colm. "Just like Denny. He wants to get away."

Smiling, Sean tweaked Colm's cheek and asked, "What do you hear about Tuck?"

Margaret replied, "Paddy told me that after O'Neil was gaoled at County Cork for the payroll robbery, the guards told him he could be set free if he told the truth about Tuck helping the Whiteboys. They finally broke him after almost a year."

Arms folded across his chest, Sean nodded. "I don't blame him for squealing after all that time."

Margaret said, "They arrested Tuck soon after O'Neil confessed. The three judges decided a week later that Tuck was guilty of helping Deck and O'Neil and that Tuck was the one who wrote all the threats to priests, middlemen, and landowners. Usually takes a couple years to transport prisoners to Australia. Took only a month to put Tuck on a ship. Sentenced him to ten years' hard labor."

"Tuck's not used to hard labor, I fear. He's a learned man. Damnable injustice."

"He's been in prison for more than a year now. No telling if he's still alive."

"God willing, he is," Sean said. "Who's the new schoolmaster?"

"'Tis Dorian Byrne. Used to be Tuck's Poor Scholar, but he left a few years ago for Maynooth Seminary. Left there to teach here."

"Why'd he leave the seminary?" Sean asked.

"Not sure. Denny told me Dorian said he didn't have enough passion to be a priest. Maybe 'twas fate. Denny wants to stay on as a Poor Scholar, but he needs a schoolmaster to keep learning himself."

"Have you seen O'Neil since he's been out?" Sean asked.

"No, but Padraigh said bad luck follows O'Neil. After he was freed, he found work as a cottier, like before, with the O'Keefes, up in Urhan. They took in O'Neil's wife and five children, too. Had just about put his spade in the ground when he was caught stealing O'Keefe's oats and barley. Arrested again. Inside a week, he and his whole family were sent packing to a prison colony in Australia. He in chains, his wife and children not bound, but all called 'undesirables.'"

Sean looked toward the Bay. "Doubt we'll see Tommy O'Neil or his family. Ever again."

CHANGE

"**D**a!" Colm squealed as Padraigh walked into the dimly lit shanty in the waning hours of daylight. Raising his arms skyward, Colm's eyes locked with his father's. "Up Da!"

Smiling, Padraigh brushed his hands across his own arms and chest, showing Colm that he was too dirty to pick him up.

Margaret scooped Colm into her arms and planted a soft kiss on Padraigh's lips. The three embraced, Colm sandwiched between his parents. He quickly found his father's beard and began tugging on it.

"Got to give me some room, laddie. You too, Maggie." Padraigh pulled back, wheezing hard.

"Sicker, are you?" Margaret asked.

Suddenly, as if the sun had sprung from behind a threatening cloud, Padraigh beamed. "Long week it was, long as a year. I missed you, Maggie." He gave her a look, a look she knew well, a look she often returned. But not today.

200

"You're wheezing worse than last week. What happened?"

"Down in the hole every day. No wonder I be struggling for air. And them sleeping quarters ain't good for breathing. Or living, neither," looking at her softly.

Taking Margaret's hand in his, he pulled her close. She put Colm down and melded into his grimy arms. "How much longer can you go under grass, Paddy?"

"Long as it takes. We're getting by. Though I hear the price of copper is down since the war's been over with them Yanks awhile. Going to hurt us because bargains will come in low."

"When're the next bargains to be figured?"

"Day after tomorrow. If they're lower, a lot of us won't go under. The cap'ns know it. Colonel Hall, Puxley and Parker know it, too. They say cap'ns have been given blunderbusses, just in case."

"In case of what? I don't want you getting shot!"

"Don't plan to, I don't. But they can't bring all that copper up without us. We got the power, Maggie. Especially now there's none of them strange workers from the hinterland, them that used to undercut us. Ain't seen any since that strapping strange worker climbed to grass after a full day below, screeched at the top of his lungs, grabbed his stomach and fell dead. Guess they thought the mine killed him."

"So being mad gives you power, does it? Strange workers who left for good, *they're* the ones with the power. Smart power."

"Think about it. Us locals got the power."

"Be telling me about your power, if you be so kind."

"If we get fair bargains, we work. If we don't, we stop work and Puxley loses money."

"Don't like the sound of it."

"I don't like it much neither, but if we do nothing, nothing will change. A lot of folks working there are desperate as Deck was, God rest his soul."

"How many are willing to stop?"

"Truth is, I don't know. Some are fired up. Others don't say much."

"Don't matter. There's enough tilling and planting and fixing to do tomorrow that I'm betting you be too tired on Monday to make it to the Gap. Never mind halfway up the mountain."

"A betting woman is what you be?"

Margaret responded with her eyes. A glint of challenge. And resignation.

CHAPTER 38

THE WILL TO CHANGE

It was a familiar scene, workers waiting for captains to emerge from the Count House to announce monthly bargains. About seventy in all stood on the dressing floor, their eyes fixed expectantly on the empty porch. But on this day, instead of captains, Colonel Hall walked onto the porch alone.

Clearing his throat, he addressed the workers in a loud voice, "As you know, bargains have been lower than usual. England's not building warships, least not now, so the price of copper is down. And mines in South America and Australia are pulling tons of copper from the ground. Prices will come up, but it takes time. I'm asking you to be patient."

"We ain't got no more patience," a worker shouted. "None. We're clean out. Ain't fair, it ain't!"

"Hear this," Hall answered. "We offer you the best wages we can, considering the current copper price, so—"

"You're lying," another loud voice interrupted. "Full of the blarney, you are!"

All eyes focused on Hall. *If these workers strike, no telling how much we'll lose. Puxley will be in an uproar. But how can I offer increased wages when there are none?*

He took a deep breath. "We don't like it either. If the price of copper goes too low, we'll have to shut down the mine and there will be nothing for any of us. Captains Glasson, Egan, Smith, Walters, Bishop and Peirce are inside, trying to get you the best bargains they can."

"We need to know what are the wages afore we work," another angry worker yelled, "or we walk!"

"Captains will be out shortly," Hall replied.

The crowd was restive, low-pitched grumbling occasionally pierced by loud obscenities. A few men paced. Many agreed that they were ready to stop work if their bargain wage was lower than the last.

Another half hour passed before the captains emerged from the Count House. Workers pressed toward the porch as the captains communicated bargains to the assembled miners. "We got nothing," one worker yelled. "Less than last month!" The angry mumbling got even louder.

Padraigh walked up to the porch and glared at Hall. "We ain't dogs, or slaves, Colonel. You be offering us slave wages. We say no. Ain't worth our time. We do better at home planting spuds."

Hall implored them. "I urge you to take your bargains and begin work."

Padraigh shook his head and turned his back on Hall.

More than half the workers also turned their backs and began walking off the dressing floor, their feet shuffling on the dressing floor's flattened stones. The handful of workers that remained, stood waiting to accept their bare-bones bargains.

"What's going on?" Puxley strutted from his carriage as workers streamed past him. They said nothing as they stepped aside to let him pass. "Where are these workers going?" Puxley bellowed to Hall still standing on the porch landing.

Hall walked down the steps to meet Puxley. "Wouldn't take the bargains offered."

"They can't do that! Get them back here, Hall!"

"How do you suggest I get them back?"

"Order them back!" Puxley sputtered.

"Would you return if your wages kept dropping?"

"I told you to tell them the reasons. Hard times!"

"I did. They don't care about hard times. If you want them back, raise their pay to Cornwall wages."

"If I do that, there'll be more and more demands until I'm broke."

Hall stood silent.

"Get them back here!" Puxley bellowed. "I won't give in to a bunch of lawless renegades! I'll go under first!"

Hall hurried toward the mass of retreating workers and shouted, "Mr. Puxley wants to speak to you! Return to the dressing floor now!"

Nearly all returned. Those who didn't jeered, calling them weaklings and traitors. Some shook their fists at the workers willing to listen to Hall and Puxley.

Puxley stomped up the porch steps and turned to the reassembled workers. "For those who accept bargains offered, there will be no penalty. Anyone refusing to work today will receive half wages for the next three bargains."

Puxley scanned the workers' faces, then stomped down the porch steps and strode to his carriage. Dillon hopped down from his perch and opened the coach door, then scrambled to his seat and drove away rapidly, with Puxley shouting, "Go! Go!"

Hall lingered on the dressing floor with the workers. Almost all remained in groups with their respective captains. About a dozen, including Padraigh, walked toward the path that led to the packed-gravel road into Allihies and Twomey's pub.

Glasson stood on the porch alongside the other captains. He spoke with a loud, threatening voice. "You Irish who want your full pay, step forward. All others, go back to your caves."

Padraigh's feet froze. Slowly he turned around, eyes narrow slits and fists at the ready. He sprinted across the dressing floor toward the porch, but Hall grabbed him and immobilized his arms. As if shedding a burning jacket, he freed himself from Hall's clutches. Hall tried again to stop him, but the other striking workers pushed him away and followed Padraigh. The distance between Padraigh and Glasson closed rapidly as Padraigh surged though the workers toward the porch.

But Glasson was nowhere in sight. Nor were the other captains. Three men stood at the bottom of the porch steps, all dressed alike. The strikers who had followed Padraigh were nowhere to be found. He stood alone, out of breath, facing three constables. Each with a blunderbuss aimed at him.

CHAPTER 39

AFTERMATH

Dirt from the lazy bed clung to Margaret's chin and forehead as she rested her hands on the long spade handle. Beside her sat Colm, busily tossing seedlings onto nearby rocky ground. "Colm, laddie, potatoes won't grow in rock. You must plant them in the soft soil." She pointed to the lazy bed row she'd just dug. With a wide smile, Colm began tossing the potato eye seedlings in the bed.

As he toddled off, Sean walked up from the O'Toole shanty. "Ain't the strike happening today?"

"Don't know. No word. If they didn't go under grass, he'll be soon home. If they got the bargain they wanted, he'll be home at week's end."

"Haven't seen Ambrose either," Sean said. "He set out with Paddy early this morning. Since Deck's been gone, Ambrose has been Paddy's shadow. He'd rather be cobbing at the mine than here doing farming chores. Thirteen years he is now. Should be helping his ma more, sure and I know."

208

"Beara, our very land is upside down. First, Paddy wanted work at the mine, four years it's been. Now he says he won't work unless he gets paid fair. I don't know what is fair, but I know what ain't fair is Paddy's breathing troubles. And he's not the only one. And me Denny's staying at the hedge school to help the new schoolmaster. Feel like I lost me husband and me firstborn."

"Denny ain't a child no more. Thinking for himself, he is," Sean said.

"He's still a child to me."

Meanwhile, Padraigh approached the beach at Ballydonegan Bay, with Ambrose at his side, when the sun suddenly gave way to clouds. The wind picked up, brushing their faces with a cold, misty breeze.

"Don't seem like many others left with us on the strike," Ambrose said.

Padraigh nodded.

"Should we go back?"

"Likely so, and we be begging to work at half wage. Sorry, lad, right now I'm thinking how our people scattered today. Stings me, just like this here beach sand scatters in the wind and stings me eyes."

"Why can't they pay us fair?"

"Because they don't have to."

"Why not?"

"'Cause we don't stand together. Too scared and weak

to stand up to threats of half wages. Needed more workers who wouldn't back down."

Padraigh pulled out his poitín flask and took three long swallows.

"Can we get more to stand with us?" Ambrose asked.

"We will someday, lad. But not this day. We lost today. We lost big."

"Didn't lose everything!"

"No? What, then, didn't we lose?"

"I didn't lose you. Constables let you go, they did."

Padraigh squeezed Ambrose's shoulder. "You feeling all right? Your face is as pale as white quartz, it is."

"Feel a little weak. Got some pains in me stomach."

"We best be moving faster, get you home."

They had just about reached the Gap when Ambrose grabbed his abdomen, bent over and dropped his pants. Instantly, he vomited and passed watery diarrhea.

For the love o' Jesus. Can't be, but 'tis. Same fishy smell, same rice water look. Oh Lord, don't do this! It's the same as me boys, Shamus, Deil and Leo.

"Don't think I can make it." Ambrose's voice was barely audible as he defecated for the third time next to the rutted trail.

"I'll help you, lad. Got to get you home."

On their final approach to the Murley land, Ambrose staggered, lost his footing and fell in a heap.

Holy Christ! 'Tis moving too fast. Bedad! How am I going to carry this wee lad all the way home? He don't weigh much, but it's too much for me short breath.

Ambrose's eyes were closed, his face contorted in pain, giving him an elfin-like look. Padraigh struggled to lift him. "Unghhh," he groaned. "I got you, lad. We headed home now. Hold on."

Carrying the sleeping two-year-old Declan, Coleen was talking to Margaret in front of the Murley shanty when they spotted Padraigh trudging toward them, his body bent forward, his head down, concentrating on each step. He held firm the bundle draped on his back, his arms entwined with Ambrose's arms and legs.

"What happened?" Coleen screamed as she and Margaret ran toward them.

"It came on too fast. Losing all his waters, he is. Seemed okay, he did, when we left the mine. Seen this before. Our three sons. Hoped I'd never see it again."

"What should I do?" Coleen asked.

"He's got to drink, much as he can. If he loses too much liquid, we'll lose him. Believe me, I know. Don't let the other chil'ren near him. Spreads fast, it does."

"He's right, Coleen," Margaret said. "Spreads like wildfire."

Padraigh carried Ambrose to the tiny sleeping room in Coleen's shanty and laid him on the family sleeping mat.

Her four other children, Odel, Camille, Mary and Margaret, followed, watching silently.

"Keep the other children away from Ambrose, you must!" Padraigh screamed to Coleen. "This sickness will kill!"

"Where can they go? And what about me wee Declan? He must stay with me and I must care for Ambrose."

"The children will stay with us," Margaret said. "All but Declan. We will pray to the fairies that your milk will be magic so he won't get the sickness."

Padraigh shot Margaret an angry look. "You mean pray to our Lord, don't you?"

"In matters this grave, I use me heart."

Padraigh shook his head. *No use saying more.* He gathered up Coleen's four other children and herded them outside.

CHAPTER 40

KILLERS

At 10:00 am, only a handful of workers were at their stations. Colonel Hall entered Dr. Mahoney's office. "Any workers report ill this morning?"

Mahoney shook his head as he put a whiskey flask to his lips, drank, then wiped his mouth with a sleeve. "One crushed foot from an underground blast. Happened about eight o'clock. I wrapped the foot and sent him home. It will heal, but not without deformity."

Hall groaned. "Since the O'Toole boy took ill and died nearly a month ago, we've got more and more sickness. Fewer than half are reporting for work. Anything you can do to help before the mine goes broke?"

"Christ Almighty, Andrew. If I could help, I'd have done it long ago. Trouble is, we don't know what causes this illness—it's cholera. You may have heard it called Blue Death. Some get it, some don't. Some have mild symptoms,

213

some die within hours. It's likely bad water, or bad food, but no way to know."

"Don't we know anything more about this cursed disease?"

"We know that when many live and work in close quarters, like the Irish workers' quarters, infections like this one spread. And we think that's where this infection began. At present, only a handful are staying there, and those few are back at work. They've either recovered from the infection or never got it. They're the lucky ones."

"Sounds like you're guessing, Doctor."

"Not entirely. I spoke with Mrs. Riley yesterday. She was in Allihies, waiting, like me, for medical supplies to arrive from Cork. After talking with her, I'd say there's good reason to expect the disease will cool down."

"Mrs. Riley, the midwife?"

Mahoney nodded. "She keeps records of all her cases. Babies keep coming. Infections like this one show no mercy."

"What does she know about the illness?"

"Like me, she knows what she sees. She told me that cases in and around Cloghfune have decreased these past two weeks. A good sign. But she has also seen a few new cases. She is watching them closely."

"So workers staying away from the mine could be infecting one another in their homes?"

"Could be."

Hall shook his head, his expression somber.

"By the way," Mahoney said, "Padraigh Murley came to the mine yesterday. Surprised me. He's one of the few still on strike, if it can be called a strike. It's been two months."

"Sick, was he?" Hall asked.

"He's got trouble. Coughing up blood, having them damned fevers and night sweats. He wants to return to work, even at half pay, because he's afraid he won't be able to work much longer. Looks like a waif, and I told him so. Looks like 'white plague,' but I spared him that for now. Man's got to have hope."

"Consumption?"

Mahoney nodded. "He's not the only one. Murley's a fighter. He may last longer than others."

"Think he's able to work?"

"Says he wants to. They fear a bad potato crop this year. He'll return next week if his wife and young son continue to get better. They got cholera, too."

"A bad crop might not be so bad if it drives more workers back here."

"Right, Colonel. It's all about survival, isn't it? The mine or the men. Can't have both. Diseases and accidents killing off our workers, and here I am, the healer. I'm no healer when I'm called to treat crushed limbs, eyes burnt from blasting, accidents that shouldn't happen. Or this wretched illness." Mahoney reached again for his flask.

"That's not what I meant."

Mahoney uncapped his flask, tipped his head back and took another large swig of whiskey.

"There's another way to look at it," Hall said. "Man and mine moving forward. We've dug deep. We're down four hundred feet. The horse windlass has reduced the back-breaking work of hauling ore up by hand. New machinery makes crushing rock easier. New rail tracks will carry ore carts from the mine to the adit. We're growing. And profits were growing, until this illness knocked so many down. Giving up now will put the Beara back where it was before 1812, filled with desperately poor families."

"Can't go back. But the road ahead will test the Irish like never before. Reminds me of the helots from ancient Greek times. Know about them?"

Hall shifted his weight a few times, as if he'd been thrown off balance.

"No equality then, and there's none today, centuries later. Helots were born to be slaves, forced to work Sparta's land, even though they outnumbered the Spartans seven to one. Sound familiar? Took a hundred years to revolt successfully."

Hall remained silent.

"A hundred years, my friend. Don't forget that. The Irish here on the Beara will remain desperately poor, though I pray not for another hundred years."

"Keep that to yourself. Would only serve to rile up the Irish again, and that means the constables will come a-courting, guns at the ready."

"The Irish are already riled," Mahoney said. "The strike didn't amount to much, but they all know what's going on. What they lack is the collective will to act on it."

"Let's hope that continues. Without the Irish worker, we can't compete with the mines in Chile and Australia."

"I thought you were sympathetic to local workers," Mahoney said.

"I am. But unless we have enough workers, we'll fall further behind."

Mahoney took another long tipple. "We are forced, then, to rely on the Irish to keep the mine in operation."

"Without them, the mine won't survive."

"If they only knew that," Mahoney said.

"I believe many do."

CHAPTER 41

POOR SCHOLAR LESSON

Nearing home, pail and milk stool in hand, Denis spotted his mother carrying a sling full of freshly harvested potatoes from their field. "Less than half a pail of milk, Ma," he called.

"Been almost a year since Bo's last calving. If she's going dry, we'll need to take her to market. Let's try longer milkings twice a day, see if she'll give more."

"I'd milk her later, but I'm going to quarters to visit Da. Hardly ever see him. Sundays when he's home, he sleeps mostly."

"Needs to, he does. Don't get much sleep in the quarters. Says he's got to keep working. Sutchins said the estate owner is going to bring in cattle and more sheep, raise the rent, and rid the land of potato fields. Us tenants, too."

"What's happened?"

"Price of spuds is unpredictable, so the estate owner is making changes. More money for him. Less of everything for us."

218

"Ain't fair."

"No, it ain't. Da's doing all he can."

Denis nodded. "I be leaving now."

Nearing the school, Denis thought about what Dorian had told the students yesterday. "A man named Stephens is coming to help cottiers and mine workers learn how to get their rights back in ways that will stun the British."

Dorian was waiting when Denis entered the empty classroom. Befitting a young schoolmaster, Dorian wore a whitish shirt with a gathered neckline beneath an old green overcoat with tails that trailed to the backs of his knees. Flaxen knee breeches met long gray woolen socks. His shoes were black, worn down at the heels. Dark brown hair that fell to his shoulders was tied back loosely with a black ribbon.

He arose from his schoolmaster's chair, carrying a pamphlet. "Stephens'll be here in a few days. One of his Rockite friends came by late yesterday and told me. Also gave me a copy of Pastorini's Prophecy." Dorian looked at the pamphlet as if it were a rare gem.

Denis glanced at it. "Schoolmaster Tucker didn't believe in Pastorini's Prophecy. It predicted Protestants would be crushed, powerless by 1825. He didn't want students to know about the Prophecy until they learned about the history of Catholics and Protestants and could judge better the truth of it."

"You have a lot to learn," Dorian said. "Tuck is a Whiteboy. He has accepted the Prophecy."

219

"No, he hasn't. Told me before he went to prison. When he was fifteen, he didn't know the Whiteboys' oath he took was forever. He's been thinking different for all the years he's been grown. He says that education will bring us out of the dark. He's heard Daniel O'Connell preach and believes if Irish unite, we'll become free. Catholic Emancipation, he calls it. Irish will run for office and vote, is what he said. And he said the Prophecy is false."

"Your learning has just begun, Poor Scholar. The only way Catholics can fight unjust laws is by rising up. With the Prophecy in hand, James Stephens will bring the Rockites, Ribbonmen and Whiteboys together. Catholics will have the power to defeat the Protestants."

"Is this your opinion? For all I know, Pastorini could be a Whiteboy himself."

Dorian swatted at Denis as though he were a fly. "Never a Whiteboy. Pastorini is a name he's chosen. His real name is Bishop Walmsely. He's Catholic, knows math, astronomy and the evil ways of Protestants. Word traveled about the Prophecy to Stephens and the Rockite, Captain Rock. With the help of Whiteboys and Ribbonmen, they believe they will defeat the Protestants. More so now, because the Prophecy says so!"

"But Tuck sits in a prison because he was bound to help two Whiteboys who thought robbing a payroll would relieve their troubles."

Dorian's eyes narrowed. "I want you to take the Whiteboys' pledge. Help us follow Pastorini's Prophecy."

Denis shook his head.

"Wake up. These words are Catholic truths. You must stay this evening to learn more about the Prophecy."

"I can't. Need to see my da. He's been sick."

"Your da's so sick that you can't be here for a few extra hours?"

"I must see him tonight."

"Little time is left."

"I'm asking you to wait, Dorian."

CHAPTER 42

CLOSE CALL

Denis arrived at the Irish workers' quarters as the cloud-veiled sun settled onto the horizon. Located in the foothills below the overarching presence of Mountain Mine, the quarters were a mile from Allihies, along a dirt road that passed scattered houses and Twomey's pub.

The large wooden quarters resembled a low-slung barn, with a door near each end of the front wall and three small windows spaced between them. A smaller, windowless outbuilding was downslope, adjacent to the quarters. Inside, five privy holes were cut in a wooden bench over a cavernous pit. A powerful stench emanated from the outbuilding.

Denis rapped on the door but got no response. He pushed it open and entered. Wooden cots jutted out from each wall of the unlighted room, about eighty in all, spaced only inches apart. A handful of men stood in the middle of the room, some with a flask in hand, talking.

222

"Good morrow!" Denis stood just inside the door, his nostrils filled with stale, musty smells of tobacco, poitín and sweat.

No one answered.

Denis walked closer. "I'm looking for Padraigh Murley."

"And what you be wanting with Murley?" one in the group shot back.

"Me da, he is. I need to find him."

"You be looking like his boy," another said. "At Twomey's he is."

Denis nodded. "Thank you. I'll find him."

"Be sure you do. He wasn't feeling well when he left, but said being at Twomey's made his breathing better."

Denis nodded soberly and turned to leave.

"Another thing," one of the men said. "There's a meeting going on at Twomey's. A new man just came to town, calls himself a Rockite, one of them violent people. He heard about our mine troubles. Trying right now, he is, to convince workers to turn against the English, not by striking like we tried, but with guns."

Denis turned toward the door.

"Didn't I used to see you on the dressing floor awhile back?"

"A ragger, I was. Past three years I'm the Poor Scholar, for Schoolmaster Tucker 'til he was arrested. Now I'm with Schoolmaster Dorian."

"You can read and write, can you? And speak the English too?"

"Yes. Needs to be a lot more of us, and not just children. I got to be going to Twomey's. If me da comes back, kindly tell him I was here looking for him."

Denis left the quarters and hurried toward Twomey's. Approaching the entrance, he heard a stern, high-spirited voice. Inside the dim candlelit pub, Denis scanned the crowded room for his father. A short, stout bearded man stood next to Twomey's makeshift bar, holding a walking stick. Men were gathered around, all eyes focused on him.

Then Denis heard a familiar voice. "How'd you find this here copper town, Stephens?" Father Murphy asked.

"With me feet, Padre." Stephens drew a few snickers. "I come from Dublin to find men who are faithful as a shamrock and who'll help me set our brethren free."

"I saw you running from them constables in Cork awhile back," Father Murphy continued. "Like a bull trying to escape castration. Looked like a war to me."

"'Twas, and it isn't over. It's your war, too, Padre, and the war of every poor Irish mine worker and farmer. We'll never be free if we don't realize what keeps you begging for tithes, and these men here begging for decent wages."

On the far side of the room, a thin red-bearded man leaned against the wall, coughing. Denis had begun to sidle toward him when a windstorm of four uniformed constables burst in, blunderbusses in hand, shoving Denis and others aside.

"Halt, Stephens! You're under arrest!"

Stephens stepped behind two men and pushed them hard toward the constables. He disappeared from sight, slipping behind others.

Denis reached the man leaning against the far wall. "Da!" he yelled.

Padraigh's face was pale, his hair damp and bedraggled. His chest heaved with each breath. His sunken blue eyes were riveted on a wide-eyed Denis. "Don't want you here. Go home."

"Ain't leaving without you," Denis shot back.

"Leave now, afore you get rounded up with me and the others."

Grabbing Padraigh's arm, Denis pulled him toward the door. Padraigh didn't resist.

At the other end of the pub, the constables threatened to shoot if the workers surrounding Stephens didn't step away. The stunned workers stepped aside.

"Cowards!" Stephens yelled. The constables pushed him to the floor and handcuffed him.

Father Murphy was moving stealthily, crouching close to the darkened perimeter of the room, inching toward the exit, when Denis beckoned. "Father Murphy, over here!"

Father Murphy hurried to Denis and grabbed one of Padraigh's arms. "These constables mean business, Paddy. Get moving or you'll soon be in gaol." Father Murphy motioned to head for the door.

Outside, Padraigh staggered behind Twomey's, with Denis and Father Murphy holding him up. Breathless, Padraigh leaned against the rear wall. "Got to rest."

Several minutes passed before he raised his head and said, "Now, let's go."

When they reached the workers' quarters, Padraigh stumbled to the nearest wooden cot and sat on it, head down. A coughing spasm doubled him over. His breathing became louder and more labored. He spoke between coughs. "Denny, go home. Now."

"I'm staying with you, Da. We got to talk."

"Not now."

Denis stood at his father's side. "I don't understand, I don't."

"Too much mine dust, doc says."

"Da, this ain't right you being here, sick as you be. You need to be home."

Padraigh spoke in short sentences. "Under grass all week. Don't know how long. Afore I be home. Tell Ma."

"Da, come back with me and Father Murphy now."

"Need to rest, is all."

Father Murphy interrupted. "Paddy, you got to leave now. They're looking for Rockite sympathizers. You'll be arrested. Denny and me'll help you get home."

"I ain't no sympathizer. Neither is me boy. I ain't going nowhere, 'cept to me bargain here tomorrow. If the Lord is willing."

"You're as stubborn as a goat. Come, then, Denis. We're going to Cloghfune."

Denis turned to his father. "I'm not leaving you, Da."

Padraigh opened his eyes. "Don't want you here."

"Leave him be, Denis. Doubt he'd make the walk home anyway. 'Sides, constables don't want an invalid on their hands."

Denis put his hand on Padraigh's shoulder. Downcast, he started to leave with Father Murphy, then turned back. "Goodbye, Da."

Padraigh took Denis's hand and gave it a weak squeeze. His eyes welled up as he watched his son leave the quarters.

CHAPTER 43

SEEKING PADDY

Margaret was sitting near the hearth darning torn copper sacks when Denis arrived home. "Where's Da?" she asked.

"At quarters, he is. I found him at Twomey's, listening to a man name of Stephens rile up farmers and mine workers. Constables came in, arrested him and as many Irish as they could lay hands on. Da and me got out, with help from Father Murphy."

"Father Murphy?"

"At Twomey's, he was."

Margaret put down the sack and lowered her head. "Evil fairies all around, stirring up trouble by the likes of Whiteboys and now that Rockite."

"No evil fairies, Ma. 'Tis Stephens himself who is evil. Stirs up more hate, he does. If not for Father Murphy, I'm not sure we'd have made it out without getting arrested."

"What about Da?"

"Resting as best he could when I left him. But breathing hard, he was."

Margaret returned to her darning. "Been two weeks already since Da's been home. Lumpers are ready for harvesting. Big crop this year, and I need Da here to help."

"I be helping you, and Colm can help. Da won't be able to."

"What do you mean? Won't be able to help at all?"

"His breathing, Ma. He's struggling more. But Sean and the rest of the O'Tooles will be harvesting their own plots, and I know they be helping us. If only Declan were here. Wish he was."

Margaret nodded. "We learn from the past, don't we, Denny?"

"If we pay attention."

"You been paying attention these past years, being a Poor Scholar?"

"The more I pay attention, the more confused I get."

"Growing up is what you be doing."

"I hated hedge school at first, but Tuck taught me a lot. And now I can't see myself doing anything else but learning, and understanding, and teaching the children."

"What confuses you, then?"

"Tuck in prison. And Schoolmaster Dorian. He's teaching things different than Tuck. Same arithmetic, English, and bookkeeping, but he wants to teach students to believe that us farmers and mine workers got to have a revolution, guns and all. No talking or discussing. Just kill Protestants. It's in the Prophecy, he says. Tuck didn't believe any of that, even though he's a Whiteboy, like Dorian."

"I be telling you, Denny, Whiteboys have no real power. Constables round them up like sheep for slaughter. Da told me forty Whiteboys was captured and tried in Cork for shooting at the king's lieges. Don't know how many of the king's men they killed. Whiteboys acted like beasts. Instead of asking for mercy at the trial, they cursed English law and King George too."

"What happened to them?"

"Hung they were, all forty of them, their bodies given away for dissection. Not a decent burial for any of them."

Denis shuddered. "Did Da say what we should do?"

Margaret nodded. "Da is convinced we should follow Daniel O'Connell, the man they call 'The Liberator.'"

"Before Tuck was sent to prison, he taught me and the students about him, too.

Margaret added, "Da says O'Connell gathers big crowds, thousands, and his name is a rallying cry to fight for a fair say. Not with guns, but with the vote. Da told me he wants to take you to one of O'Connell's meetings, monster meetings they're called, so you can hear him and see for yourself."

"See why I'm confused? I don't want to take the Whiteboy pledge, but if I don't, Dorian will push me out. When he told me about Pastorini's Prophecy yesterday, he leaned on me again to take the pledge, but I didn't."

"You were smart. Da said you'll have a short life if you take the pledge."

Early the next morning, Margaret, Colm, Denis and all the O'Tooles gathered outside the Murley shanty with potato sacks to begin the long-awaited harvest. Margaret looked over the Murley fields of splayed potato stalks with fragile drying leaves. "'Tis a good day to start digging. Lumpers be full grown and ripe for harvest."

Coleen gathered her children around her. "Never thought we'd be here today without me precious Ambrose."

Katherine agreed, "A gentle boy with quiet ways who loved his kin."

"I always looked up to Ambrose," Camille said. "'Cept when he pulled my braids at Mass Rock."

"I miss him a lot, I do," said ten-year-old Odel. "And I miss Da too. Been three harvests now he's gone."

"When we miss people so much it hurts, sometimes hard work eases the pain," Sean said.

"Digging'll be our balm for the next few days." Denis said. He turned to Sean and added, "This year will be one of our best 'cause of them wooden bins you made. No more digging pits out back for storage, and using straw for cover. No more watching the crop get wrecked by the weather and chewed up by creatures."

"Maybe no more summer hunger!" Coleen exclaimed.

"Maybe. I was sure and enough hungry this summer," Denis said.

"Getting better, we are," Sean said. "We're learning to grow lumpers that are mighty big so's they fill us up."

"Our lives depend on them," Margaret said.

The Murleys and the O'Tooles all nodded, then went to their plots to dig with their hands and spades beneath the rows of harvest-ready potato plants. They easily filled their sacks with large, knobby light brown-skinned potatoes. After hours of toil with the sun near the horizon, they bid each other tired goodbyes and headed home. Denis and Sean each carried a final full sack of potatoes for their families.

Denis raised the lid of the new bin and emptied the potatoes, with Margaret and Colm standing close by. "I'll make some stirabout with our rich crop," Margaret said. "When you be visiting Da after hedge school tomorrow, you can take him some."

CHAPTER 44

THE FIGHT

When Denis approached the school, Dorian was outside pacing. "I fear everything is ruined. Stephens arrived yesterday. Soon as he started to speak at Twomey's, he was arrested."

"You mean the Rockite we were talking about yesterday?"

"You know he's the one, Murley."

Denis stood passive. *Yes, I do know he's the one.*

"The constables must have found out about his travels here," Dorian said. "Probably hid out near Twomey's waiting for him."

"Were others arrested?" Denis asked.

"All they could haul away is what I heard."

"Just like it'll be for us if the constables find out we're teaching Pastorini's Prophecy. It's dangerous to start teaching it now."

233

Dorian's eyes narrowed to slits. "If you can't support me by teaching the Prophecy and taking the Whiteboys' pledge, I have no use for you. Don't return tomorrow unless you support me and the pledge."

"I won't be taking the pledge," Denis said. "I won't be teaching students about maiming or killing Protestants. And I won't be here tomorrow."

Dorian spat on the ground and walked toward the school, his final words delivered over his shoulder. "You're no longer my Poor Scholar!"

"Nor do I want to be! If you follow the ways of Whiteboys, or them Rockites, I feel sorry for you. But worse for our students." Denis didn't wait for a response. Shaking with anger, he burst into a run, headed to the workers' quarters.

Richard Glasson stood by the north adit, his attention riveted on the three Irish workers standing in front of him. "Kelly, where in blazes are Shea and Murley?"

"Heard the constables were called to Twomey's last night. Big ruckus. Ain't seen Shea since. He maybe got arrested."

"What about Murley?"

No one answered.

"Tell me where he is," Glasson blustered.

"Saw him in quarters late last night," Kelly volunteered. "Breathing poorly, he was. Nowhere around this morning."

"Taking up space in quarters, is he?"

"Ain't like that," Kelly said. "He's been working every day, wants to finish his bargain. Sick, he is, with the breathing."

"That's not how I see it. You three go under grass to yesterday's level, finish loading the ore you left there."

The men turned and walked toward the adit, lunch pails in hand.

Minutes later, Glasson marched into Colonel Hall's office. "Shea and Murley didn't show up for the bell today. They're off my bargain."

"Shea was arrested last night at Twomey's. Let's find Murley," Hall said. "Doc Mahoney says his breathing problems are worse. He may be in Doc's office."

"Get Murley and Shea off my bargain," Glasson demanded.

Hall didn't respond.

The waiting room at the clinic was quiet except for harsh wheezing coming from behind the closed door of the exam room. The door opened and Dr. Mahoney appeared. "Looking for Murley? He's in here. One of the men in quarters found me late last night, worried about Murley's gasping. I managed to get him here a few hours ago. Gave him opium so he could sleep."

In the exam room, Padraigh was sitting on the edge of the table, leaning forward, his arms rigid, hands resting on his thighs. His breaths were rapid. When he exhaled, his lips made a circle as if he were going to whistle. His skin was pale and clammy.

Glasson looked at his truant mine worker. "Hall, I need a replacement."

"You have eyes, my friend, but you cannot see," Hall said. "That makes you a blind man. Return to your crew and finish your bargain. You're down two men. So be it."

Glasson scoffed, gave a nod and walked away.

Mahoney took his hollow wooden tool and listened to Padraigh's chest inch by inch. "You're more congested than a few hours ago."

"Felt... better... yesterday... Doc... at quarters."

"Chest hurts?" Mahoney asked.

Padraigh nodded.

Mahoney pulled a brown bottle from his pocket and uncorked it. "You're wearing out your heart, Murley. You can't keep going under grass if you want to keep living."

Padraigh looked at the stone floor and shrugged.

Mahoney put the bottle to Padraigh's lips. "Take a swallow. Will help your breathing."

He opened his mouth and swallowed.

"Here. Take another swallow," Mahoney said.

Padraigh's hands shook uncontrollably as he tried to take the bottle.

Mahoney again put the bottle to his lips. "Swallow. Now rest while I talk to the Colonel."

Padraigh's breathing slowed slightly but remained loud and congested.

Stepping out of earshot, Mahoney spoke in a low voice. "Not much I can do but give him opium, and I'm running low."

"How bad is it?" Hall asked.

"It's serious, Andrew. I've told you I believe he has consumption. His lungs have been weakened by the soot and dust he breathes. It's hit him harder than many these past four years. I suspect he has pneumonia again on top of his troubles. Lungs can only take so much."

"Will he get better?"

"Truth is, he's been getting sicker and sicker these past months."

"But some with consumption get treatment, like Puxley's wife, Sarah."

"True, some go to places of rest for illnesses like Murley's, and a few recover, for a while. Mrs. Puxley has been in a sanitarium in Wales for a year. No place like that for local Irish."

"I'll see to it he gets home," Hall said.

"I advise you to hurry."

"For the love of Christ, Daniel, we're killing these men. Why can't we treat them?"

"Science hasn't caught up. All we know about consumption is it kills, and it runs in families and where people live in crowded places. It hits the poor hardest. And it's worse for those like Murley, who breathe in dust and soot every day. How soon can you get him home?"

"I know a couple of copper transporters who'll take him home for a price."

The two men returned to Padraigh, who had raised his feet onto the table and was sitting nearly upright, his back resting against the wall.

"Opium's taking effect," Mahoney said. "His breathing's not as labored."

"How're you feeling, Padraigh?"

"Like a huge weight is on me, but I can bear it."

"We're going to get you home in a transporter's wagon," Hall said. "Maybe today."

"Finish me bargain first."

"There'll be more bargains. You'll get paid for the work you did."

"If I leave, I fear I won't be making it back."

Mahoney intervened. "Murley, the air in the quarters isn't good for you. You've got pneumonia again. Your chances are better on your farm."

Padraigh closed his eyes and shook his head, his chest rising high each time he took a breath.

"Putting me out to pasture, you are. Won't be able to feed me family."

CHAPTER 45

RETURN AND REPOSE

The quarters were empty when Denis arrived. *Da couldn't have gone under grass today. Got to find him.*

Following the path to the dressing floor, Denis spotted Colonel Hall in the distance, striding rapidly away. Denis began to trot. "Colonel Hall!" he called.

Hall turned around and waved.

"Looking for me da, I am. I was here yesterday and he wasn't doing good."

"Your father's on his way home, in a transporter's wagon. He needs rest."

"For how long?"

"Doctor Mahoney says as long as it takes."

"I'd like me old job back."

"I thought you were the Poor Scholar at the hedge school."

Denis shook his head, then looked at the ground.

Hall waited.

"If me da is too sick to work, I want to finish his bargain."

"But your father didn't want you to work in the mine. He wanted you to be educated."

"Yes, sir, he did. Truth is, Schoolmaster Dorian and I had a disagreement. He's not wanting me back."

"There's a place for you here. Under grass is where I need you. You're about eighteen, aren't you?"

"Not for a while. Soon maybe."

"Talk with your father first. Then return and let me know."

"Thank you, sir."

On his way home, by Ballydonegan Bay, Denis sat down on a rock partially protected from the wind by a row of low-lying bushes. He took the cup of gruel and jar of sweet tea from his lunch pail, then ate and drank as though it were his last meal. When he finished, his eyelids grew heavy, and he stretched out on the soft sand near the bushes and closed his eyes.

He was awakened by taps on his shoulder. "Denis, lad, Poor Scholar. What you be doing? Truant are you?"

Denis bolted upright. "Da?" He turned and looked over his shoulder toward the voice. "Tuck? That you? How can it be you?"

"I'm no ghost." Tuck smiled. "Though at times I wished I was. Be telling me now, you've become schoolmaster and have sent Dorian on his way."

Denis shook his head and embraced Tuck's now-thin frame. "Tuck, what did they do to you? How'd you get here?"

"'Tis a long story, lad. Judge sent me where he sends everybody who had anything to do with Whiteboys. New South Wales, Australia's where I was."

"But, Tuck, you're not a real Whiteboy. You don't kill or maim."

"True now, but I can't change the past. On the trip over, I was locked in steerage with the other convicts. When you've been in that hole once, you know you'll never be there again, because you'd rather die. We lived in slab huts with tree bark roofs. Worked the soil morning 'til night, like slaves. I got very sick, almost died. The magistrate who handled my case learned I was a schoolmaster. That saved me. When recovered, I taught the children of prison guards and convicts for two years."

"But, Tuck, I thought you'd be gone for eight more years. Feared I'd never see you again!"

"Well, me lad, I earned my release." Tuck pulled a flask from his pocket, took a long drink and offered the flask to Denis. "You like this med'cine yet? Better 'n' poitín."

"Got a taste for poitín, I do, but me da's the one who makes it. Never showed me how."

"Try this."

Denis took a large mouthful and his eyes widened. "'Tis burning all the way down." He blinked and swallowed a few more times.

"That's enough for you. Now I want to hear why you haven't challenged Dorian to take his place. Been more than three years now."

"Don't know enough to challenge him," Denis said, then he told Tuck about being fired from hedge school that morning.

"Dorian's young yet," Tuck said. "Maybe how I was at his age. He sees only one way to undo years of injustice. Having the Rockite, Stephens, here only makes Dorian more impatient."

Denis lowered his head. "I know, Tuck, I know."

"Taught you well, I did. We must always be learning to find the right answers. But I'm believing you will not find answers here."

"Here? What do you mean?"

"I mean here in Ireland. There's change a-coming, and it may be fast. Soon may come a time when you should be leaving Ireland with your family."

"Where would we go? How could we go? Anyways, I got to get home, see about me da. Why don't you come with me?"

Tuck nodded and took another swallow of whiskey.

Padraigh and Colm sat on the birch bench outside the shanty in a cool autumn mist. Padraigh's eyes were closed, and his head lay back.

Colm slipped off the bench and ran to Denis, wrapping his arms and legs around one of Denis's legs.

"Colm, what you be doing?" Denis walked with an exaggerated limp, with Colm hanging on his leg.

"I be with Da," Colm said.

Denis turned toward his father, "Da, Schoolmaster Tucker's here. He's back from Australia."

Padraigh raised his head and nodded. His chest heaved with each intake of air.

"Saints and angels welcome you, Thomas Tucker," Margaret said from the shanty doorway.

"Ah, Margaret! A welcome sight you be!" Tuck said.

Margaret smiled broadly. "You must stay with us, close to the hearth."

"Just for this evening. Must be going on the morrow."

Padraigh held his hand out to welcome Tuck.

"Saints in heaven, Paddy. You be getting better?"

"If God... is willing, Tuck... I be willing."

"He's willing all right," Margaret said. "Don't know yet if he's able."

After a supper of potato gruel, dulce and poitín, Padraigh, Margaret, Denis, Colm and Tuck sat around the hearth. "Tuck, will you return to your rightful place as schoolmaster?" Margaret asked.

"Wouldn't be hard to challenge Dorian. His youth is against him, even though he trained some at the seminary. Takes time to learn, doesn't it, Denis?"

Denis nodded and looked at Padraigh sitting in a chair, his head resting against the wall. "I was at the mine today, Da, looking for you. Told Colonel Hall I wanted to finish your bargain. He said to ask you first."

Padraigh sat straight up. "Look at me, son." His voice was unexpectedly strong and angry. "This how you want to be?"

Denis explained, "Dorian gave me a choice today. Sign the Whiteboys' pledge or no longer be his Poor Scholar. I said no to the pledge. I'm not going back. Going to work at the mine, I am."

Padraigh closed his eyes, then began coughing. Tight and constricted at first, the cough gradually increased in pitch and intensity. Like a tidal wave far out at sea, its momentum increased as the wave headed toward shore.

Then Padraigh vomited a sea of blood. Margaret hurried to him. Their eyes locked, as they had thousands of times before, but only for a second. Padraigh crumpled.

Denis, Tuck and Colm rushed to him.

"Da!"

"Paddy!"

"Da!"

"You be all right."

"We here for you!"

"Don't suffer."

Padraigh's heart stopped beating. His worldly toils finished.

CHAPTER 46

GRIEF

Sharp gusts of wind assaulted Denis, Seamus and Ryan as they stepped from the adit after climbing up vertical wooden ladders from three hundred feet below. The sun had already set. After receiving their pay from paymaster Parker, the trio joined other workers in a ragtag queue headed to Twomey's pub.

"Our bargain ends today," Denis said. "I heard they're looking for workers for Number Three shaft. Either of you know about it?"

"A new cap'n's been hired for it," Seamus answered. "Don't know more."

"No way to know if he'll be fair or not," Denis added, "until the bargain's made."

"Too many bastard captains," Ryan growled. "He's like that devil, Glasson, that's all I be hearing."

"The only good thing about Glasson is he ain't got any of his men blown up, like some others. Yet," Denis said.

The three pushed their way to the bar, where Frank Twomey and his wife were taking shouted orders. "Three whiskeys. Make 'em tall!" Seamus yelled.

Twomey focused his piercing blue eyes on Denis. "What you be doing here again, lad? You should be home with your ma."

"Like everyone else, Mr. Twomey, I come for refreshment. Me ma knows I'm here. Told her I would be."

"You been in here too much since your da passed. God rest his soul."

Denis shook his head. "I don't see it that way."

"Hmph." Twomey set three tin tumblers on the waist-high bar plank and poured three shots of whiskey.

The workers paid Twomey two pence each and took their cups to an empty table and sat down.

"What's wrong with Frank Twomey?" Seamus asked.

"Don't know," Denis answered, looking into his cup.

The din inside Twomey's rose, like the hum of a swarm of worker bees.

"Twomey knows the midwife, Mrs. Riley," Denis said, "and I suspect he heard how me ma took to lying down for weeks after me da died. She couldn't take care of Colm, or herself. Mrs. Riley was afraid she would die. I was, too."

"She was sick?" Ryan asked.

"Too much grief, Mrs. Riley told my ma and it made her feel like dying herself. When I came back to the mine, Coleen O'Toole took in Colm and cared for him like her own."

"So, did your ma get up one day?"

"Took a long time. Father Murphy visited and prayed over her a lot. Evenings and Sundays I'd play the fiddle and sing, like I used to with Bridgee. Bit by bit, Ma got better. Told me she was finally able to get up because the Cross of St. Brigid helped drive the evil fairies from our house."

"Just like me ma and da," Ryan said. "Still believing in fairies even though Father Murphy says they're wrong."

"Used to make me da angry when Ma talked about fairies," Denis said. "Now I think she be believing Father Murphy a little more."

"Hard to know what to believe," Seamus added.

"True, but one thing that's easy to believe," Denis said, "is that the Beara is changing."

"What you mean, changing?" Ryan asked.

"More workers at the mine making money. More laborers coming to work the farms. And now it isn't against the law for Irish children to go to school, there may be a national school here one day," Denis explained.

"But we still be poor as dirt," Ryan said.

"Don't have to stay poor, we don't," Denis said. "Tuck's been telling me about America, where there's lots of copper and coal mining jobs."

Hours had passed when Denis, Seamus and Ryan dug into their pockets for the fourth time.

A fiddler and tin whistler sat on the other side of the pub, playing Celtic tunes. Denis sang loudly as he walked unsteadily to the bar, coins in hand, his eyes unfocused. "Three more whiskeys." He leaned over the bar, face-to-face with Twomey.

"Why am I seeing you here too often, Denny? You know your da wouldn't allow it."

"Me da ain't here. Ain't never going to be here."

"No, but he be looking down on you. You, your ma and Colm."

"Don't know about that, I don't."

Twomey shook his head.

Denis swung his arm toward the animated pub patrons singing and laughing. "That's why I'm here. See if what they got will rub off on me. Look at 'em."

"Nay. Look at you."

Denis crossed his arms in front of his chest. "And who might you be? My father?"

Twomey poured three more whiskeys. Denis laid six-pence on the bar, picked up the drinks with both hand and performed a clumsy about-face. He returned to Seamus and Ryan, but they weren't alone. Sitting with them were two women buddlers from the mine, both about seventeen. They were all talking and laughing.

Denis put the tin cups on the table, then downed his in one swallow. Without a word, he put down his cup and stumbled out of the pub.

Early next morning, Margaret returned from the brook carrying two large pails of water and stoked the hearth ashes before adding more peat. Colm sat on Denis's back, teasing him to wake up.

Margaret looked over at the pair. "Father Murphy be saying Mass soon. You forget?"

"Didn't forget. Not feeling so good, I'm not."

"And what be wrong?"

Colm maintained his perch on Denis's back. "Denny just come home not so long ago."

"You be at Twomey's?" Margaret asked.

"Like I told you. Me, Ryan and Seamus 'd be there awhile after work."

"How much of your pay's left?"

"Most. Some."

"Blue Bell's udders are full. She ain't patient like Bonine Bo was. She be needing you now, Denny. And I told Father Murphy we'd be at Mass Rock this morning."

Denis sighed and arose with Colm's arms clamped around his neck.

Two hours later, Margaret, Colm and Denis stood close together along with other huddled families at Mass Rock. The wind whipped through the shivering congregation as Father Murphy read the Gospel and began his sermon. "We know from Epiphany that God has given us his only Son, our Savior. His light will never waver, but we must always look for it. During my five years as your priest, many of you have lost loved ones. Some of you have lost faith because of your loss and are consumed by bitterness and grief. If you keep faith, you will never be alone. Do not be afraid. Your work is not yet done here on earth."

Denis looked down and closed his eyes. Father Murphy's voice faded until Denis could no longer hear him.

CHAPTER 47

PAYDAY

Margaret bent over in front of two gravestones at the makeshift cemetery beyond Mass Rock on a cold, damp afternoon. Six-year-old Colm stood next to her. The surfaces of the stones lay flush with the ground, only a glimpse of badly carved letters visible through the dirt and leaves.

"I want to see Da's stone," Colm said.

Kneeling, Margaret said, "Brush the leaves and dirt away from Da's like I do for Bridgee's." They brushed nature's cover away and Colm ran his fingers over the carved letters on his father's stone.

"Yours says, '*Padraigh Murley died 1817 age 39.*' Mine says, '*Bridget Murley died 1813 age 3.*'" Midsentence, Margaret's eyes filled with tears.

She blessed herself. *Fairies in my silent world, keep me dear Paddy and me dear Bridgee safe from evil spirits.*

"Is Bridgee scared like me," Colm asked, "when it rains bad and there's thunder and lightning?"

251

"Never scared. She's happy in heaven."

"Will Denny have to go to heaven to be happy?"

"I pray no. Not soon, anyway."

"Why can't Denny ever be home?"

"He works hard, like Da used to. Don't leave much time, 'cept on Sunday when he comes home from the mine."

"I miss Denny and Da."

"I do too," Margaret said as she put her arm around Colm.

While Margaret and Colm were at the graves, Denis was under grass, working with a crew of four. A five-hole blast had been successful, leaving a cloud of soot and loose dust that had almost settled at the base of a ten-foot square, wood-framed work space, a stope.

Almost twenty, Denis had lost all semblance of his adolescent frame, replaced by his father's once-rugged build and stature. At five feet eleven inches, Denis moved with a swiftness, balance and awareness that had been less evident in his father. His freckled, boyish face had grown handsome. Unruly brown hair fell to the nape of his neck and sprouted from his miner's hat. He had a three-day growth of beard.

Denis stood with pick and sledge alongside Seamus, Ryan, and a fourth, older worker from Cloghfune, Thomas O'Brien. They waited for the all-clear from mining captain, James Bishop. "Damn good thing we build air tunnels between sites," Bishop said. "Dust cloud's already clearing up. Bring down them big blocks from overhead. Get every piece you can."

Each worker took up a position a few feet from the others, candles affixed to their leather caps, chiseling, hammering, picking and sledging large blocks of copper-laden ore for hours. After catching his breath from a violent coughing spell, Ryan said, "Nearly time for the bell, ain't it?"

"Believe it is," said Thomas. He groaned as he tried to stand up straight. "Payday it is."

The four began to stack their tools.

Bishop returned from the shaft, pushing two empty ore carts, and shoved them into the stope amidst the piles of ore and the four workers.

"Decent day's work, men. Before you hear the bell, fill these carts, take 'em to the shaft and load 'em into the kibble for transport. Raggers are expecting more ore afore day's done."

"How many loads?" Ryan asked, his thin face weary.

"Many as you can 'til the bell rings. I'll get another cart."

The four workers finished the workday an hour later, picked up their week's wages from paymaster Parker and headed to Twomey's pub. Crowded with patrons drinking pints of beer and shots of whiskey, the pub was noisy until Colonel Hall and Doctor Mahoney entered. Heads turned as the two men walked toward the bar.

"What brings you here, sir?" a worker asked Colonel Hall.

"We're thirsty. Not minding, are you?"

"Certainly not, sir. Just want to make sure there's no constables coming in behind you." The worker smiled.

Hall returned the smile.

"Be singing soon, we will," said the worker.

"We'll be joining you," Hall said.

Twomey greeted the men and set two tin tumblers of whiskey on the bar.

Hall looked about the pub. "No trouble so far, Dan," he said to Mahoney. "All I see is men relaxing."

"Won't stay that way long." Mahoney replied. "These men are drinking their paychecks, getting beat up, some too injured to work."

"I'd be a heavy drinker too if I never saw the light of day, worked twelve-hour shifts in the hole, plagued by danger, and for my troubles got paid less than Cornwall workers."

Hall continued, "Progress comes at a price, according to John Puxley. Would Irish farmers be better off without the mine? Depends. For Puxley and his investors, it's worth the trouble. It'll take years to know if the Irish efforts will be seen as industrial progress or a thinning of the ranks. Have you told Puxley about the Irish workers getting drunk after work, especially on payday?"

Mahoney nodded. "He's known for a long time. John believes the Irish have a character flaw and nothing can be done about it."

"Do you believe that?"

"No. These men are trying to keep hope alive. This is their respite."

Nearby, Denis stood unsteadily and reached for a tin fiddle on the bar, but his reach fell short. He stumbled and plunged forward. His three companions and most of the other patrons laughed loudly at him. He smiled sheepishly and grabbed the fiddle.

"That lad hasn't been the same since he lost his father," Mahoney said. "He's in danger, Andrew."

Hall sighed. "I know."

CHAPTER 48

PROFIT AND LOSS

John Puxley sat at the head of the conference table in the Count House, next to his largest shareholder, David Eyers. Also seated were Colonel Hall and mine accountant and paymaster James Parker. The hearth's peat fire dulled the chill of the rainy afternoon. It had been raining all week.

"Good afternoon, gentlemen," Puxley opened. "We're here to talk about annual sales and dividends." The men listened intently to Puxley.

"Unlike the losses of '13 and '17 and the meager profits of '14, '15 and '16, we've earned a nice profit this year because of risks we took and damned hard work. New equipment has increased the productivity of our three hundred workers. We're ready to install another horse whim and stable underground."

"Horses underground?" Eyers asked.

"Pit ponies. They're small, sturdy, and sure-footed, and valuable for hauling ore. After it's blasted and sledged, the ore is loaded into carts. Ponies haul the carts to the adits for raggers to unload."

"What about the water that collects down under?" Eyers asked.

"Pit ponies are helpful there, too. Like the windlass aboveground, ponies are tethered to a large circular wheel. As they walk round and round, kibbles attached to a cable lift the underground water to above grass."

"Horses live in the dark?" Eyers asked.

"They do. Pit ponies have been working in coal mines since the mid-1700s."

"Live a long life, do they?"

"Five years if we're lucky, but they do the work of a dozen men," Puxley answered.

"We've also installed a large water wheel," Hall added. "It powers heavy cast-iron slabs to break ragged ore chunks into small, pea-sized pieces."

"How was it done before?" Eyers asked.

"Women and children—by hand."

"How are the Irish workers faring?" Eyers asked.

Puxley raised his eyebrows toward Hall.

"John has given them the opportunity to prove themselves." Hall said. "We believe we provide the Irish with a decent living, not dependent on the potato."

"Countryside still looks damned hopeless to me," Eyers said.

"Takes time, Mr. Eyers," Hall answered.

"This has been our best year yet," Puxley interjected. "Even with costs for labor, equipment, buildings and supplies, we earned a profit. Shareholders will receive ninety pounds per share."

Eyers nodded approvingly.

Colonel Hall and Parker sat stone-faced.

Puxley rose abruptly. "Now that business is done, we'll take a look at the mine."

After a hasty tour, the four men returned to the Count House porch.

"Paymaster Parker will pay your dividend in cash," Puxley said.

"You're a fine leader, John." Eyers said. "Pleasure to do business with you." The two men shook hands.

As soon as Eyers was paid, he mounted his horse, waved goodbye and rode toward Allihies.

Puxley summoned his post boy, Dillon, with a whistle. Dillon drove the carriage slowly toward him.

"John, before you leave, I want to talk with you about the Irish workers."

"I don't have time, Hall."

"Please, sir. Last week, I went to Twomey's with Doc Mahoney to see for myself the drinking, rowdiness and violence, especially after payday. I agree with Daniel, we need to stop this senseless behavior somehow."

"Moving this mountain would be easier," Puxley said.

"Daniel knows of a Capuchin friar, Theobald Mathew. A humble man, I'm told, with no fear of political or religious penalties. He preaches and workers listen. He sells temperance and men buy it. They take the pledge on the spot."

Puxley scoffed. "Irish workers won't change their drinking ways."

"Their health and their livelihoods are at stake. And the mine's success depends on them."

"Look, Hall, I don't want to see these men get maimed or die. We've lost too many already. Do what you think is needed."

"I'll ask Daniel to check with Father Murphy. He'll know where to find the friar."

CHAPTER 49

LEARNING

Parishioners lingered after Mass at the Rock on an unseasonably warm Sunday morning. Father Murphy walked toward Margaret and Colm and tousled the boy's blond hair, prompting giggles. Father blessed them with a sign of the cross, prompting another giggle.

Admonishing Colm with a stern look, Margaret said flatly, "Thank you, Father."

"I pray the Lord be with you."

Margaret nodded.

"Haven't been seeing Denis for many a Sunday."

"I know, Father. Nothing I can do. Needs rest on Sundays, he does."

"Denis is gone all the time," Colm said.

"Where's he gone, Colm?" Father Murphy smiled and bent down face-to-face with Colm.

"Under grass, like me da."

260

Margaret put her arm around Colm's shoulder. "He's too young to understand. Sometimes it's hard even for mothers."

Tucker interrupted the trio. "Good morrow to all this fine day. Thought I'd be finding Denis here."

"Denny's at home," Margaret said. "Mine work's wearing him out."

"Hard work, I know it is. I want Denny to return to be my Poor Scholar."

"But Dorian is still schoolmaster, isn't he?" Margaret asked.

"I challenged Dorian, earned back me schoolmaster position. And to be sure no false voices, Father Murphy here was present to judge our answers."

"Yes, I was," Father Murphy said. "Dorian's knowledge did not nearly match Tuck's. Not on Virgil, Homer, Plato or Socrates."

"In fairness to Dorian," Tuck said, "he has learned Latin and English well. But even after his studies at Maynooth, he knows languages no better than I."

"Now you are schoolmaster again, what will become of Dorian?" Margaret asked.

"As is custom, he is ready to leave and find another schoolmaster to challenge."

"You've no Poor Scholar," Father Murphy reminded Tuck.

"I want Denis back. I still have much to teach him."

"Please come home with us to eat," Margaret said, "and talk to Denis."

"I would like that," Tuck said.

They reached the Murley shanty at midday. "Wait here on the bench," Margaret said, "while I fetch Denis."

Minutes later a sleepy-eyed, disheveled Denis appeared.

"Taking you from your rest, I am," said Tuck.

Denis shook his head. "No matter, no matter."

Tuck pointed at Colm. "You've been hiding your young brother from me. Needs to be at hedge school."

"Been meaning to, Tuck."

"I want you to return to learning, too. It's what you must do."

"Truth is, I can't for now. Me family needs me earning money. Rent has gone up again and lumpers are low."

"Something else holding you back?" Tuck asked.

Denis paused before he answered, "I didn't do what my da wanted when he was alive. Wanted me to be learned, he did, like you do. I want that too, but my mind won't let me. Under grass I can bear it. Feels like we're together, my da and me. Doing what he did, so we can live tolerably."

"You and Father Murphy talk?"

Denis shook his head. "He's good at preaching, but I'm not good at listening. 'Sides, the lumper crop is uncertain. End of summer 'twill be ready, but no telling how good it'll be."

"Who's tending them lumpers?" Tuck asked.

"My ma."

"Who else?"

"I help her when I'm home."

"Tired are you on Sunday?"

"'Tis true, but I can't change that right now."

Margaret appeared at the doorway. "Come inside for stirabout. Tuck, you sit close to the hearth."

"I may have to do some traveling in the months ahead," Tuck said after they were all seated.

"To America?" Denis asked.

"Not sure."

"But you came back—only a year ago."

"If I leave all of a sudden, it'll be for an important reason."

"Makes no sense."

"I'll be telling you more when you return to your rightful place as my Poor Scholar. In the meantime, have your ma bring Colm to school soon."

Denis smiled at Tuck. "I will, Tuck, I will."

CHAPTER 50

FALLING

Denis, Seamus, Ryan and Thomas were about to begin a new month long bargain. Each laden with a metal lunch pail, hammer, axe and chisel, they hustled for cover, heads bent low, protecting themselves from the cold, pelting rain.

Captain Bishop stood waiting as they ran to the adit. "Men, this here north shaft is deeper than the one you've been working. We're way below the water table."

"We get extra pay for bailing?" Ryan asked.

"Look at it this way—sooner water's gone, the more ore will fly your way."

Ryan turned both palms up, as if to say, nothing I can do anyway. Without warning, he began coughing hard, a harsh raspy sound.

"You with us, Ryan?" asked Bishop.

Face reddened, Ryan nodded.

Inside the adit, they began the four-hundred-and-twenty-five-foot descent down the ladder into the dark, dank mine. Waiting at the bottom was a foot of standing water.

264

Bishop pointed to Denis. "The pony's in the stable yonder, next to the shaft. Bring him here, harnessed, and lash him to the whim. Start hauling up that water straightaway."

"Yes, sir." Denis headed for the stable while Bishop continued explaining the bargain to the remaining three workers. "Big blasting today, men. Get your hammers and chisels moving so we can pack gunpowder deep in them holes."

Before Denis untethered the pit pony from its stable, he pulled a flask of poitín from his pocket and took a long swig. The pit pony's empty eyes reflected the candlelight from Denis's cap. "Buck up, Peetie. You got a long day ahead. Don't let us down." Peetie loped slowly along, prodded gently by the butt of Denis's hammer.

Hours later, after countless kibbles of water had been hoisted to the surface, Peetie stood immobile, eyes closed, still harnessed in place on the whim's circular path. It was early afternoon. The four workers had chiseled out deep blast holes. They stood outside the stope as Bishop prepared the explosives. He inserted the blasting caps and inspected the fuse lengths. "We're using a new blasting cap to set off the powder. S'posed to be much better."

"Why 'tis better?" Ryan asked.

"Uses some kind of mercury so the reaction is faster. Wait here."

Bishop again checked the blasting caps and fuses, then walked back to where they stood.

"Dangerous, is it?" Denis asked.

"Sure 'tis. You need to show proper caution. Could save your life. I'm going back in to light the fuse now. Stand by."

Without warning, a loud explosion came from the direction of the east lode. The workers looked at each other in wide-eyed alarm. Seconds later, Bishop strode toward them, hands covering his ears. "Fuse lit!"

An ear-piercing blast was followed by a black cloud of dust that filled the stope like dense fog. "Stand by here," Bishop said. "I'm going to check on that other blast. Didn't sound right. No hammering or chiseling 'til I return."

The stope was still so clouded with rock dust particles that the workers couldn't see into it. Suddenly, a flame shot out. "For the love o' Jesus!" yelled Seamus. "Fire's a-coming at us!"

"No! Will stop soon. I've heard about these flames."

Ryan squinted at Denis. "You think you're so smart, Murley, think you know everything. So you know everything about the new blasting cap, do you?"

Denis didn't answer. He and the others kept their eyes on the fire. It spontaneously disappeared seconds later, replaced by an irritating metallic odor. The four workers cupped their hands over their noses and mouths.

"I got to get outta here!" Ryan yelled, gasping for breath. His lips had a blue hue, his face ashen. He bent over and vomited.

"Bishop's coming back. Stay here."

"Can't. Got to get out." Ryan continued to gasp, still bent over, hands on his knees.

Denis turned to Seamus. "Can you help him get out? Thomas and me'll wait here for the captain."

"Might take two of us to get him up the ladder, Denny," Seamus said.

"Might," said Thomas.

Denis nodded. "Fume's getting worse. Tommy, go up top with Seamus and Ryan. I'll stay." Now pale and breathing rapidly himself, Denis said, "Get out of here—so you can get some air."

"What about you?" asked Seamus.

"I'll wait for Bishop, long as I can."

"You're crazy, man. Come with us," Seamus urged.

"No! Now go!"

They left. Denis stood alone, staring into the stope. After a while, the dust cloud and the noxious odor had dissipated enough so that breathing was easier. *Won't get me pay standing here. Looks clear. I'm going in. But first...* He pulled out his flask of poitín and drained it.

Adjusting the candle on his cap, he picked up his hammer, chisel and axe and walked into the stope. *Bedad. Never seen so much loose ore from a single blast.*

He loaded the ore into tram carts, pausing occasionally to take a few deep breaths. After filling several carts with the largest chunks, Denis turned his attention to the ceiling. He struck the loosened rock with his axe, careful not to stand directly underneath. At first, nothing. Then, a light rain of rock dust began to fall from cracks in the ceiling. Denis waited for layers of the ceiling to break loose, as had happened so many times before. Nothing.

The sprinkle of rock dust stopped. Warily, Denis prepared to strike the ceiling again. A burst of light rock and dust fell on his face. And then the ceiling came crashing down.

CHAPTER 51

SEARCHING

One-hundred-ten pound Ryan looked like a sheep draped over Seamus' bulky shoulders. Seamus said, "Hang on, Ry, we're gonna get you out."

"Can't make it." Ryan gasped. "Need air."

"Good air's up top. You gotta make it, else what'd we do without your griping every day?"

Grasping the highest rung he could reach with one hand and holding Ryan's arm with the other, Seamus began to ascend the first of many ladders from the four-hundred-and-twenty-five-foot level. Thomas followed, keeping an eye on Ryan's upside-down face.

Halfway to the top, Ryan cracked. "Stop! Can't take this."

"Hold on. Step-off coming up." Seamus stepped onto an uneven outcropping and stumbled forward, out of breath, still holding on to Ryan.

Ryan rolled off Seamus' shoulder, wheezing loudly. The two lay on their backs, looking up at Thomas. "You two all right?"

"Aye," Seamus answered. "Just got to catch me breath."

"I'm gonna go ahead," Thomas said. "Climb to grass and let Doc know you're bringing Ryan up. And also tell the Colonel about the east lode explosion that sent Captain Bishop over there to find out what happened."

"Go on, Tommy. I'll come up with Ryan."

Seamus turned to Ryan. "Better air'll help you up top."

Ryan nodded. His chest heaved as he took one painful breath after another.

When Seamus and Ryan finally emerged at the adit, Thomas, Colonel Hall and Dr. Mahoney were waiting. Ryan's eyes pleaded for relief, his mouth open, gasping for air. Mahoney looked at Ryan. "Breathing better up here?"

"Maybe a little," Ryan said, bending over, resting his hands on his thighs.

"Go to my office and rest. Wait there until I return."

Ryan began walking slowly toward the doctor's office.

"We've got to go down." Hall said. "The other crew at the east lode may have had problems, too. Doc, I'm going to need you, Seamus and Thomas to go with me."

Meanwhile, Captain Bishop had returned to the north lode site, where he'd left his team after hearing the first explosion. His face, cap, bibbed overalls, shirt and boots were blackened by soot and dust.

Bishop looked at the massive pile of rock and rubble at his work site and put his head in his hands, reeling. "This is worse than I've ever seen."

His thoughts spiraled. *Glasson and one of his workers are bad off. Two other workers are helping them to topside. And look here at this rubble. If Seamus, Thomas, Ryan and Murley didn't get out, it's their grave. Got to get help.* As Bishop neared the ladder, he saw Hall, Mahoney, Seamus and Thomas descending. Bishop sighed in relief at the sight of them, then asked. "Where's Ryan and Murley?"

"Ryan is topside, Cap'n. We left Denis here," Seamus said. "He wanted to wait to tell you about the fire and fumes from our blast."

"This is a cave-in like I've never seen. Massive."

"Denny must've gone topside," Seamus said. "He wouldn't 'a gone in alone, for Christ's sake. He knows better. But we didn't pass him coming down."

"If Murley's under this rubble because he waited for me, he's a fool." Bishop ran his dirty hands through his hair. "No sense trying to dig him out. It's a tomb."

"What about Glasson and his men?" Hall asked.

"It's not good," Bishop answered. "Glasson and one of his workers were burned. They'll need your attention, Doc. Two of Glasson's workers who escaped the fire are helping them up to grass."

"Were you able to talk to Captain Glasson?" Hall asked.

"'Fraid I was," said Bishop. "He told me they used the new mercury blasting caps for the first time. Same as I used here. Glasson was in a lot of pain. Arms and face blackened where his skin should've been. His worker was burned too, but not as bad as Glasson."

"Forget about the blasting caps, at least for now," Hall said. "Doc, Bishop, and I will go to the east lode ladder to help the rescue workers and treat the injured. Seamus and Thomas, you stay here and dig for any sign of Murley."

"We'll need all hands at the east lode, Colonel," Bishop protested. "Those men are hurt bad."

"Murley may be buried alive. I can't give up on him. Not without knowing for sure," Hall said. "Let's get moving."

CHAPTER 52

SUFFERING

"Jesus, if Denny's in there, no telling what shape he's in," Seamus said.

"May not be alive," Thomas replied.

The stope's wood-framed ceiling had collapsed, its timbers broken and interwoven with jagged chunks of ore. The nearly impregnable debris was waist-high.

"You believe in miracles?" Seamus asked.

"Never did, but I'm starting right now. We don't have much time if he's bad off."

"Murley, we're coming to get you, you son-of-a-bitch!" Seamus yelled. "You hear me, Murley?"

Silence. Without a word, Seamus and Thomas began lifting the heaviest rocks and beams with their bare hands and tossing them aside. The work was backbreaking. "Can't stop now," Thomas said after an hour. "Hope's gone if we stop."

Seamus rubbed the back of his hand across his forehead. "Aye, Tommy. We stay at it, long as we can."

Another hour passed. Their hands were bloodied. As much debris lay in front of them as they'd removed.

"Seamus, look!" Thomas shouted. "A damn boot!"

The men furiously cleared rock and debris, Thomas pulled on the boot, first gingerly, then with more force. A sharp yank freed it from its tight space. It held moist, caked blood, but no foot.

"'Tis Denny's boot, it is." Seamus said.

"Murley! You there, Murley?" Thomas yelled at the pile of debris.

Silence.

"He's here. I know he is."

"Let's get 'im out."

With renewed strength, they cleared more rubble from around the site of the boot. No further sign of Denis.

"Cave-in must've thrown him," said Seamus.

"But who knows where?" Thomas added.

"Say a prayer. And let's dig in a bigger circle."

After still more digging, Seamus stopped, bent over. "Chances of finding Denny are getting slimmer every minute, Tommy."

Thomas looked down at his bloodied hands, then pointed toward the stope's entry. "What about over there?"

"If he's under all that, he's dead." Seamus stared morosely at the rubble, ten feet beyond where they'd found the boot.

"Got to try, Seamus, got to try."

A half hour later, Thomas picked up a jagged piece of ore and showed it to Seamus. "Jesus. More blood."

"Murley! Can you hear me?" Seamus yelled. "We're coming in."

Together, Seamus and Thomas hoisted large pieces of rock from the pile until they saw a bare foot. And a bloodied pant leg. Seamus touched the foot, lightly at first, then firmly. No movement. No sound. "Foot's still warm. Gotta find his head."

Like wild men, they threw off piece by piece until they saw a bibbed overall strap, and then, a miner's cap. Finally, they uncovered a large timber, nearly split in two, folded like an inverted V over Denis's head. His face was barely visible, the timber inches from his nose and mouth.

"Denny! Can you hear me?" Seamus yelled. "We're going to get you outta here!"

Denis didn't answer.

Thomas placed his fingers on Denis's neck. "It's there! I can feel the beating. He ain't dead!"

"His chest. Got to get his chest free," Seamus said.

Thomas shouted in Denis's ear. "Murley, you smell like a poitín still. I see you breathing, so you better wake up, you drunken lout."

"Maybe poitín saved him," Seamus said.

"Or made him do something stupid, like go where he shouldn't and not see danger."

Seamus pleaded with Denis. "Murley, wake up. You gotta wake up!"

As Thomas and Seamus labored, Denis moved his head slightly. "For Christ's sake! Open your eyes, Murley!"

Denis did not open his eyes. He moaned, then fell silent again. Seamus and Thomas continued to pull away debris that still lay on him.

"Oh, Christ," Seamus whispered. "Look at his leg." A bloody, bony protrusion below his right knee had pierced his pant leg. It stuck out like a branch of a tree. His lower leg was twisted at an unnatural angle. Thomas turned away, retching.

"Tommy, get up to grass. Find Doc. I'll finish digging Murley out. We'll need Peetie and the whim to get him up top."

Thomas shook his head. "We just got one miracle, Seamus. Now we need another." He ran to the ladder and began the arduous ascent to find Doc Mahoney.

CHAPTER 53

THE BREAK

Seamus was sitting in darkness, next to Denis, when flickers of light bounded off the walls of the shaft. "Over here! Over here!" Seamus yelled.

Dr. Mahoney, Colonel Hall, Thomas and Captain Bishop came into view.

"Thought I'd seen the last of anyone. Candles gone hours ago. Denny ain't said nothing, but he's still breathing. Moaned a little before, he did, but nothing now."

Mahoney maneuvered over the rubble to look at Denis's ashen face, lit up by the glow of candles from their caps. He checked for a pulse. "Murley! Open your eyes!"

No response.

"Open your eyes, open your eyes!" Mahoney repeated.

"Been like that since we found him," Seamus said.

"He won't survive if we don't get him up top." Mahoney lowered his eyes to the jagged shin bone protruding through Denis's bloody pants. "Can't move him without a splint."

"I knew he was bad off, 'specially his leg. So I grabbed this here board from the dressing floor afore we come back down."

"Good man, Thomas." Bishop turned to Mahoney. "Only way to get him up top, Doc, is to haul him up with the horse whim."

"Got a kibble big enough?"

"Believe we do. I'll get it set up."

Mahoney faced the others. "First, his bone needs to be set straight, or he'll never walk again. Seamus, get up by his head, hold his shoulders and arms. Thomas, you hold on to his hips, so he can't move. Colonel, lift his right leg. I'll place the board under it."

Hall gaped at Denis's injury.

"I'll tell you when I'm going to set the leg," Mahoney said.

"Will he make it, Doc?" Seamus asked.

"No way to know. He's in shock. Quiet now."

They all stood still, watching intently. Mahoney pulled a knife from his pocket and cut the pant leg away, revealing more protruding bone. He tore the pant leg into narrow strips, then took hold of Denis's right foot. "Seamus, Thomas, hold him fast. One, two, three."

Mahoney pulled hard. Still holding Denis's foot with one hand, with his other hand he pushed the protruding shin bones firmly into place, forcing them together underneath the skin. The onlookers gasped.

Denis did not react.

As if preparing to darn a sock, Mahoney threaded a thin wire into the eye of a three-inch curved needle. He sewed the jagged skin wound until it was closed, twenty stitches in all. Then he tied the torn pant strips around Denis's leg and splint.

"He ain't looking good, Doc," Seamus said.

"I know. We must get him above grass straightaway."

"Kibble's ready," Bishop announced. "Hooked up to the whim. Peetie's on the path, ready to get the prod."

On Mahoney's cue, Hall, Thomas, Seamus, and Bishop lifted Denis in one motion and placed him in the kibble, his head resting against one side, his feet and splinted leg dangling over the other. Mahoney leaned over him. "We're taking you up. Hang on, lad."

Denis did not respond.

As Denis's body was hoisted in the kibble, Mahoney whispered to Hall, "Doesn't look good. If he'd been awake, he'd have fought like a madman. No protest. That's a bad sign."

Hall nodded.

Mahoney turned to Thomas and Seamus. "Get up the ladder quickly. The men up top will help you carry him to Parker's office in the Count House. My office is full. Ryan, Glasson and the other burned man are there, families too. Word travels fast." Heavy-footed and dust-covered, the pair hurried to the nearby ladder.

Darkness had fallen by the time Seamus and Thomas reached the adit. Still unconscious, Denis lay in the kibble, surrounded by workers.

"Has he moved or talked?" Seamus asked.

"Been moaning some," one worker answered. "That's all. What the hell happened?"

"Cave-in," Seamus answered. "Bad one. Lift him like a log, support his arms and head. I'll carry his bum leg. Tommy, you take the other leg and hold up his arse."

The men lifted Denis in unison, carried him to Parker's office, and carefully laid him on the cot.

"Never seen nothing like this afore," one worker said.

Another shook his head. "Bad luck runs in some families. That's Padraigh Murley's boy."

"I knew Paddy, rest his soul. Didn't know his boy here."

"Can't leave him here alone."

"We ain't leaving him," Seamus said. "One of you go to Doc's office. Tell him we're here and we need him."

Another hour passed before Mahoney and Hall entered Parker's office. "Couldn't come sooner," Mahoney said.

"Been moaning a little, he has," Seamus said.

"Every now and then he grits his teeth," Thomas added. "Turns his head some, then goes back to sleep."

"Has he drunk any water?" Mahoney asked.

"Ain't awake enough," Seamus said. "Tried to give him some, but he choked."

Mahoney looked down at Denis for a few minutes. "The lad's in a coma. He shouldn't be moved tonight. If he makes it to sunrise, we'll get him home."

"Home?" Hall raised his eyebrows.

Mahoney paused. "It's better he be at home. Infection is sure to set in his leg, his lungs, too. No avoiding it. Healing is out of my hands now. No telling how hard his head was hit."

"You mean we just see if he makes it through the night and haul him home if he does?"

"Nothing else I can do." Mahoney turned to Seamus and Thomas. "Can one of you stay 'til morning, see if you can get him to drink?"

Together, Seamus and Thomas said, "Yes, sir."

"We ain't leavin' him," Seamus added.

CHAPTER 54

UNJUST CAUSE

John Puxley stood at the head of the table in the Count House, surrounded by Colonel Hall, Dr. Mahoney, Parker and four mining captains. He waited for the men to settle in their seats. They stared at their boss, grimly, silently.

"Yesterday's explosion was caused by too much niter in the blast mixture. It came straight from the Cork Gunpowder Factory. Some say it was the mercury blasting caps. Not so."

"How can you be sure, John?" Hall asked.

Puxley's stiffened. His eyes lingered on Hall a few seconds, then he looked at the group. "Because I know explosives. Only Bishop and Glasson used the new black powder yesterday. Others used the blasting caps with no problem. We must move quickly. Send the injured workers home today."

"That's not possible, John. Three of the four injured live in Cloghfune. All were severely hurt. Both Glasson and his

282

worker have serious burns. Glasson, at least, can be taken home to Cornwall housing nearby."

"If word gets out about the explosion and cave-in, our profit margin will suffer. I can't afford it."

"Word is already out," Hall responded. "Workers are upset. They're afraid."

"I want the injured Cloghfune workers gone today. Glasson stays here with his family."

"Have you seen Glasson's burns?" Doctor Mahoney asked.

Puxley nodded stiffly, "Yes, I have, and I am concerned for him and the others, but I remind you I run this business for a profit."

Captain Bishop interrupted. "Sir, after the explosions and fire yesterday, there was a strong metallic smell. One of my workers collapsed, had to be carried up. Fumes near killed him."

"Truth is, that lad already had bad breathing," Doctor Mahoney added. "Being under grass for five years has made it worse."

Puxley shot stern looks at Bishop and Mahoney, then turned to Hall. "Take a sample of the gunpowder to the Cork Factory. Find out why they used too much niter. I can't afford to compensate these men. The factory will pay. None of the injured men will return to the mine anytime soon, if at all."

"Do you really think the gunpowder factory will admit to incorrectly mixing explosives?" Hall asked.

"I'm not paying for someone else's mistake," Puxley said with an exasperated sigh. "Our investors expect a profit."

Mahoney stood, his face reddened. "The four injured men are in grave danger. One is near death. Two others, Captain Glasson included, suffered severe burns of their arms and face. The lad overcome by fumes is better, but still very ill."

Puxley placed his fists on the table and leaned forward. "For the last time, I'm running this business to make a profit. For the men who take the risk to earn a living, the good outweighs the bad."

"We'll not prosper if able-bodied men can't or won't work," Hall responded, "and it's not only men. Women and children have accidents on the dressing floor, too. A Royal Commission has been set up to interview workers under twenty, see how they're treated, find out how many are enrolled in the national school here on the Beara."

Puxley took in a deep breath. "I'm well aware of the Devon Commission. That's all for today, gentlemen." He gathered up his top hat and overcoat and headed for the door.

Hall rose quickly and intercepted him before he reached the exit. "Wait, John. I must talk with you."

"I have no time."

"You need to take time, sir. The gunpowder factory won't pay these injured men. Traveling there will be a waste of my time."

"You may know the workers, Hall, but you don't know explosives. I know what happened. Too much niter."

"We need proof."

"Goddamn it! I looked at the gunpowder last night. That's proof enough for me and it will be for them. That is final, Hall."

The two men stared intently at each other. Neither wavered until Puxley seemed to tire of the face-off and started to leave.

"I'll go to the gunpowder factory," Hall said. "For the injured men I'll have to hire a horse and carriage."

"No. Have their families come get them."

"I doubt any family has a horse, much less a carriage. Remember, John, these men can't walk."

Another period of silence.

Finally, Puxley said, "My driver, Dillon, will return with one of my carriages and take them."

Hall nodded.

"Colonel, I want you to accompany the carriage on horseback to Cloghfune. Speak to the families. Then go to the gunpowder factory in Cork."

"That may take a few days, John. Who will be in charge while I'm gone? The toxic odor below ground lingers. I'm worried there is danger lurking. We can't afford another explosion."

"The lingering odor is harmless. The captains will be in charge while you're away."

Parker interrupted. "I looked in on Murley," he said to Hall. "You better go see him. Doc is in there now."

"Carry on," Puxley said to Hall. "Be sure you pack a sample of the new black powder. That's your evidence. The factory must take responsibility and compensate these men."

Hall followed Parker into his office. Dr. Mahoney and Seamus stood over a shivering Denis, his face sweaty and ashen, his eyes closed. He was breathing rapidly.

"Infection's already set in. It could finish him off," Mahoney said.

"Can you do anything else?"

"Done all I can."

"He took a little water and sweet tea when we roused him," Seamus said. "Choked some, but kept it down, mostly."

"Keep offering him sips. Make sure he doesn't choke. And remember, he can hear you."

"Where's Thomas?" Hall asked.

"He went back to quarters late last night," Seamus answered. "Thomas and I figured one of us needed to work our bargain today with Cap'n Bishop."

"Has Denis spoken?" Hall asked.

"Not yet, sir. Opened his eyes a little and moaned some, then back to sleep."

Hall told Seamus about the plan to transport Denis, Ryan and Malcolm to Cloghfune. "I want you to ride along to help, especially with Murley. I'll follow on horseback to talk to their families."

"Cap'n Bishop won't take me off me bargain, will he, sir?" Seamus asked.

"No. You can be sure he won't."

"I'd stay with me friend no matter what, but me family needs money. Rent's been hiked and ain't hardly enough to eat."

"I'll speak to Captain Bishop myself."

A few hours later, Hall heard the clip-clop of hooves and saw Dillon pull the carriage up to Mahoney's office.

CHAPTER 55

UNCERTAINTY

On the long bumpy ride to Cloghfune, Denis lay crumpled on the cushioned carriage seat, moaning now and then. Seamus, Ryan and Malcolm sat cramped together on the floorboard. For miles, the only sounds in Puxley's carriage were Ryan's labored wheezing and Denis's moaning. Malcolm's arm and hand burns were covered with cheesecloth bandages soaked in vinegar. His swollen eyes were closed, his face and head blackened.

Then Denis's teeth began chattering. His shivers had returned. Seamus tried to soothe him, crossing his arms over his chest and covering him with a blanket. "We're going to get you home straightaway, Murley."

No response from Denis.

"Don't you be worrying about copper, our bargain, or none of that."

Seamus turned to Ryan and Malcolm. "You're all going to get better. And if you don't know why, I be telling you.

288

You're Irish, that's why." Seamus blinked back tears, then lifted his head and forced a smile at Denis. "'Sides, Murley, you been eyeing that pretty buddler on the dressing floor. She's ripe for picking, with them freckles and blue eyes and, oh my, them long braids. I seen you looking at her, and just so you know, I been looking at her, too. So you better wake up, for Christ's sake, or I'll have no choice but to take her, and you, my friend, will lose out."

Denis fell into a deep sleep for a while, then began moaning again, turning his head from side to side. "We be home soon, Denny. Can you quiet some? Ryan's struggling to breathe, he is. And Malcolm got burned real bad at the east lode."

Denis quieted.

"Doc was right. Maybe you be hearing me."

Dillon delivered Ryan and Malcolm to their homes, accompanied by Colonel Hall, then drew the carriage up to the Murley shanty. Colm was playing in the early evening light when he saw the carriage lumbering along the narrow path. "Who that be?" he yelled. "Maybe tinkers! Or, maybe Denny!"

He sprinted toward the carriage as Margaret came rushing outside. "What has happened? Is it me Denny?"

Hall dismounted and walked toward Margaret. "It is your son, ma'am. Several were injured in an accident yesterday. Doctor Mahoney thinks Denis's best chance to wake up is here with you and your family."

"He's not awake?" Margaret asked.

"No. Doctor Mahoney thinks he's trying to, but it's hard to say."

"I can't lose me Denny." Margaret's eyes pleaded with Colonel Hall.

"His head was hit hard and his right leg was broken. He's got stitches and a splint. But there is hope. He's alive and breathing strong. The doctor wants you to give him as much broth, porridge and sweet tea as much as he can take, soon as he's able."

Hall handed Margaret a small vial. "The doctor also gave me some opium. Give it to Denis when he wakes if the pain is bad. And ask Mrs. Riley to check on him tomorrow."

Unnoticed, Colm climbed into the carriage and stared at Denis lying still on the carriage seat. Seamus put his hand on Colm's shoulder. "Your brother got hurt at the mine. Should be waking up soon, now he's home."

Colm leaned toward Denis's ear. "Wake up, Denny, you home. Schoolmaster Tucker wants you to come with me to hedge school. Can you? Please?"

Denis half-opened his eyes and looked at Colm. Then, his eyes slowly closed again.

Dillon, Colonel Hall, Seamus and Margaret stood ready to lift Denis from the carriage seat and carry him into the shanty.

"All together now," Hall commanded. With one motion, the four of them lifted Denis, carried him inside and laid him gently on a pallet near the hearth.

Dillon knelt on the earthen floor next to Denis. "If you are a sinner, may the Lord forgive you now if a priest is nowhere near."

Margaret's cheeks were streaked with tears. "And who be you to say this?"

"No harm intended, ma'am. I was a young boy when my parents died. Quick it was, no priest present to forgive their sins. The nuns at the orphanage said my parents went to hell, or maybe purgatory, a place almost as bad. Worst I ever felt. I'll never forget it."

Margaret shuddered. "Me Denny must have the last blessing, in case he don't..." She looked outside for the banshee woman of death.

"I pray he awakens," Dillon said, "but I can drive me master's carriage to fetch the priest."

"Father Murphy will come if you can find him." Margaret said. She placed her hands on Colm's shoulders and looked into his eyes. "You must find Mrs. Riley. Run to her house. Follow the path near the brook. Tell her what has happened and ask her to come first thing tomorrow."

Solemn-faced, Colm nodded to his mother, then turned to Denis. "Wait for me, Denny. I be back soon."

Hall, Seamus, Dillon and Colm left. Tears continued to trickle down Margaret's cheeks. "Denny, me firstborn, strong of mind and body, me heart will break if you are taken. Evil fairies show your mercy, not to me, but to me loving boy. Let him taste the sweet with the bitter, and fulfill his promise in this life."

Denis's head moved slightly. His eyes opened, but he said nothing.

"Keep your eyes open. Stay with me."

CHAPTER 56

BUT FOR A SPARK

"Hurry, afore the fire dies," Margaret warned Colm. She wrapped a shawl around her shoulders, drawing it tight.

"'Tis raining. Peat will be soggy."

"Don't matter. Hurry along now."

Denis hoisted himself from the hearth ledge and dropped into the chair, using his uninjured leg as a pivot.

Margaret moved the rickety table closer to him. "When you going to use your hurt leg? Mrs. Riley talked to Dr. Mahoney, and he says you should try to walk more normal."

"Easy for him to say."

"Mrs. Riley says if you don't use your leg, it'll get weaker. Been almost six months."

"'Tis me penance."

"And what cause have you to say that?" Margaret asked.

Denis fell silent for a few minutes, staring at the cold hearth. "Father Murphy told us if we been sinning, and we die without being forgiven, we go to purgatory, maybe forever."

"He be saying that. I heard him too."

293

"I'm in purgatory now, falling down a dark hole and nothing I can do."

Margaret took a deep breath. "If you think it is so, it will be so."

"Look at me, Ma. Can't go back to the mine. Can't help till the soil. Can't take a step without killing myself." Denis pulled a flask of poitín from his pants pocket and drank.

"And what sinning caused you falling in that dark hole?"

Denis's stringy hair fell to his shoulders and an unkempt beard covered his sunken cheeks. His face was drawn and pale, his eyes blank. "Me sinning is me own." He slumped over the table, laying his head on his forearm.

"Don't know so much about sinning or Father Murphy's purgatory," Margaret said, "but I know about them evil fairies. They make you crazy sometimes."

Denis didn't respond.

Margaret picked up her tools and carried them outside, along with a bag of seed potatoes for planting, but she returned to Denis's side a few minutes later. "Them fairies trying to kill you, lad. You must stand up to fight." Margaret joined her hands together. "I lost me Paddy, lost me three boys, lost me Bridgee. I'll not lose you too, Denny. I won't let them fairies have you, I won't."

Colm walked toward home carrying a large cloth bag full of wet peat, oblivious to the rain rivulets falling freely from his wide-brimmed hat. On the pathway that led to the cluster of shanties, he met Father Murphy. The priest's wool cap did little to protect him from the rain nor did his lightweight black overcoat. "Good morrow, Master Colm. Going home?"

"Yes, Father. Got this here load of peat and some kindling." Colm rested his heavy bag on the ground.

"I'm on my way to visit Denis. Been a while now since I've seen your brother. How's he doing?"

"Still trying to walk, he is, but hurts too much. He mostly hops."

"Does he have a walking stick?"

"No, Father. We help him."

"You help him a lot, do you? 'Tis a big job. How old are you?"

"I be seven years old, pretty sure."

"You're at least seven. Maybe eight by your looks."

Colm hoisted the bag of peat onto his shoulder and smiled up at Father Murphy.

"Know how to read and add numbers, do you?"

"Some. Been learning with Schoolmaster Tucker. Since Denny been hurt, I don't go too much 'cause I'm helping me ma take care of him."

"Like school, do you?"

"Sure 'n' I do. But if Denny don't get better, I be staying at home. 'Specially now 'tis planting time."

When the drenched pair arrived at the Murley shanty, Margaret was kneeling at the hearth with a black iron poker, pushing the dying embers about. "Thanks be to heaven you be back. And Father Murphy, too. Good morrow to you."

"Good morrow, kindly, Margaret." Father Murphy glanced at the cold, dark hearth and at the slumped-over Denis.

"Father, how nice of you to visit," Margaret said. "Step close to the hearth. I'll soon get it stoked again."

"Mind if I stoke it?" Father Murphy replied. "Truth is if there's but one spark, I'll find it."

"Thank you, Father. I pray there is one."

Denis remained slumped over the table. Colm whispered into his ear. "Wake up, Denny. Father Murphy's here."

Denis began to stir.

"Best let him sleep, Colm," Father Murphy said.

"No," said Margaret. "Better he's awake. Drinking too much poitín, he is. Makes him sleep too much."

"He make poitín himself?"

"Seamus and Ryan help. Day after he come home, he woke up in bad pain. Thrashed about, couldn't stop moaning. Nay, yelling he was, and shaking, too. Colonel Hall gave me opium, but it soon was gone. And then Colm and me could hardly take care of him. Mrs. Riley said poitín would help. When Seamus, Ryan and Thomas saw how bad off he was, they fixed the still that Paddy made. Used the last of our potatoes. The lads brought the barley and yeast. Took a few days, but the poitín helped. He ain't crying out no more. Problem is he ain't doing much of anything."

Colm tugged at Denis's shoulder. "Denny, wake up. Father Murphy's come to give you his blessing."

Denis raised his head enough to meet Father Murphy's gaze. "H'lo, Father."

"Greetings to you, Denis. Praying for you. So are a lot of others."

Denis nodded and slumped again, his head resting on the table. "See what I mean, Father?" said Margaret.

Father Murphy gave his blessing to the top of Denis's head. "We must pray that Denis will return to us, that he will accept what has befallen him."

"He won't return to us if he keeps drinking," Margaret responded, "not caring whether he lives or don't."

"I'd like Denis to meet Friar Mathew," Father Murphy said. "He's a young man, earnest. Not a great orator, but I've seen him talk with ordinary men, high and low. He's a gentle man, but not gentle about lives wrecked by alcohol. He helps men stop drinking."

"How does he do that?" Margaret asked.

"He has a calling. I heard it in my heart when he spoke. Felt his spirit, his force. Truth is, all Ireland is awash in poitín, making once courageous men cower. Friar Mathew speaks to large crowds. A few weeks ago he spoke to the workers at Mountain Mine. Dogged, he is, about being a real man. A real provider, protector and defender. He professes that men need courage to trust in the Lord. Men are riveted when he speaks. Women, too. He asks them to take the pledge, a temperance pledge."

"Do they?" Margaret asked.

"Most do. He kneels, asks them to kneel around him and recite the pledge together. 'I promise, as long as I am a member of the Abstinence Society, to abstain from all intoxicating liquors, except for medicinal or sacramental purposes.' After, he gives a blessing to each person who took the pledge."

Margaret put a hand on Denis's shoulder. "I must believe there is hope. Otherwise, he is lost."

CHAPTER 57

A LEAP

Margaret refreshed the fire and stirred the pot of potato gruel left over from the previous evening. "Colm, you be off to the brook. Need water straightaway to thin the gruel. Hurry now, so we won't be late for Mass."

"I'm going," Colm replied.

Denis lay on his pallet in the sleeping room.

"You be rousing, Denny," Margaret called. "Seamus and Thomas will be here soon. They'll take you to Mass and to the meeting with Friar Mathew."

"Can't. Me leg's worse today than it's ever been."

"You must try."

"Can't. Tell Seamus and Thomas I can't go with them."

"You best tell them. Father Murphy asked me to make today's Communion bread. It's ready, so I must be taking it to him now. I left some bread for you to have with the gruel."

"I don't care about bread. And I don't want them seeing me like this." Denis looked down at his misshapen right leg. A

299

knot the size of a fist protruded from the wound Dr. Mahoney had stitched. And his right leg was an inch shorter than his left. He took a few swallows from his flask. "Not today."

"Father Murphy is waiting for the Communion bread, Denny. Be sure that Colm gets on his way to Mass soon's he's back." Margaret waved goodbye and left.

Denis took another swallow. Dropping the flask on his pallet, he rolled onto his left side and used his left arm for leverage, pushing himself to a sitting position. Then he used both arms to raise himself up, standing with all his weight on his good leg. "Arrgggghh."

He stood motionless, listening for Seamus and Thomas. *I can't go with you. That is all I have to say. Won't say no more. They'll understand.*

No sooner had Denis decided what to say to his friends, Colm returned, smiling, with a pail full of water. "How's this, Denny?"

Denis nodded and smiled.

"Ma said I must be helping you get ready for Mass and the meeting after."

"Can't go. I told her so. You go along."

"Guess I better, else I'll be late. Ma said she was going to put water in the gruel for thinning."

"Okay, wee brother, leave the pail on the hearth."

A few minutes after Colm left for Mass Rock, Seamus and Thomas arrived. Thomas carried an ash walking stick under his arm. Seamus carried a flask of poitín.

300

"Good morrow, Denny," they said in unison.

"Can't go with you," Denis said.

"Murley, what are we to do? Drag you? Push you? Or maybe you want us to carry you?" Seamus asked.

"Don't want you to do nothing. I can't go, and you be knowing it."

"No, you be knowing it," Thomas chimed. "We think you be wanting your ma to take care of you cause you're too weak to do for yourself."

Denis flushed. His neck muscles tightened. "Yeah, that's right! How'd you know? So get the feck outta here."

"Don't matter, ma's boy," Seamus said. "We ain't leaving until we leave with you. Mass Rock and then to the gathering with Friar Mathew."

Denis snatched the walking stick from Thomas and threw it at the stone hearth. The stick whacked the side of the black iron pot, sending splashes of potato gruel onto the hearth, narrowly missing Seamus. "For Christ's sake, Murley! You're coming with us even if we have to drag you. 'Tis up to you."

"Git outta here!"

Thomas retrieved the walking stick from the hearth, wiped off the potato gruel and returned the stick to Denis. Denis immediately flung the stick again. Thomas retrieved it again and returned it to Denis. "We're walking out the door here, Murley, and you're coming with us. So get yourself ready."

"You're crazy. I'm done. Will never walk again. Just hop around."

"If you say you won't, you won't."

"You sons o' bitches. What do you know? Nothing!" Denis grabbed a chair and flung it with all the strength of a ragger. It broke into three pieces that ricocheted off the stone hearth and crashed into the wall.

"You done?" Seamus asked.

"No, I ain't! You want to know what 'done' is? Watch me." He hopped to the wall where pieces of the chair had landed.

"Okay, so you ain't done," Thomas said. "Aim your fit out the door, for Christ's sake. Your ma and brother need a home to come back to."

"Leave me alone. Get the feck out!"

"Can't. Here's the walking stick."

"Won't do me no good."

"'Fraid to try it?"

Denis yanked the walking stick from Thomas, held it by the shaft in one hand, took four wobbly steps outside and flung the stick like a javelin.

"No I ain't 'fraid to try it. I just ain't going to."

"Finally giving up, you are?" Seamus asked. "Wait for your ma to hold your hand while you hop around like a damned rabbit."

"If I could reach you, you'd be yelping for your own ma."

"You're too much of a dosser to try," Seamus said.

302

Denis lunged toward Seamus, but fell short. Seamus walked backward, egging Denis on. "Better wait for your ma."

Denis advanced until the foot of his good leg struck a mound of dirt and he tumbled to the ground. He lay there for a few minutes with his eyes closed.

Seamus stood nearby, waiting for Denis to speak, while Thomas retrieved the walking stick. "Going to get up, Murley?" Seamus asked.

"Only to beat your arse."

"Not if you're dragging yourself on your belly."

"Here." Thomas handed the walking stick to Denis again. "You'll need this."

Denis's jaws tightened. "I'm gonna teach you feckin' arses a painful lesson."

Thomas started to giggle first, then Seamus. Soon Denis gave in to the infectious laughter. Seamus and Thomas laughed so hard they dropped to the ground, but then a different sound took over. Denis's laughter morphed into a guttural whimper, then into loud, uncontrollable weeping.

Seamus and Thomas looked on helplessly. "Think he might die?" Thomas asked.

Seamus shook his head. "No. He'll pull through. He got through the cave-in, didn't he?"

Denis kept crying.

"Murley, we'll wait for you," Seamus said, "long as it takes."

CHAPTER 58

THE PLEDGE

Ten men knelt in a semicircle at Mass Rock. Friar Mathew anointed the forehead of the last member inducted into the Abstinence Society. "Reward James O'Reilly with the gift of temperance and the will to reap the reward of mental clarity."

The friar turned a broad smile to the group. "Here we go in the name of God! Rejoice with each other as you come to the altar to make your mark in the Abstinence Pledge Book."

Smiles and handshakes were interrupted when a trio of young men approached Mass Rock. Father Murphy leaned into Friar Mathew. "The lad in the middle is the one I've told you about. It's a miracle he's alive. Another that he came today."

"Let's see if we can turn the young man to a different life."

"That would be still another miracle, Friar."

Denis stood between Seamus and Thomas, his weight on his left leg, using the walking stick for balance. Despite the cool morning, his face and hair were sweaty.

Colm stood beside his mother, then began to sprint toward his brother. "Denny!"

"Heads up, Murley," Seamus said. "We won't let him knock you over."

"May not matter. The big force coming at me ain't Colm. Mass Rock is coming at me like a cyclone. I'm going to get crushed." Denis's arms began to shake.

"Relax," Thomas urged. "Look how far you've traveled these past two hours."

"Me legs ain't going to hold me," Denis said. His eyes rolled upward and his legs gave way as he dropped to the ground.

Friar Mathew knelt beside Denis. "What are you feeling, lad?"

Denis's whole body shook. He closed his eyes. "Mass Rock's about to flatten me. Kill me, it will. I deserve it."

"Deserve it, do you now? Could be you're suffering for a reason."

"Don't know. But I'm scared, is what I am."

"Of what?"

Denis didn't hesitate. "Afraid I'll die. Too weak to stop it."

"I can help you be stronger."

Colm sat on the ground next to Denis. Thomas and Seamus hovered on either side.

"I know what has happened to you," Friar Mathew continued, "and I know what it's like to fear for your life. Before

I went to seminary I drank every day. Couldn't live without poitín. I resigned from Maynooth after two years because I was about to get thrown out, whether I stopped drinking or not. Wasn't until an evil birdman threatened me that I took the path to the friary. Without alcohol."

Denis's eyes remained closed. Friar Mathew grasped Denis's hand and said, "I am asking you to take the path of abstinence with me."

Eyes still closed, Denis shook his head. "I need to find my father. When I reach for him, he turns away. When I talk to him, he disappears. When I ask him to forgive me, blood spews from his mouth." Tears seeped out of Denis's eyes.

"Trust me to help you. Seamus and Thomas, too."

Seamus raised his eyebrows. "How will you help us, Friar?"

"Irishmen have learned that poitín dulls pain, makes people laugh and dance, makes the heart and head forget about the troubles of the past and the pain of the present. But, over time, alcohol takes away right thinking. The men here today took a pledge to live without alcohol and, if necessary, with pain."

"You mean forever without poitín?" Seamus asked.

"You have free will. The pledge will help you abstain from drink. And I will pray for you to keep your pledge."

Denis opened his eyes and raised his head, focusing on Colm. "Ma still here?"

"She's praying the Rosary over yonder." Colm pointed.

"Go tell her I couldn't get to Mass, but I'm going to stay here and take the pledge. Tell her I can't see my way ahead, but this is what I will do today."

"I be telling her." Colm got up and ran to his mother.

CHAPTER 59

AN ACCOUNTING

Colonel Hall, Daniel Mahoney and James Parker were seated at the Count House table when John Puxley flung open the heavy oak door.

"We've a lot of work to do this morning, gentlemen. Not enough time to do it all unless your reports are ready." He took the chair at the head of the table.

"Good morning, sir." Hall turned in his seat to face Puxley.

"Morning, Colonel. Good morning, James, Daniel."

"Morning, John," Daniel said.

"Yes, sir, good morning," James said.

"Colonel, have we received compensation from the Cork Gunpowder Factory for the injured workers?"

"Not yet. Cork's three-judge panel heard the case only a month ago."

"A month ago? Why, Hall? Tell me why there's been a five-month delay."

"The trial calendars were packed because of Whiteboys, Rockites, and other gangsters."

"Damnable situation. What happened when the case was heard? I trust you were there."

"Of course I was there. The factory owner produced the amounts of niter, charcoal and sulfur used to make the explosive, and a sample proving, he said, no error in the mixing. I presented the sample of the tainted powder, lighter in color than the owner's sample, and answered all questions about the explosions and injuries."

"What did the judges say?"

"They need to study it, and consult with someone who knows more about explosives."

"If only I could've been there," Puxley sputtered. "I was in Wales. My wife's had a setback."

"Sorry, sir. But we should hear from the panel soon."

Puxley abruptly turned from Hall to Parker. "You have the Investors Report?"

Parker handed it to Puxley.

The room went quiet as Puxley read the four-page report. When he finally looked up, he shook his head. "I'm concerned about all these expenses. Why are the numbers so high?"

Parker sat forward in his chair. "The cost of sending Glasson and his family back to Cornwall was considerable. And he's been in the Prince of Wales Hospital since his return. It's in the report, sir."

"Six months and still in the hospital? Why? What happened?"

"Glasson's doctor wrote several weeks ago," Mahoney answered. "Glasson's infection had already set in by the time he got there. The doctor feared the arm might have to be amputated. Glasson's fingers and elbows were frozen because of the terrible pain. I've not heard more since then."

Puxley jabbed his finger at Hall. "We'll go out of business if we don't win the claim against the factory. Shouldn't take this long, damn it all."

"What does Glasson's care cost?" Hall asked.

"One hundred pounds a month," Parker said.

Puxley sat ramrod straight on the edge of his seat. "What about the local workers who were injured? What did that cost me?"

"Nothing," Mahoney answered. "But they've suffered mightily. The worker burned alongside Glasson is healing slowly, according to the midwife. The worker who had severe breathing difficulty is not able to work, though Mrs. Riley tells me he is somewhat better."

"And the third worker?" Puxley asked.

"Denis Murley," Mahoney said. "No one thought he'd live, but somehow he did. He's about twenty and crippled. He'll never go under grass again."

Puxley returned to the Investors Report. "What are all these charges under 'Other'?" He pointed to a list of entries:

Blasting powder, 90 pounds
Candles, #85
Hammers, #26
Shovels, #18

"Missing equipment and supplies," Parker answered. "We figure they were stolen by the Irish workers. We have to account for the cost."

Puxley turned to Hall. "What do you intend to do about these thefts?"

"A lot of pilfering happens at night. I'll hire a night watchman, perhaps an off-duty constable."

"Then do it," Puxley ordered. "I won't be surprised if the investors pull out, given the stealing, accidents, bad weather and lousy morale. I've never seen so many problems. Aside from the weather, all caused by the Irish."

Mahoney stood. "Take a look at my report, John. We've hired an additional hundred workers these past six months. We had another explosion just a month ago. Two men are sitting at home in darkness because of it. Both are blind."

Puxley snatched the report from Mahoney's hand. "I am running this business, or trying to. Dammit, you are the physician. You tell me. What should we do?"

"Start a savings account," Mahoney said. "Have workers and management contribute monthly, give workers injury compensation."

"And when will this end?" Puxley asked. "When I am broke?"

"It may never end," Mahoney answered. "Not until we can protect our workers from accidents that maim and kill."

"That's your job, Hall. Yours, too Daniel."

"I assure you," Hall said, "we are doing all we can to keep the workers safe."

"We're shaving at least fifteen years off the lives of those who go underground." Mahoney was angry. "Do you know that, John?"

"Of course I know it. Some days, like today, I wish I'd never set foot on the Beara. But there is no turning back. We all know that."

"Hold it, John," Parker said. "You haven't looked at the last page of the report. Despite our problems, the investors' profit is up to fifty-six pounds per share, more than last quarter. For now, at least, you can afford to compensate injured workers, if you choose to do it."

Puxley studied the last page of the report. "Well, that is some relief. We can pay a small amount to the injured workers. But no more than six months. And not retroactively. I will set the amount. The investors, I believe, will approve my generosity."

CHAPTER 60

THE CLIMB

Aided by his walking stick, Denis walked alone through Bealbarnish Gap on the trail to Ballydonegan Bay, wincing when he encountered uneven ground. The trail ahead lay beneath a nearly cloudless sky. *Come on, Murley, get your arse to Bally Bay, or die trying, you dosser. You've never gotten through the Gap since you took the pledge. You used to run through it all the way to Allihies, headwinds or no. Now a headwind like never before. Don't matter. Do it! Do it for Da.*

Denis's thoughts were interrupted by a faint conversation that gradually grew louder. Denis listened closely.

"I hear when friends go to high places, they don't care no more about their old friends."

"I be hearing that, too."

"Shame, 'tis. 'Specially when the no-more friend had a chance to meet a pretty lass at Twomey's."

Denis stopped and turned to see Seamus and Thomas, both grinning. Denis's face relaxed into a broad smile.

"How you be doing, Denny?"

"Doing okay. Been walking, I have, trying to get strong again so I can go back under grass."

"'Fraid we'd never see you again," Seamus said, "with you at home, taking the pledge, and us at the mine all day and night."

"Living at the quarters now, are you?"

"Decided to, once space opened up."

"Maybe when I'm back at the mine I'll be able to stay there with you."

"Think you'll be able to go back?" Thomas asked.

Denis leaned on his walking stick. "Don't know. At first, when I woke up, I wanted to be dead. For a long time I felt like that. These past few weeks, something has changed inside me. One thing I know is that you two saved my life."

The three young men spontaneously embraced. Seamus patted Denis's back. "And we ain't going to forget our friend, Mr. Twomey."

"Right," Thomas said. "Ain't no fun if he ain't scowling about our loud singing and playing the fiddle bad."

All three laughed.

"Hey, Denny. We're on our way to Twomey's. Can you come with us? Me 'n' Thomas didn't take the pledge."

"I might like to, but I haven't made it to Bally Bay since my leg was broke. I'd never make it another mile to Twomey's."

"Going to keep the pledge, are you?" Seamus asked.

"Going to keep it today. Not sure about tomorrow or any other time except now."

"What's not drinking done for you?"

"Cleared my head, it has. I decided there was no sense living if I didn't try to get back on my feet, gimpy leg, pain and all."

Thomas asked, "How'd Friar Mathew convince you to take the pledge?"

"Spoke to my heart, he did. Pushed me to surrender without me knowing it. That wouldn't have happened if you and Seamus had let me stay in my sorrow."

"Jesus, Denny, you knew how to fight us, you did!"

"Thanks for not letting me win."

"But you did win. Won big. Now you're not thinking about going to a friary, are you?"

"Nothing like that," Denis laughed.

"Never going to Twomey's again?"

"Not today."

"You best hurry up with your walking," Seamus said. "Remember Sarah, the pretty buddler I told you about? She likes me a lot."

"Afore I was hurt, Sarah liked me. I think you should worry. A lot."

Seamus grinned. "I got a challenge for you. We'll race you to Bally Bay, just beyond the next stand of trees, then all downhill to water's edge. You man enough, Murley?"

"I'm man enough, but I think you're pushing me."

"Truth is, I am. But you've come a long way since you took the pledge. Forget the race 'til you say you're ready."

Denis nodded.

"Let's get going," Thomas said, "to Bally shore. Seamus and me on to Twomey's. You, Denny, back to the Gap and home."

The three young men fell in line on the narrow path, Seamus, Thomas and Denis.

CHAPTER 61

BREAD AND FLOWERS

Margaret stood over the black pot, stirring potato gruel, adding strips of dulce, giving color to the off-white daily offering. A shaft of sunlight lit the hearth through the hole in the roof. Denis limped through the door, walking stick in one hand, a pail of water in the other. "Here 'tis, Ma," he said, putting the pail on the hearth.

"Plants are puny, need manure," Margaret said.

"I saw the plants, too," Denis replied. "Soon's I get home from hedge school, I'll manure them. Colm will help."

Margaret nodded. "I be going to Mass Rock to give Father the Communion bread and pick flowers for the altar."

"Flowers for the altar? Ma, what happened to the fairies, pookas and leprechauns? Have you forsaken them for Father Murphy and Pope Pius?"

Margaret sighed. "Maybe I have taken a side. Been at war, I have, trying to understand why your da, your sister and your brothers were taken from us."

"I think about it too. I miss them awful."

"When you almost died last year, I felt hopeless. Soon I realized it was no use to beg or bargain or be angry with Father Murphy, or them fairies neither. I cared for you. Father Murphy prayed over you, and I did too, some. Mostly, I just gave thanks each day you were alive.

"Once I knew you would live, I brought flowers for Mass Rock altar and made Communion bread, though Father never asked. Truth is, that quieted my aching heart and brought light to my soul."

"Is a soul like a window?" Colm asked.

"No, but Father Murphy says we all have one," Denis answered.

"What is a soul?" Colm asked.

"Father Murphy says a soul is a part of life that we can think about, but not until we get older."

"Why?" Colm asked.

"Because by then, our thinking is connected to God and the Church," Denis said.

"It takes a long time," Margaret said to Colm.

"And takes learning from Father Murphy," Denis added. "But for now, I need learning from Schoolmaster Tucker, so hurry and get ready for school, Colm. I'm coming with you."

"Why you going to see Tuck?" Margaret asked.

"Da's words keep coming back to me, about learning and being a Poor Scholar. Remembering the bad things I said to Da is much worse than the pain in my leg."

"You can't erase pain from the past, but you can learn from it. That's what Da would want," Margaret said.

Halfway to the school, Colm turned to see Denis limping behind him. "I'm going to run ahead," Colm said. "I'll tell Schoolmaster Tucker you'll be there soon."

"Sure, wee brother, don't be late."

Minutes after students began a reading lesson with Poor Scholar, Luke Flaherty, Denis arrived.

Tuck greeted him. "Good morrow, Denis, me lad, 'tis a bright spot in me day to see you."

"Good morrow, kindly, Schoolmaster Tuck. It's good to see you, too. Can we talk in your room?"

They passed the students listening to Luke, while others sat on floor mats using stones to write on their slates. Tuck and Denis entered Tuck's room and sat on his cot.

"How you be doing, Denis? What about your leg?" Tuck asked.

"I'm better getting around. Maybe one day I won't need a walking stick. What about you, Tuck, how you be doing?"

"Like always, teaching as many as I can. Your Colm has learning in his blood, just like you."

Denis's smile was tentative. "Can you teach me to be a clerk, Tuck?"

"My students are usually no older than fourteen. Tell me why you want to be a clerk?"

"Can't go under grass again, but I want to work at the

mine. Learned a lot about numbers from you. And I like numbers, I do, but I need to learn more."

"Would Colonel Hall hire you?" Tuck asked. "Irish are workers, not bosses."

"I'd not be a boss. But Mr. Parker might need help because there are so many more workers."

"You're right, the mine is growing."

"Think Colonel wouldn't hire me?"

Tuck shook his head. "Not sure, but I know you're smart enough. Fact is, we'll have to start soon because I may be leaving for America."

"Why?" Denis asked.

"When I came back from prison, I told you I was a free man because I taught the children of prison guards and prisoners."

Denis nodded.

"Well, that wasn't exactly what happened. Truth is, when I was teaching, I escaped, with the help of natives and prisoners. Now, they're cracking down on agrarian violence again—hard. A military group in Cork has been ordered to arrest Whiteboys, Rockites and other groups. Been working on it for months, I'm told."

"Why didn't you tell me the truth before?"

"You were too young, and I was too proud."

"But what's to become of hedge school, and the students?"

"Poor Scholar Luke has a gift for teaching. Like Dorian, he came from Maynooth after two years of seminary study.

He's from humble beginnings, but brilliant. And loves the children."

"How soon will you leave?"

"Time is nigh. As I told you before, I won't return to gaol. If I must leave suddenly for America, I will get word to you."

Denis stood up and leaned on his walking stick. "America is the place you told me about a long time ago?"

"Yes, the same. Your da was right about you needing to be a learned person. Clerking is a good place to begin. I'll teach you all I can, long as I'm here."

"Thank you, Tuck. How much for my lessons?"

"Nothing, Denis. You have been loyal to me since we first met years ago. I will teach you to be an excellent clerk. Maybe one day you will come to America."

CHAPTER 62

TUMULT

Margaret sat on the birch bench scrunching a potful of barley ears, knocking the delicate chaff off the grains. Keeping one eye on the path, she waited for Denis and Colm to return from the peat bog.

It was Saturday, a day after the end of the potato harvest and the beginning of the barley harvest. Margaret easily worked the barley ears, but the rhythm of her fingers slowed as she focused on memories of Padraigh. *If only you were here, Paddy, my heart would stop aching. You'd see them large lumpers filling our bin to the brim. You'd see our barley field all golden and ready for harvesting. You'd hear Colm talking English more every day, almost as good as Irish. And our Denny, you'd hear him talk about debits and credits and general ledgers. A clerk's language, he tells me. He's writing with a lead pencil and parchment paper, thanks to Tuck, but more to you, for he'd be scything the barley if you hadn't pushed him like you did.*

"Margaret." The voice was familiar. "Good morrow. Denis here?"

322

Startled, she looked up. "Good morrow, Tuck! Was just thinking about you."

He carried a brown satchel in one hand, his arm straining with its weight. "Must tell Denis something," he said, unusually terse.

"He and Colm just left for the peat bog yonder." Margaret pointed.

"Don't have time to go there. Can you give him a message?"

"Of course, but why not sit and visit?"

"Not today. Not ever again, I fear."

"Not ever? You must tell me why. What has happened?"

"It pains me, but I cannot tell you. I beg you tell Denis he has learned enough bookkeeping. He is ready to be a clerk."

Tuck's flushed face accentuated his snow-white hair. With the back of his hand, he mopped sweat from his forehead. His clothes were rumpled and damp. "I be going. Need to travel."

"No, please be staying."

Eyes hyperalert, looking left and right, he reached into the satchel and pulled out a blunderbuss.

"Oh, Tuck! Something *is* awful wrong."

"'Tis. Don't say you saw me, I beg you."

With that, Tuck fled, heavy satchel in one hand, pistol in the other. He ran behind the O'Toole shanties, taking the worn grassy path to Bantry Bay.

Minutes later, four constables approached on horseback. The horses snorted to a halt directly in front of Margaret as the riders yanked hard on their reins. Each constable had a blunderbuss in a holster at his side.

"We're looking for a fugitive," the rider closest to Margaret yelled. "He's been living in these parts. Seen him? Tucker's his name. Calls himself a schoolmaster."

Margaret shook her head and answered in English. "I 'aven't seen 'im. Don't know 'im."

"No wasting time here. He can't be far ahead."

Margaret gave him a cold stare.

"He's likely to try to get on a fishing boat leaving Bantry Bay," the constable said. "Can't let him get that far."

The constables rode on.

An hour later, Denis and Colm returned with two heavy sacks of peat. Margaret told Denis about Tuck and the constables.

"I was afraid this would happen," Denis said. "Tuck told me he might have to leave quick."

"This ain't right and you know it," Margaret said. "Ain't nothing wrong with teaching children how to read, write, speak English, work math and a lot else."

"I'll tell you about it later," Denis said. "Right now I've got to find him - quick."

"I want to come, too," Colm said.

"No, Colm. You stay here with Ma. Lots of barley needs thrashing."

"Better I come, in case you fall."

"Come, then."

As the two made their way toward a lookout spot over the Bay, three shots rang out in quick succession. The two bolted toward the sounds, running along the path to Bantry Bay, Denis moving faster than he had since his injury. Up ahead were four constables. Two on foot, two on horseback. They were looking down at a body. It was Tuck.

Denis was breathing hard when he reached Tuck. One of the two constables held Tuck's empty satchel, its contents of books and a few pieces of clothing were strewn on the ground.

"Jesus, no!" Denis fell to the ground at Tuck's side.

Tuck was ghostly white, blood oozing from his neck and chest. His eyelids fluttered.

Denis put his face close to Tuck's. "Tuck, don't give up. Please!"

Tuck opened his eyes. "Told them. No prison. No choice."

"Tuck, please don't die."

"Make Eire proud," Tuck whispered, "in all you do."

Tuck's eyes closed. He died. Free.

CHAPTER 63

DEATH AND LIFE

News of Thomas Tucker's death traveled fast. Most of Cloghfune attended his wake, held at the hedge school the night before his burial. Father Murphy declined to go to the wake, his practice since becoming a priest six years earlier. When he arrived at Mass Rock early the next morning to prepare for the Sunday funeral, a horse was tethered to a tree, harnessed to a low-backed carriage. Four pallbearers stood nearby. *At least someone had a mind to get a horse and carriage ready to carry the casket to the cemetery.*

In flowing black vestments, Father Murphy looked out at the large congregation, the warm autumn morning muting the palpable sadness. Margaret walked quickly toward him with a basket of Communion bread.

"Sorry to be late, Father. 'Tis a sad day, it is. I be thinking there isn't enough bread. I be seeing more people here than ever before."

"There will be enough," Father Murphy said. "Only a small piece of Jesus needed to feed the soul."

Margaret gave a somber nod and started to turn away.

"Don't see Denis and Colm," Father Murphy said.

"They be coming."

"I pray they come soon."

Denis and Colm arrived toward the end of Mass, slipping behind the last row of standing parishioners, in tall weeds that grew amid the stony terrain. Denis's lower right leg bulged and throbbed. He shifted his weight to his left leg, balancing with his walking stick. Both Colm and Denis had sad faces and swollen eyes.

"We were blessed to have Schoolmaster Tucker among us for many years," Father Murphy announced at the end of Mass. "His only desire was to instill the gift of knowledge in Irish children. And in their parents, too."

No one stirred until Sean O'Toole spoke out from the middle of the congregation. "Tuck was more than schoolmaster. After Declan died, Tuck helped me get me brother a proper burial. Saved me from despair."

Katherine Callahan spoke up. "If not for Tuck, I wouldn't have a home or family. Years ago he helped our parents stop feuding, allowing Jack and me to marry. Now our family is welcome here in this church." Seven-year-old Mary stood between her parents, holding her father's hand.

"Not only a teacher and peacemaker," Mrs. Riley said, "Tuck was a friend. He had a way of finding books. Gave me two—a medical book and one about birthing. I am grateful."

Soon another voice was heard. "Six years ago I met Tuck for the first time, behind a hedge, giving a spelling lesson. Tuck's faith in helping the Irish and English understand each other made Mountain Mine a success, and provided jobs for many of you." Colonel Hall's voice started to break.

Most everyone nodded.

Rose Doyle spoke up. "When I was seven I told Schoolmaster Tucker me parents couldn't pay to keep me in school. He said I had best keep coming 'cause nothing is more important than learning. Now, I be speaking English and learning arithmetic. And I be helping me ma and da with learning English, too."

Ryan stood next to Rose. "I been knocked down by bad lungs. Can't work in the mine no more. Schoolmaster Tucker came to me house, told me I must return to school so I can make a living, if I can't grow potatoes all my days. Didn't care so much about learning before, but I do now."

"After me Paddy died," Margaret said, "and me drowning in sorrow, he helped me get the death papers recorded so I could keep leasing our land. Saved me family."

"Hedge school will never be the same without Schoolmaster Tuck," Poor Scholar Flaherty said. "But lessons will go on because of him. He taught not only students, but his Poor Scholars, too. Grateful I am to have studied with him, but for too short a time. Rest in peace, Schoolmaster Tuck."

Father Murphy waited. He had spotted Denis earlier, but no sign of him now. "Please gather in the cemetery for burial prayers," Father announced. "Tuck's soul has risen. He is in heaven."

Margaret turned to look for Denis and Colm. Mrs. Riley was with them, looking at Denis's leg. Margaret hurried to them.

"Needs to be drained," Mrs. Riley said. "The leg is weeping. Too much fluid." She brushed her fingers on the hard, swollen leg. Rosy fluid oozed from the skin.

Denis stared with downcast eyes at his swollen leg. "What else can happen to me?"

"It can get worse. 'Tis an infection, and serious, it is."

Denis put his head in his hands, then crossed his arms, pulling them tight around his chest, as the chills began their inexorable rise. He began to shake.

Colonel Hall arrived a few steps behind Margaret. "Can't you treat him?"

"Only way to get bad humor out is with a needle. No other way."

"Can you do it?" Margaret asked.

"Birthing babies is me job. Denis must be treated soon, else he'll lose his leg. Or worse."

"Knew his leg was bad," Colm said, "but said he had to come anyway."

"Stop the pallbearers," Hall yelled to Father Murphy. "We need the carriage. The Murley lad needs to be taken to Allihies." *Can't lose him. Not without a fight. Though it will be a fight of another kind when Puxley learns Mahoney treated him.*

Colm jumped up. "I'll stop them!"

"I best go too," Margaret said, "to be sure Father Murphy understands."

Father Murphy stood behind the casket in front of Mass Rock, a long line of parishioners queued up behind him. The four pallbearers were about to lift the casket onto the carriage when Colm stopped squarely in front of Father Murphy. Before Colm or Margaret could speak, Father put his hand on Colm's small shoulder. "Today we honor the dead and the living. Turn the horse and carriage around and carry Denis to Allihies. With God's grace, Dr. Mahoney can help him. We pray for Denis as we carry Schoolmaster Tuck to his final resting place."

"Thank you, Father," Margaret said. "We are grateful."

Together, Margaret and Colm led the horse to Denis. Still shivering, he hoisted himself onto the floorboard in the back of the carriage. Colm jumped in beside him. Mrs. Riley and Margaret climbed upon the carriage seat and Margaret took the reins.

"I'll take you straightaway to Dr. Mahoney," Hall said.

"I remember Dr. Mahoney well," Margaret said. "I pray this time his healing will be different."

CHAPTER 64

A BEGINNING

Colm left for hedge school and Margaret, now a birth helper, was on her way to assist Mrs. Riley. Denis set out for Mountain Mine, the first time since the cave-in more than a year earlier. He walked with a severe limp, gripping his cane like a vise. A few hours later, he neared the dressing floor. *Same sounds I heard seven years ago, when I came first time with Da.*

When Denis approached the four steps that led up to the porch of the Count House, he stopped abruptly. *Now go ahead, climb that mountain in front of you.*

He tossed his cane to the porch and used his three strong limbs to scoot up the steps. At the landing he picked up his cane, stood up straight, took a deep breath and opened the heavy oak door.

Nine well-dressed men sat at the conference table, John Puxley at its head. Hall sat to Puxley's right, Parker and Mahoney to his left. Also seated at the table were five of the mine's shareholders.

331

They all stared at Denis.

"Murley?" Hall asked. "Is that you?"

"Yes sir. Excuse me, but I was wanting to find you."

"How're you doing?" Hall asked.

Puxley raised his eyebrows. "See here, Colonel, this is no time for a social visit. Have him wait outside."

Hall nodded and turned to Denis with a smile. "I'll find you. Stay close by."

"Yes, sir."

Avoiding the stairs, Denis walked to the far end of the porch, out of view.

"Let's get on with the report," Puxley said.

"Wait a minute," investor Eyres said. "Is he a worker? Looks like he's a cripple. What happened to him?"

Puxley gave Hall a look.

"Name's Denis Murley," Hall said, "a local from Cloghfune. Started work here when he was thirteen. He survived a cave-in a year ago."

"I remember that report," Eyers said. "What about the others?"

"Gentlemen, everyone survived," Puxley said. "It's getting late. We have much more to discuss."

"I would like to hear about the injuries," another investor said. "How much did it cost the company?"

Puxley shot a glance at Hall. "As you know," Hall said, "we've set aside money from workers' pay, and some of our profit, to compensate when needed."

"How much did this young man receive?"

"He didn't receive anything," Puxley said, "because he lives with his family, farming."

"That's why he didn't receive anything?" Eyers asked, his voice rising at the end of the question.

Puxley quickly replied, "Fact is, we were not able to get a settlement from the Cork Gunpowder Factory, though it was clearly at fault. We didn't have enough money in our fund at the time to help all the injured."

"Hardly seems fair," an investor said, "if they were injured as badly as this Murley lad."

"Are the others back at work?" Eyers asked.

"Not yet," Hall replied. "Captain Glasson is still recovering at home in Wales. Two other locals won't be coming back."

"We are making progress keeping workers safe," Puxley said, "and also producing at a high rate. Your dividends today will show that."

"We walk a fine line," Hall added, "hauling up ore, being competitive, and keeping our workers out of harm's way. As you just saw, this business can be cruel."

The meeting ended an hour later. Puxley gave generous dividends to the shareholders.

Hall, Puxley, Parker and Mahoney were still in the meeting room when Denis reappeared at the door. "Just want you to know I'm still here, Colonel," he said.

Puxley was gathering his papers, ready to go.

"Have a seat here at the conference table," Hall said to Denis.

Dr. Mahoney stood at the doorway, inadvertently blocking Puxley's departure. Denis and Puxley made eye contact for a few brief seconds.

Hall facilitated the accidental encounter. "Denis, I'd like you to meet Mr. Puxley, the mine's owner."

"Never thought this would happen, sir." Denis said. "Pleased to meet you. My name's Denis Murley."

"Yes, I know," said Puxley.

"Me da worked here also. Passed now, he has."

"Yes, I know that, too," Puxley said. "You had a sister?"

"Yes, I did. Dr. Mahoney here tried hard to save her."

"I know," said Puxley.

"Why'd you come here today?" Hall asked.

"I want to work. My body may look crippled, but my brain isn't. Schoolmaster Tucker taught me clerking. Brilliant teacher, he was. Before he died, he said I was ready for bookkeeping. Was hoping I could help Mr. Parker."

"Unheard of," Puxley said.

"Unheard of?" Denis asked.

"What Mr. Puxley means is the Irish are hired as workers," Hall said, "not clerks."

"But I know bookkeeping. Double entry, debits, credits, net profit, net loss, quarterly reports and a whole lot more."

"It's just not done," Puxley said. "Least not in this mine."

"But I speak Irish and English. I can translate, especially on paydays."

"Mr. Parker manages the books," Puxley said. "No need for another bookkeeper. Maybe in time."

"That's not exactly true, John," Parker said. "We've grown considerably. Now over five hundred strong. I'm hardly able to keep up. Sometimes I feel like I'm drowning in numbers."

"You never told me this."

"I'm telling you now. Copper production is growing, even though we complain things aren't moving fast enough. I want to hear what Murley has to say, why he thinks he can help, what his skills are."

Hall, Puxley, Parker and Mahoney turned their eyes to Denis, who stood balanced on both legs, his cane at his side.

"When I first came here to the mine, my father and I were turned away because we were Irish. Next thing I knew, Colonel Hall was telling my father how much the Irish were needed. I didn't understand it. But when we started working here, me a ragger, I felt a strength I hadn't known. My father saw things different. He raised me to learn and understand more than he ever did. After a while, he made me stop working at the mine and go back to hedge school as a Poor Scholar with Schoolmaster Tucker. That's where I learned what I know today, about math, bookkeeping, reading, and literature, too. Schoolmaster Tucker told me I had a gift for numbers.

"Over two years ago my father died and I got lost in sorrow. One day, Friar Mathew found me and after a time, the wounds healed in my body and in my mind. I'm twenty years old. I want to earn a living as my father wanted.

"Mr. Parker, if you hire me, I will be your able assistant. I will take what I've learned and add to it. I know you need to test my bookkeeping skills and I'm ready anytime.

"Dr. Mahoney, you saved my life—twice. I don't remember the first time, but I remember long after the accident, if you hadn't been there to drain the infection in my leg, I'd have lost it. You eased my father's suffering, and Bridget's too. I will always be grateful to you.

"Colonel Hall, you were always fair to me and all workers, no matter whether we were from Cornwall or the Beara. I have always looked up to you.

"You started this business, Mr. Puxley. I've no idea how, but many are thankful to you for the opportunity to live a better life here on the Beara. I know there've been problems, but without the mine, we would have to depend on the spud. And without Irish workers, your mine would not be profitable. I want to use my experience and education to help the mine continue to be a success for all of us."

Silence prevailed as the four men contemplated Denis's words.

"I'm a businessman, Murley," Puxley said at last. "When I opened the mine, I had no intention to hire Irish. Farmers all, lazy, too. But as you say, we needed you Irish to make copper mining successful. And you did. You, your father and hundreds of others.

"I see the sacrifice you've made. And while I wish the cave-in had never happened, that can't be a reason to hire you."

"I wouldn't want it to be a reason, sir," Denis said.

"Colonel Hall has proven me wrong many times about the Irish. The company is grateful for his perseverance. I will leave it to him again, and to Mr. Parker, to decide if we need a clerk."

"Thank you, Mr. Puxley. If I am hired, I promise you will have no regrets."

Puxley suppressed a smile. "I must be going. Carry on, gentlemen."

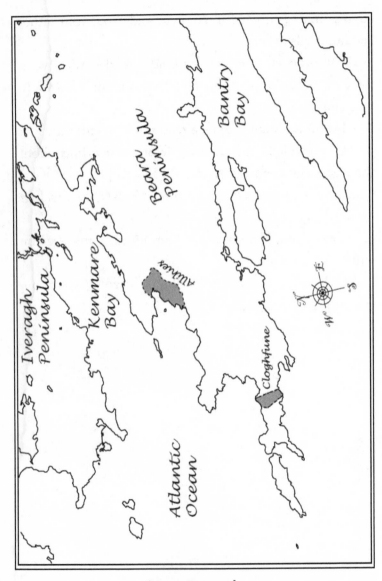

Beara Peninsula

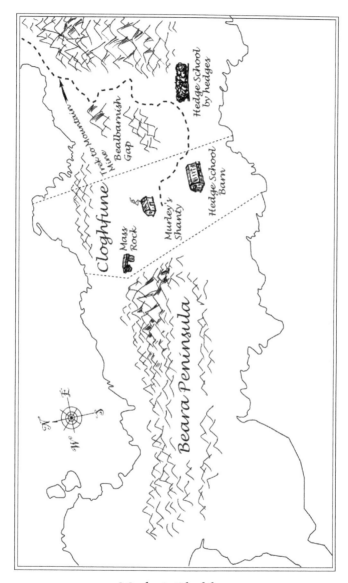

Murley's Cloghfune

Cloghfune to Mountain Mine

GLOSSARY

Adit – An entrance to an underground mine, used for extracting, hauling ore, ventilation and water drainage.

Banshee – From Irish mythology, a spirit in the form of a wailing woman that appears to or is heard by family members as a sign that one of them is about to die.

Bargain – A contract for earning wages, bargained monthly by a skilled miner, who represents a number of workers.

Bedad – An Irish minced oath, a corruption of be gad, for by God! Used to express surprise or for emphasis.

Blunderbuss – A muzzle-loaded firearm with a short, large caliber barrel, flared at the muzzle and used with lead shot and other projectiles.

Bucker – A mine worker who uses a flat-faced hammer to buck or grind "cobbed" ore to about 10 mm diameter.

Buddler – A mine worker who separates metal bearing sand from waste sand by use of a buddle (an inclined trough through which water flows).

Changeling – Typically described as being the offspring of a fairy, troll, elf or other legendary creature that has been secretly left in the place of a human child. In Ireland, looking at a baby too intently signified envy resulting in the baby becoming ensnared as a changeling in the power of a fairy.

Cobber – A mine worker who breaks rocks with a long-headed hammer to gravel size (3 cm) to enable picking out waste. This process is called cobbing and is followed by bucking.

Cottier – An Irish peasant farmer who grows crops (typically, potatoes) in exchange for the right to live in a cottage/shanty on the land and pay rent in the form of a portion of the crop grown.

Count House –A term that is shortened from its proper name, Account House, where financial accounts are maintained.

Cross of St. Brigid – St. Brigid, founder of an Irish monastery in County Kildare, born in 450 AD, developed a uniquely styled cross, using rushes or straw. Found in many Irish homes even to present day, its purpose is to protect the home from evil, fire and hunger. Origins of the story of the cross vary.

Dosser – A person known for avoiding work, is useless, a lay-about.

Dragoon – A blunderbuss in handgun form.

Dressing Floor – An extensive ground level surface area of a mine, where varied ore crushing activities take place after unrefined ore is excavated from underground or an open pit.

Drumlin – A small hill, narrow or elongated, formed over time by glacial ice acting on rocks and sediment. From the Irish word, littlest ridge.

Dunboy Castle – Originally a stone tower house, it was a stronghold of O'Sullivan Bere and his clan, to guard the harbor of Berehaven. It was destroyed in 1602 by the English to suppress an Irish insurgency. In 1739 Henry and John Puxley built an English manor house near the remains of the original structure. It is variously known as Dunboy Castle, Puxley Castle, Puxley Manor and Puxley Mansion. In 1921 the castle was torched by the IRA, it remains in ruins.

Evil Eye – A curse or hex placed on a person or an animal by staring at the person to an abnormal degree, including staring, glaring, or better known in Irish culture as being "overlooked." There are numerous countermeasures to offset, or prevent, the effects of the Evil Eye.

Gaelic – The Irish language is sometimes referred to in English as Gaelic, Irish Gaelic, or Erse (originally a Scottish word), but is more generally referred to in Ireland as the Irish language or simply Irish to avoid confusion with Scottish Gaelic, the closely-related language spoken in Scotland.

Griffith's Valuation – A 17-year project (1847-1864) to establish a uniform guide to the value of land throughout Ireland, for the purpose of developing a tax rate to support the poor and destitute. In over 300 volumes, the valuations include the name(s) of persons leasing a property, property description, acreage, value of land and buildings.

Gruel – A type of cereal (e.g., oat, wheat, rye) mixed with boiling water or milk that can be drunk or eaten. Gruel for the Murley family consisted of potatoes boiled in water or milk.

Hedge Schools – Clandestine schools established to educate Irish children who were denied schooling because of Penal Laws enacted by the British in the late 1600s. Penal Laws were repealed by the early1700s, but hedge schools persisted until the mid-1800s.

Horse Whim – Mechanical power generated by a horse walking around a circular platform, tethered to an overhead winding drum or windlass.

Kibble – A wooden or iron bucket used in wells or mines for hoisting water, ore or refuse to the surface.

Linhay – A shed with a lean-to roof and an open front beneath which mine workers were sheltered from the weather.

Lode – An area of mineralization underground of valuable ores. Also known as a vein or seam. Generally, the lode is vertical or near-vertical and can extend for long distances.

Lumper – A variety of potato grown in Ireland beginning in early 1800s and associated with the potato famine. It was easy to grow, tolerating poor soil and requiring little manure. Consistency of the lumper was waxy.

The skin was lumpy, and light brown, the flesh yellow. Nutritional value was healthy with adequate protein, carbohydrate and vitamin B and C.

Open-Cast or Pit Mining – Mineral lodes that are located on the surface or opened to the surface and excavated directly. Similar to stone quarrying.

Ore – A mineral and mixtures of minerals that have value and are worked for profit.

Peat – A deposit of semi-carbonized plant remains from a water-saturated environment, such as bogs or moors. It is considered to be the early stage in the natural process of the development of coal.

Picker – A mine worker who separates stone and trash from copper bearing ore called the "picked" ore.

Pookas – From Celtic folklore, a mischievous but not malevolent Irish spirit or goblin. It can take the form of an animal, e.g., a dog, rabbit, or goat.

Poor Scholar – An Irish student, typically male, with a strong desire for learning, but too poor to pursue his studies at his own expense. In a hedge school, he usually assists a schoolmaster with education of younger children in return for being schooled in advanced studies.

Poitín/Poteen – A traditional Irish alcoholic beverage traditionally distilled in a small pot still usually from malted barley, grain, treacle, sugar beet, potatoes or whey. The term is a diminutive of the Irish word *pota*, meaning "pot."

Pricker – A long brass or copper rod that was pushed into packed gunpowder in a blast hole and removed to leave a hole in the powder for inserting a fuse.

Ragger – A mine worker, usually strong young men, who used sledge hammers to break up large blocks of ore-containing quartz into pieces ("ragged" ore) for further processing.

Ribbonmen – An agrarian secret society similar to Whiteboys and Rockites. They carried out vigilante acts against unjust landlords and clergy demanding tithes. They were called Ribbonmen because they wore as a badge a green ribbon attached to their clothing.

Rockites – Another agrarian secret society, headed by mythical leader, "Captain Rock" who led the Rockite rebellion of 1821-1824 against agrarian wrongs to poor Irish.

Smelting – The process of subjecting mineral ores to heat, combined with chemical reducing agents in a furnace, to liberate base or precious metals as liquids.

Spaller – A mine worker who breaks ore into smaller pieces, each about 15 cm in diameter, using a long handled hammer. The spalling process follows ragging.

Sphagnum Moss – A type of peat moss that can store 16 to 26 times as much water as its dry weight.

Stope – An excavated area resulting from the extraction of ore-bearing rock, often narrow, deep and elongated, reflecting the former position of a lode. The ceilings of stopes are sometimes supported with timbers.

Spalpeen – A poor migratory farm worker in Ireland, often viewed as a rascal or a mischievous and cunning person.

Under Grass – A term used to identify mining below ground level.

Union (Act of Union of 1801) – The unification of England and Ireland on January 1, 1801. Many Irish thought they would gain emancipation by this act. Instead the Irish parliament was dissolved.

Vervain – A hardy wildflower perennial with small pale violet, blue or white flowers. It has a long history of use as a magical and medical herb.

Whiteboys – A secret agrarian group of Irishmen organized in the mid-1700s, who took vigilante action to defend tenants' land rights to subsistence farming. Their name derives from their penchant for carrying out crimes wearing white shirts.